'I like this one, Higgy,' Vaughan said. 'Look at her eyes, the way they go all distant. Ye gods, but she must have sensitive tits. I'd like to take her out tomorrow, if that's okay?'

'Well, er . . .' Higgy hesitated. 'I'll have to check that, sir. She's still only a novice and we have strict rules about letting them out to guests too soon.'

'I'll accept responsibility if anything goes wrong,' Vaughan chuckled. He leaned forward and brushed a kiss across Amaarini's lips. 'I get the feeling this one may be worth it!'

Amaarini closed her eyes and bit hard into the rubber between her teeth. Her nipples tingled and she knew that her body was on the verge of betraying her. To her relief, Higgy intervened. 'Best leave her for the moment, sir,' he said gently. 'Can't have her losing it just before a race. The more experienced ones can handle that, and even coming during a race don't seem to affect them but, same as you said, Diamond here is raw. You take her over the top now and she'll be useless out on the track.'

SLAVE ACTS

Jennifer Jane Pope

This book is a work of fiction.
In real life, make sure you practise safe sex.

First published in 2002 by
Nexus
Thames Wharf Studios
Rainville Road
London W6 9HA

www.nexus-books.co.uk

Typeset by TW Typesetting, Plymouth, Devon

Printed and bound by
Clays Ltd, St Ives PLC

ISBN 0 352 33665 X

Author's Preface

When I began work on *Slave Genesis*, some little while ago now, I knew that the story would need at least two volumes in order to tell it properly and I suspected it might even need a third, though I did wonder how my readers would react to such a large work.

However, two years on and here we are with the fourth book, with a fifth planned and still, it seems from my mailbox, you haven't tired of the saga one little bit and remain as eager as ever to hear more from our disparate bunch of heroes, heroines, villains and villainesses. One fan in the USA has even gone so far as to suggest that this series could grow to rival John Norman's *Gor* adventures, though I think that could be both premature and presumptious on my own part to even consider that possibility. After all, there were nearly thirty books in that alternative Earth opus . . .

But enough of that.

For the moment I'd simply like to take this opportunity to thank you all once again for your support and enthusiasm, your suggestions and criticisms and for what I hope will be your continued interest into the future. I'd also like to apologise to those of you who have already read books one, two and three, for the prologue which follows this – you can skip it if you want and go straight back into the story.

And to those of you coming fresh to this series, I hope the prologue explains everything that needs explaining, so that this volume will stand complete in itself. If you enjoy it, I'm pretty sure that *Slave Genesis*, *Slave Exodus* and *Slave Revelations* are all still available out there somewhere, either in the shops, or else somewhere on the good old Internet. I'm sure you'll find copies if you really want them and hopefully Nexus will consider reprinting before too long.

But I'm keeping you from the nitty-gritty, aren't I? So I'll just close by saying that I trust you'll enjoy this book as much as you've enjoyed the previous ones, or that eventually you'll enjoy the previous ones as much as I hope you're about to enjoy this one.

If you understand my meaning . . .

All the very best,
Jenny Jane Pope
June 2001

Prologue

Somewhere on the remote edge of the already remote Shetland Islands, many miles north of mainland Scotland in the North Sea, two small and desolate little lumps of rock hide a sinister secret that itself masks an awful, almost unbelievable truth.

Carigillie Craig, the larger of the two islands, is the home of an exclusive health and fitness operation owned by the multi-national company *Healthglow*, and is patronised exclusively by the mega-rich set. However, these fabulously wealthy clients are not drawn by any normal ideas of keeping fit, for on the nearby smaller island of Ailsa Ness lies the real reason for their regular pilgrimages: a secret fetish and bondage operation where almost anything goes and the female submissives rival the most beautiful women in the world.

The fact that so many of these unresisting lovelies appear to be twins, triplets or even quadruplets merely adds extra spice to the fun and not one of the unwitting visitors has ever come close to suspecting the true secret of the islands.

However, a series of apparently unrelated deaths elsewhere in the Shetlands and also on the mainland itself (not to be confused with Mainland, the largest island in the Shetlands group), leads pretty young

Detective Sergeant Alex Gregory to suspect that all may not be as it should be. When her superior refuses to give any credence to her suspicions, she decides to take individual action.

She enrols the assistance of a former college friend who now runs an air taxi service and parachutes on to Ailsa by night, where she finds herself confronted by the most bizarre sight imaginable – a moonlight pony race featuring human pony-girls. Whether or not all this is illegal, Alex never has time to discover. A careless accident leaves her lying in the bottom of a gully, her neck and spine broken and damaged beyond repair in several places, her body paralysed and useless.

When she finally recovers consciousness an even greater shock awaits her, for the body in which she now finds herself is not her own and she herself is now a captive pony-girl, available to anyone and everyone who can afford the asking price. Meantime, her old body has been returned to Mainland and cremated – the story about an unfortunate accident accepted by the authorities – so that Alex cannot even hope that anyone will still be looking for her.

However, another chain of circumstances leads her former colleague, Detective Constable Tim 'Geordie' Walker, to become involved in an investigation being organised by his own former colleague – an investigation that points to the two islands having somewhat more to them than the respectable facade they present might suggest.

When billionaire Andrew Lachan's luxury yacht *Jessica* is destroyed by a mystery explosion, initial reaction from official sources puts his death down as a tragic accident. However Colin Turner, a member of an elite police department which looks out for the safety of the rich and important, is not convinced and enlists Geordie's assistance to pursue the matter further.

Along with Lachan's former personal assistant, the beautiful Sara, they discover Lachan's dedication to the pursuit of pony-girl racing. Sara, as much to her astonishment as to anyone else's, finds herself strangely drawn to this world of leather tack, rubber bits and hoofed boots. Following a lead via Celia Butler, one of *Healthglow*'s most regular clients and suppliers, the trio find themselves at Celia's remote farm, caught up in a world of bizarre fetishism and bondage. Sara becomes Sassie the pony-girl and Colin and Geordie become even more confused.

However, still unable to uncover evidence of any actual criminal activity, their only course is to try to get on to the two islands and when they receive a report that a young Andean girl has been found, dressed from head to toe in rubber and drifting at sea only a few miles from Ailsa and Carigillie, matters become more urgent.

Thanks to Celia's reluctant cooperation, Colin – accompanied by Sara, Millie (Geordie's recruit from the Butler farmstead) and Anna, a police inspector from Norway – go undercover as novice clients, whilst Geordie waits not far off shore aboard the trawler *Essie*, whose curious skipper makes it clear to him that this operation goes far beyond an investigation into a possible suspicious death.

Ironically, the man whose 'death' has brought matters thus far is actually very much alive on Ailsa – though far from happy – for he is now the unwitting and unwilling tenant of another of the fantastic clone bodies and appears condemned to spend his life as the spitting image of the beautiful pony-girl Jess, having failed in an attempt to abduct her from her creators and keep her exclusively for himself.

On their first evening, Melinda (better known as Millie) and Anna (using the alias Ingrid), are left in tight rubber bondage by Celia, whilst Sassie, under her expert driving, wins through a pony-girl tournament to general acclaim.

Alex Gregory, meanwhile, as pony-girl Jangles, has aroused the interest of the beautiful but cold Amaarini – one of the people responsible for running the *Healthglow* operation – and is astonished to learn the truth that the Askarlarnis, as they call themselves, are actually part of an ancient alien culture, and that their cloning/breeding program essentially began as a way of preserving their own females beyond their mid-twenties.

All the while, in the background lurks the more-than-sinister Ramon Valerez, South American drugs baron and mass murderer, anxious to buy the Askarlarnis' skills in order to create a line of human pony-women to transport his evil cargoes across the secret Andean mountain routes to be shipped out all over the western world. But do Valerez's interests stop at just that and will the Askarlarni leaders be naive enough to trust him?

And will Colin and the girls manage to discover anything on the secret island other than the intricacies of their own sexualities?

4

One

SASSIE

The best way I can explain it would be as some sort of a personal extension of mass hysteria, if that makes any sense. No? Well, I know what I mean – at least, I think I do.

Everything that happened at that race track was like a kind of madness; I was was swept up in it and seemed completely to lose myself. Sara was another person altogether, left in some other world that was no longer anything to do with me. I was just Sassie the pony-girl, that's all, and whatever personality I now had was utterly subservient, yet really strong in that I knew exactly what it was I wanted.

That weird rubber face mask that Celia put on me at first – that started it all. That wasn't me, was it? That was some exotic female from . . . well, I don't know – name any one of a few dozen eastern countries and you could be right. I just looked at myself and saw someone else, and it was like throwing a switch. Anything I did now, especially as I was quickly cuffed under that cape, was outside my own responsibility.

And Celia knew what she was doing all right, as we already knew from that visit to her own place. As we were being blindfolded to pass through into that underground monorail system, she leaned close to me and whispered in my ear so nobody else could hear. Well, I don't think anyone else could hear, anyway.

'This is the only true freedom for a slave, Sassie,' she said. 'Now you have abandoned free will, choice, and your own needs, and given them willingly into the hands of your masters and mistresses.'

There was just one moment of doubt after that, during that rail journey itself, when I wondered just what the hell I was doing. I was completely naked under that cape and helpless to protect myself. Before the blindfold hood came off I felt hands under the material, hands fondling my boobs, playing with my nipples. It could have been Celia and probably was her on one occasion, but there were other hands, too.

They seemed to be evaluating me and it felt so impersonal – as if I was just another piece of livestock. Then another hand went down between my thighs, and fingers began to probe me. I heard a man sigh – just a sort of grunt, I suppose – when he discovered I was already aroused and wet and then he just patted me, like you would a dog, only you wouldn't pat a dog there, for sure.

As I say, I very nearly lost it about then and it was all I could do to stop myself from shouting out that I'd changed my mind and wanted to go back, but I knew the danger that was likely to place the rest of you in, so I kept my mouth shut and thought I'd wait until I could say something quietly at the other end. I didn't realise I wouldn't get the opportunity again.

The stables were awesome. To think that someone could build a complex like that, and underground, too. The atmosphere just took my breath away. I could smell leather and sweat and rubber and all manner of other things I couldn't quite identify and suddenly I was back to being Sassie again and the scary feelings were going away.

Then, of course, I was handed over to the grooms and my last chance to back out swept away, especially when they fitted that thing across my back teeth and over my tongue. Even before they put the bit on me I was deprived of speech and the way they handled me was all so calculated. At the time it seemed so impersonal and offhanded, but I realise now it was far from that. Everything they did, everything they said, was intended to reinforce my status as a pony-girl and something inside me just responded automatically.

I stood there so obediently as they harnessed and bridled me and fitted those hooves and my tail and then all those various bells, and when they led me out I felt like I was walking on air. That other mask, the horse-snout shaped thing, and the blinkers, meant that I couldn't see very much at all, except for straight ahead. The collar kept my head up anyway, but even without it I know I would have walked proudly.

No, 'walk' isn't right at all – I pranced and everyone saw me, but I knew I was now just one pretty pony-girl among a whole string and there were some beautiful girls there. I didn't expect to win anything, to be honest, but there was a fire burning in me now that made me determined to give my all. When I ran, that was something else.

My boobs bounced so much it should have hurt, yet there was no pain now, simply a craving for victory, for admiration and, above all, for final fulfilment. I lost count of the number of times I came. There were proper orgasms and there were little mini ones and then there were multiple ones that just went on and on and I just carried on running throughout them.

The whip flicking my shoulders and back just added to it all and I remember wishing Celia would use it properly on me instead of just as a sort of symbolic action. I wanted her to thrash me, to show me and everyone else that I was her pony-girl; that I was the sort of animal who would do anything for the right mistress or master. Of course she wouldn't have done anything that would have left me permanently marked.

After the racing had finished, after I had won and when all the excitement was subsiding, then I should probably have felt deflated and the reality should have come back again. And yet it didn't. The moment that young groom took my reins and started checking to make sure my girth was still tight I knew what was going to happen. Everyone else was going to go off to whatever celebrations were planned back inside and I was simply going to be left to the hired help, the way a horse might be after the hunt is over. Except that real horses don't get handed over to grooms who intend to fuck them as soon as they get the chance.

His name was Jonas and he seemed to be the youngest of the grooms apart from maybe the one called Sol, but he'd apparently gone off somewhere else. I got the impression, from snatches of conversation I managed to pick up among the other grooms, that Sol was in some sort of trouble. Apparently he'd taken a pony-girl out without proper authority and she'd got away from him, but that's all I heard and I may have got it wrong.

Jonas had made it clear from the very beginning what he intended to do with me when the chance and time came, even though the older one, Higgy, kept going on about seniority. The crazy thing is, I ought to have been really upset that they were discussing who was going to have me first and yet the only thing on my mind was that I wanted it to be Jonas, if possible. The other crazy thing is that, when it looked like Higgy was going to exercise his privileges first after all, I accepted it quite placidly, like it wasn't any right of mine to choose.

In the end, Higgy was called away somewhere. There was a tall woman – she had weird eyes, a bit like a reptile I thought – who seemed to be in charge and all the grooms were scared stiff of her, I could tell. She wasn't there much, but when she was about she had a sort of presence, an aura. It wasn't evil, I don't think, more a sort of neutrality. Coldness, that was it. She was really cold, as if she had absolutely no feelings at all, like a machine on legs.

My nipples were still in their clamps, I was still belled and everything else about my rig was exactly as it had been throughout the races. The girth corset no longer seemed tight – though my legs were beginning to ache from standing on tiptoe in those hoof boots for so long – but I knew Jonas wasn't going to worry about my immediate comforts.

He led me into an empty stall – I think it was the one where I had been bridled earlier, though I'd gone past recall or caring anyway – and just hitched my rein to a hook on the wall, then unclipped one end of my bit and took it out. The tongue plate remained – he didn't want me speaking, after all.

'You know what's going to happen now, don't you, Sassie?' he said. He was so nonchalant about the whole thing, standing there, hands on hips, but he was also so good looking and strong that the nonchalant attitude just added to the feelings I was getting of being so completely in his power. Not that I knew it at the time, but without one of those special personal master tags, it meant I was available for anyone who took a fancy to me, visitors or staff alike.

I looked at Jonas and nodded. My mouth felt dry, but I was making up for that between my legs and I knew he could see that. The rubber body suit was keeping my exposed nipples aroused above and my pussy lips thrust well forward down below. It was crude and yet not crude, a simple emphasising of availability and, I suppose, surrender.

Jonas must have understood, but then he was probably very experienced, even though he didn't look very old. He took a plastic bottle and held the nozzle up to my lips, squeezing to produce a thin jet of water. I drank, gratefully, greedily almost, but he was wary of letting me drink too much all in a rush. Instead, he grabbed my bridle and kissed me and I couldn't believe the length of his tongue. It probed everywhere inside my mouth and into the top of my throat, and I thought I was going to choke.

I kissed him back, though I couldn't respond with my own tongue, but he held my bridle so that I couldn't exert any real pressure with my lips, either. It was the most bizarre kiss I had ever experienced and yet probably the most erotic. He was kissing me and yet I wasn't allowed to kiss him, at least not in the normal way, though the lack of anything normal shouldn't have surprised me any more.

The kiss lasted a long time, and then he started on my nipples and I saw just how long his tongue actually was. I was really suffering now, grunting and groaning, scraping the ground with my hooves, like a mare in heat, I guess. I wanted him to take me straight away, but he wasn't going to be hurried. Instead, he kept flicking his tongue from one nipple to the other, making those little bells jangle as he did it and my nipples just carried on getting bigger and harder and throbbing like they were going to burst at any moment.

And then, without a word, he broke off, stood back, unhitched my rein and turned me around to face away from him. Instinctively, I knew what was expected of me and I bent forward, until my back was parallel with the ground, my buttocks thrust back and I knew my sex was just so visible and available. I could hear him doing something with his clothing, but the blinkers meant I couldn't see backwards and I tensed myself, waiting to be entered, except that at first it was his tongue that pushed inside me, and it found its target first time.

I came immediately and I would have fallen forward if he hadn't grabbed me by the hips. Now I started to push back, thrusting myself into his face, but he didn't seem to mind. Instead, he just kept going with his tongue and I squealed and whinnied as one orgasm blended with another until it all just became one. I was vaguely aware when he finally stopped, for he cried out something, but before I could react, or even start to come back from the peak, he fucked me.

It sounds crude, saying it that bluntly, but that was exactly what he did, without ceremony and without further ado. One minute he was using his tongue, the next he simply pressed himself against me and slid straight in, filling me with the longest cock I had ever known, and then pumping in and out until he came, a torrent that filled me and at the same time, pushed me completely over the edge.

I must have blacked out then, though only for a few seconds, and I did not fall, presumably because he kept hold of me. When I came to again, I was standing upright once more and he was holding my bridle. I peered down as best as the collar would let me and saw that he was still rigidly erect. The sight of that shaft was as awesome as it had felt.

He was built like a stallion – truly magnificently endowed beyond anything I had ever believed humanly possible. His cock had to be at least a foot

11

long and he was only too well aware the effect the sight of it was having on me.

'Now you've been properly broken, Sassie,' he grinned. He patted my cheek and then kissed it. I simply stood there, shaking all over, my knees weak. 'Ready for some more?' he asked. I think I nodded, though I don't suppose it would really have made much difference whether I had or not. He turned me around again and I bent forward, powerless to resist even had I not been so rigidly and helplessly bound . . .

Detective Constable (Acting Sergeant) Tim 'Geordie' Walker stared moodily into the bottom of the empty coffee mug and leaned back against the rear of the bridgehouse. Outside, beyond the plexiglass screens that kept the spray and the winds at bay when the weather was far less clement than it was on this strangely calm night, the first fingers of a new dawn were appearing on the eastern horizon.

'What do you mean?' he asked. 'That's it? That's nothing – we haven't done anything except chug up and down and around in circles in this same bit of ocean for the past several hours.'

Angus Frearson, the aging master of the trawler *Essie*, shrugged and began turning the wheel to port.

'We've done as much as we can for the moment, laddie,' he announced. He jabbed a finger at the small radar screen. 'That little blip there is the *Mollie Blair*,' he said. 'She'll take over from us for a few hours, whilst we head back and take on some more fuel.'

'But we should have plenty of fuel left,' Geordie pointed out. 'These things are designed to be at sea for days on end, not hours.'

'Aye, that's true enough,' Frearson agreed. 'But we might as well take advantage to top up. Never know when we might need full tanks.'

'But why now?' said Geordie with frustration.

'Because,' Frearson replied, 'we've been around these waters for long enough. If they are watching us from over on yon islands – and our detectors say they're radar sweeping regularly – then let's not do anything to arouse their suspicions. We'll just leave the nets out and make a slow headway back towards the main islands and let the lads on the *Mollie* listen out for your friends. After we've refuelled, we can come back up – from a different direction, probably – and resume trawling on a different stretch over the other side, but still within range.'

'Why not just call up the cavalry and go right on in?' Geordie snapped. 'We know that sub was unloading something, so why not go in and find out what? They won't be delivering rice puddings by submarine, so whatever they were carrying should be enough to charge them with something worthwhile.'

'Possibly,' Frearson agreed. 'But there's always the bigger picture to consider, son, believe me.' He brought the wheel back to dead ahead once more and peered through the screen ahead of him. 'This operation – the main operation, that is, not just our little jaunt tonight – has been going on a long time and our lords and masters won't thank us for maybe just blowing the lot for the sake of a few bags of heroin or cocaine.'

'You think that's all they'd have been carrying?' Geordie challenged. 'Seems like a lot of trouble to smuggle in a few kilos of narcotics.'

'Who's to say it was only a *few* kilos?' Frearson countered. 'Could be many millions of pounds worth and probably is, but that's not the point, is it? We grab whatever they've just delivered and aye, I'll grant you we'll save a lot of misery, but our friends over there'll simply find another way in and the whole

13

thing starts over.' He paused. 'Besides, we don't know it's simply drugs. Could well be there's far more involved, which is why your pal Colin has gone in there to have a snoop around. My orders are not to move unless we hear from him, or unless those orders are changed directly from main base.'

'So we've wasted a complete night?' Geordie groaned. Frearson raised one white and bushy eyebrow.

'Maybe,' he said. 'And then again, maybe not. Let's wait and see how young Colin and your other pals got on, shall we?'

'I thought you wanted to keep me completely to yourself, mistress?' Alex stared at Amaarini through eyes made round by surprise, but the tall Askarlarni female's beautiful features had resumed their normal impassive, impenetrable state, her hooded eyes deep and unblinking. In her tight, shiny black catsuit and high-heeled boots, she presented an imposing figure. And yet the power she radiated, Alex realised, came from far beyond her mere external appearance, which Amaarini maintained solely in order to present the sort of image the island's patrons expected.

'It will not hurt you to earn your keep, Jangles' she replied, silkily. 'We have two particularly large parties of guests arriving today and we would have been far from slack even without either of them, so all the slaves will have to work even harder in order not to disappoint them. Besides, I have many duties that will keep me busy for a while and I should not like you growing idle and fat.' She continued briskly. 'Now, stand up and place your arms by your sides. At least I'm sparing you the usual routine of being pawed about by the grooms.'

Alex rose as reluctantly as she dared, only too well aware that the alien woman's moods could change

14

even quicker than the notoriously unreliable North Sea above and outside. The small bells hanging from her nipple rings tinkled as her full breasts swayed in time with her movements and, as she automatically lowered her eyes in the accepted slave manner, she found herself staring down at her recently aquired body with even more distaste than when she had first seen it.

The one who called himself Doctor Keith Lineker had perfected his science to an incredible degree, she had to admit, but to what purpose? Her own body, vertebrae shattered by her fall into that steep gully, had long since been destroyed; cremated, so they had told her, by grieving family and colleagues who believed the evidence of their eyes when the corpse was returned to Mainland. And yet the real her was now forced to live on like this.

In many ways, of course, her new body was a great improvement on the original: taller, stronger, fitter, her features now would be the envy of even the most beautiful fashion model, but although she inhabited it, this stunning creation was hers for one reason only and even then they could control many of its functions by means of one of those devilish remote control units.

Her pain level could be raised or lowered at the press of a button, on the whim of whoever held the device, and her voice could be switched off similarly, rendering her either mute, or else capable of making only those awful whinneying sounds. Also, her new eyes did not blink and she could not cry – tear ducts were unnecessary in any case now, something to do with the fact that her lenses were only part biological and contained some mechanical components.

At least now, she thought, she could see things in colour again, unlike the majority of the other Jenny-

Anns, whose vision remained in monochrome only. The colour was not perfect – she was reminded of early Hollywood colour films – but at least it *was* colour.

Perhaps the worst aspect, from Alex's point of view as a formerly independent and strong-willed woman, was that it was not just the level of her pain threshold that could be governed from outside this body. Her pleasure threshold was equally slave to Lineker's diabolical science and the little control box, so that the simple flicking of a button could reduce her to a level where even the slightest touch of her breasts, or the stroking of her buttocks or shoulders, would begin a process deep within her that would normally require a combination of both desire and patient response.

'Open your mouth, pony-girl.' Amaarini's curt order broke into Alex's brief reverie and she found herself dropping her jaw without thinking. A moment later, Amaarini was reaching past her lips, fitting the cunning tongue plate across her lower molars, adjusting the clamp screws that kept it in place and rendered intelligible speech impossible. Alex wrinkled her nose and grunted.

'Yes, I know you don't like the tongue snaffle,' Amaarini said. 'None of you ponies do, but we don't want to take chances. Your voice will be de-activated, naturally, but we don't want to arouse curiosity. After all, most of your fellow J-As don't have that new voice technology, so the guests tend to expect what they've grown used to. There, that's got it. You can close your mouth again until it's time for your bit.'

The night before, Amaarini had finally removed Alex's boots, but now she began refitting them to her helpless slave's long legs, drawing them high up to the tops of her thighs and lacing them tightly from bottom to top, so that they now clung to each limb like an additional skin. They also lent extra support to muscles that now had to contend with the grossly elevated position of her feet and the additional weight of the thick sole and heel combinations in their cunningly hoof-shaped forms, that were complete down to the metal horseshoes with which they were permanently shod.

'I shall teach you to be proud of your new status,' Amaarini smiled, as she moved round to check the tightness of Alex's girth corset and its attendant web of harness strapping. 'To be a pony-girl full time is the ultimate achievement among slaves here. At least now you are admired properly and there are strict rules as to your treatment.' She moved back around in front of Alex and leaned close to her, her lips brushing Alex's own.

'I really don't understand some of your fellow humans,' she said. 'I can understand why to look at something as fine as you now are should excite feelings and passions, but some of their other fetishes really defy all logic and are most uncivilised.' She let out a low snicker as she stepped back.

'For instance,' she continued, 'why should wrapping a beautiful female in layers of rubber, even covering her face and then filling her mouth with a gag, excite a human male to orgasm, eh? We have men who come here who do little more than that, who can achieve all the satisfaction they need simply by keeping a female cocooned and in bondage. Be thankful you do not have to endure such torture.

'Or are you perhaps like one or two of the female humans who come here, eh Jangles?' Her eyes narrowed as she fixed Alex with an unnerving stare. 'Perhaps you would *enjoy* such treatment, though why anyone would willingly submit to be treated so

17

is beyond my understanding.' Alex shook her head fiercely, her eyes wide with consternation at the suggestion.

'No?' Amaarini smiled and Alex began to relax again. 'Well, you humans are a strange race, so nothing would surprise me. Fancy volunteering to spend a day at a time with your jaws stretched around a rubber pear, unable to see and available for anyone to use as they see fit, even down to whipping you. Unbelievable!' She shook her head, her mane of dark hair shimmering.

'Bridle time,' she announced. Alex barely stifled a sigh of resignation, but at least the posture collar would mean that she no longer felt compelled to stare down at her hairless sex, bulging between the V-straps of her lower body harness; the rings in her labia glinting like tiny eyes, proud and ready for the attachment of even more bells, if required.

Carefully, Amaarini lifted the intricate arrangement of leather and metal over Alex's head, positioning her plumed ponytail in its tight cylindrical clasp so that it rose between the split crown straps and cascaded down over her shoulders. The head harness settled so that one large blinker sat alongside each eye, restricting Alex's vision to straight ahead. Amaarini quickly tightened all the small buckles that drew it tightly about her forehead, cheeks and chin, finishing with the three rear straps that closed the collar itself about her throat.

'Beautiful,' Amaarini said. 'And more beautiful with the knowledge of what you once were, I think.' She paused for a moment, gazing into Alex's face. 'You must have been quite clever, I suppose,' she conceded. 'Detective sergeant and still so young, but then it was the foolishness of youth that brought you to your fate, was it not?'

18

Alex realised she would not have tried to contradict that statement even had she been able to. It had been rash, an act of bravado, parachuting on to the island as she had done. It had been this complete disregard for her own safety, combined with gross carelessness, that had led to the accident that in its turn had brought her to this.

'Arms behind, please,' Amaarini ordered, with unusual politeness. Alex folded her mitted and gloved arms behind her back and stood whilst Amaarini drew the tight little pouch up over her elbows and secured it to the back of her collar. Her arms were now caught up in the pouch, forearm to forearm, her shoulders drawn back so that her breats were thrust into even more prominence.

'Yes,' Amaarini said, nodding approvingly, 'I can understand why a male should desire to have you dancing on the end of his cock or at the end of his whip. If I was a male I think I should want to have you on my organ quite a lot.' She smiled again.

'Males,' she said, almost resignedly. 'They are not really so different in any species, I think. Even our own leader is eventually showing signs of yielding to his baser nature, did you know that? No, of course you didn't, Jangles, but I shall tell you.' She turned away and opened a drawer, taking out a long black dildo, the sides of which, Alex saw with a shudder, were covered in a myriad of elongated rubber pimples.

'Legs apart,' her captor instructed. Alex shuffled to obey, knowing that resistance was futile and would lead only to punishments far worse than having to endure even this monstrous phallus stimulating her at every step. She groaned slightly as the head of the thing was pressed between her puffy nether lips and gave silent thanks for the fact that her pleasure level was currently set at its minimum, for otherwise, she knew, she would further add to her humiliation by coming even before the cock was fully within her.

'Our leader, Jangles –' Amaarini was saying, as she began working the length up into Alex, '– has decided that he needs to procreate again and, as you now know, many of our males have interbred with both human females and you cloned ones, in order to produce a better blood line.

'Until now, all the clones have been fully female, so the results have been easily predictable.' She pressed the flanged base of the dildo firmly against Alex's denuded mound and quickly snapped across the leather triangle that would prevent its expulsion.

'However, in the past weeks, the doctor has added two quite interesting newcomers to our stable; two who were originally male and now find themselves in fully functioning female clone bodies. This, as you may imagine, has come as something of a shock to the two subjects in question.' She stepped back again and Alex saw that she was now grinning maliciously.

'Quite a shock,' she repeated, shaking her head slightly. 'However, the shock will be even greater for one of them when he or she discovers that she is carrying the offspring of Rekoli Maajuk. She has been told it is to happen, but of course she probably refuses to accept that it is really possible, so only when her belly starts to swell will we be able to gauge her true reaction.

'An interesting sociological experiment, Jangles, don't you think?' Amaarini said. 'I almost feel sorry for poor Tammy, especially as her arrival here was not of her own volition . . . Perhaps it would have been easier if her original body had been drowned and swept out to sea, but then few of us can choose our fate, can we, my sweet little horse-girl?'

* * *

The moonlight was filtering through the high, broken cloud as Colin turned the pony-girl Jess round to replace her bit. As he reached out, she obediently opened her mouth to receive the rubber-covered tube, but he hesitated.

'Are you happy here, Jessie?' he asked. She blinked, her huge dark eyes two pools in which tiny sparks gleamed.

'Of course, master,' she answered, her voice low and husky. Colin shook his head and stood back, studying her carefully, although by now he thought he knew every inch of her magnificent body and beautiful face. He caught the flicker of a smile crossing her lips and realised that she was enjoying his appreciation of her.

'You are very beautiful, Jess,' he murmured. She made no reply this time, simply continuing to stand there, perched on the bizarre hoof boots, her arms bound up behind her, her waist so impossibly narrow within the confines of the broad girth corset, her hips so invitingly wide, her breasts so impossibly firm and high for their size.

In truth, he realised, she was no more beautiful than his own Sassie and yet there was something about this dark-haired pony-girl that was so totally different. Sassie had quickly taken to the bit – had instinctively adopted the correct demeanour – but there was something so much more natural about the way Jessie carried herself and appeared to be so proud of her harness. It was, Colin thought with a sudden insight, as if she had been born to that harness and knew nothing of any life without it.

Perhaps that was part of the magic she had exerted over Andrew Lachan. The Scottish billionaire had clearly been besotted with her, even naming his ill-fated yacht in which he had apparently died after her. There was, of course, Colin knew, no hard and fast proof that this was the same girl – even though there was plenty of evidence to suggest it was – but now, standing so close to her in the near darkness of a late Shetlands Islands evening, there was no doubt in his own mind.

The file on Lachan showed a man used to having his own way; single minded, brilliantly innovative and successful beyond the dreams of most other mortals and yet even his sort of money could not usually buy total subservience and devotion. Even Sara, who had served him so devotedly in her professional life and who had, at least for a while, thought herself in love with him, could not have provided Lachan with the sort of total power that any man would surely feel in the presence of Jessie.

Colin glanced furtively back to where the gig stood, leaning forward, its shafts in the grass. He was convinced that one of the ornamental brass studs was actually a concealed microphone – their hosts here on these islands evidently liked to monitor what individual guests might be up to – and there was no way of knowing what its effective range might be. The cart, from which he had earlier unhitched Jess, was at least forty metres from them, but the air was unusually still and quiet, with few other sounds to disrupt whatever they said.

Besides, he thought, there was no way of telling whether or not there was a second microphone concealed on Jessie herself. Despite the overall brevity of her outfit, the various harness straps, girth corset and thigh-high hoof boots were covered in enough studs, rings and fittings – any one of which could be a bugging device. He decided to keep the conversation as neutral as possible, asking only the sort of questions a novice newcomer might be expected to ask.

'How long have you been a pony-girl, Jessie?' Her eyes rolled slightly, her full lips twitching.

'A long time, master,' she replied. The twitching became a smile. 'All my life, perhaps,' she added. 'All the life that matters to me, anyway. I was reborn as a pony-girl, I think.'

'And what were you before you were "reborn", Jess?' The smile remained.

'Unhappy, I think, master.' She seemed to consider this briefly. 'Yes, I was unhappy, but now I am very happy.' She spoke in the simplistic way of a child, or of a foreigner unused to English and yet, Colin's trained ear deduced, there was no trace of any accent, nor of any hesitation over the choice of words. If Jess spoke in a child-like fashion, it was as natural to her as a Cockney accent would be to an East Ender in London.

'You are happy because you are a pony-girl, is that it?' Did she raise her chin just a fraction higher?

'I am happy because I am a *beautiful* pony-girl,' she replied, 'and because my beauty as a pony-girl pleases my masters and mistresses.'

'Do you like to please, Jess?'

'That is what a pony-girl does, master.' Was there just a hint of amusement in her tone now? 'A pony-girl serves and pleases.'

'And fucks?'

'If that is what a master or mistress desires, yes.'

'And you like to fuck, Jessie?' Now there was more than a hint of amusement beyond her simple smile.

'Yes, master. Yes, I like to fuck.' Yes, Colin thought, the memory of their coupling only a few minutes old and already only too vividly burned in his brain, yes, Jessie certainly liked to do that. He looked again at her perfect breasts, rising and falling slowly in time with her slow, steady breathing –

a total contrast with the way in which his own lungs still fought to bring in sufficient oxygen to bring his body systems back to some sort of normality. Despite this, he could feel himself stirring again, his semi-limp organ beginning to grow as if of its own volition.

'Would you like me to fuck you again?' he asked hoarsely, reaching out to gently touch her swollen nipples. Jess let out a low sigh as his fingers touched the engorged teats.

'Oh yes, master,' she breathed. Almost imperceptibly she shifted her legs wider apart, the shod hooves scraping at the earth beneath them the only betrayal of her movement, the odour of her musk and arousal strong in Colin's nostrils . . .

Time was passing at an agonising crawl for Sol. The young groom, usually so arrogant, so quick to take advantage of the helpless pony-girls in his charge, was now getting the opportunity of seeing life from the other side of the bridle and he was not enjoying a single second of it. Things would have been bad enough even without the presence of the Charles woman, and now he was beginning to believe they could not get any worse, as she gleefully accepted the opportunity to take her revenge for his treatment of her during the short time she had once spent in the stables herself, as the result of losing a foolish bet with one of the other VIP visitors.

He had been careless, Sol knew, and he had expected to be punished for that, especially as his actions had led to the loss of one of the Andean girls intended for use in the doctor's cloning experiments. But he had done nothing that the other grooms had not done a thousand or more times before, and the girl Samba, docile up until then, had surprised him with the ferocity and speed of her attack so it really had not been his fault. A severe reprimand and maybe a suspension of his privileges would surely have been more than enough, but no, Rekoli Maajuk had seen fit to make an example of him – probably as a sop to the greasy South American fellow whose money seemed to have elevated him to a status well above that ever enjoyed by guests in the past.

A month in the stables, experiencing exactly the same conditions as the pony-girls he had previously held such power over. Sol had protested at the seeming injustice of the sentence, but the leader had been adamant and that haughty bitch Amaarini had taken great delight in seeing to it that his punishment was executed with ruthless efficiency and then, apparently, had been more than happy to accept a bid from the Charles cow to have almost exclusive rights to him for the next week or so.

Fiona Charles. Sol winced at the very echo of her name and wondered just what the millions of fans of the beautiful darling of television magazine programmes would think if they knew what their goddess was really like. If only he had known what was in the future, he thought, he most certainly would have given her a much easier ride during her own time as a pony-girl. Hindsight, he was just beginning to realise, was a perfect science, but of absolutely no practical use.

Sol leaned back against the wall of his stall; he could not sit, as the short chain from his collar had been locked to a metal staple on a level with his head, allowing him sufficient scope to take but a single step in any direction and no more. Not that he enjoyed walking – not with his feet and legs now encased in these awful hoof boots, arching his instep until he was forced to perch virtually on tip-toe and clamping the muscles of his calves and thighs in an unyielding embrace.

Around his waist he now wore the same leather corset girth that enhanced the already superb figures of the pony-girls, cinched deliberately tightly so that he could scarcely breathe. He had no breasts to pass through the circular straps that were used to force out the girls' ample charms, but Fiona had insisted that his nipples be pierced and ringed, and now they were hung with the same regulation-style bells that heralded the approach of his female counterparts.

His penis, thanks to periodic injections, remained permanently erect, but encased in a tightly-laced leather sheath and either held tightly against the stiffer leather triangle that covered his stomach by a series of four straps that kept it tautly upright, and two further straps keeping his testicles separated so that every step produced a persistant pressure on them, or else, as was the case at the moment, fitted inside a metal prosthesis, in turn covered with rubber, that made his already impressive endowment seem even bigger, yet totally prevented any sensation or enjoyment when he was required to use it to service the various females Fiona selected for him.

Behind his back, his arms were drawn up uselessly and uncomfortably – the individual sleeves having been laced tighter than he would ever have considered lacing in the case of the female ponies – and then bent so that they fitted inside the pouch that kept them in the middle of his back.

From the neck upwards, his bridle arrangement was standard, but Fiona had added a few refinements of her own. Firstly, she had ordered his head shaved, leaving just a single band of hair running from front to back over the centre of his head in what most people mistakenly referred to as a Mohican cut, but which Sol knew was really a style favoured by either the Mohawk or Huron Indians of old North America.

Into this had been woven extensions and the entirety had now been bleached, providing a mane-like effect. The areas around his eyes had then been painted black and his lips glossed, using the same robust cosmetics that he had spent so many hours applying to his female charges in the past. His ears had also been pierced and ringed and more bells added. Then had come the bridle itself, but not before Fiona had seen to it that a spiked tongue snaffle had been clamped over his teeth and one of the peculiar rubber snout extensions fitted to his lower features to produce the pony-like appearance so many of the more discerning visitors found appealing on the pony-girls who provided their usual fare.

Now, finally bitted, the straps tight around fore-head and cheeks, blinkers blinding his peripheral vision, all Sol could do was stand and wait, shifting his weight occasionally from hoof to hoof, wondering what else Fiona Charles was planning for him and not daring to even try to imagine the limits of her cruel ingenuity. In his back passage, the stubby butt plug which held his white tail in place seemed to be growing larger with every passing minute; his pierced nipples throbbed as the weight of the rings and bells kept trying to distend them further and his lungs ached with the effort of breathing.

A month, he thought, bitterly. An entire month of this. It was surely more than he would be able to bear. Already he felt as if he had been like this for a week and yet, despite the lack of clock or watch, he knew only too well that not even twenty-four hours of his torment had passed. Miserably, he hung his head as far as the rigid neck collar would allow and, had he been able to, Sol, the first resident pony-boy in the underground stables of the island of Ailsa Ness, would have wept tears of frustration and despair.

Two

Colin stood frozen in the doorway, staring at the scene on the huge bed before him. Only the fact that he already knew their identities told him that he was watching Millie and Anna, for both females were completely covered in tight rubber catsuits, their heads and faces hidden beneath hoods and masks, with added blindfolds covering even the usual eye apertures.

The two lay entwined together, harnesses about their hips keeping them pressed tightly there, groin to groin, and their arms wrapped about each other's torsos and cuffed in an unbreakable embrace. Even their faces seemed joined at the mouth, though Colin could not see how, for they seemed locked in a permanent kiss. Only when he stepped closer did he see the thick flange between them and the thin straps that held each end of a double gag upon which they sucked from time to time.

He guessed that their ears had probably been plugged beneath the thick latex helmets, for they showed not the slightest indication that they knew anyone had entered the room, and so he continued to stand for some while, watching the languid contortions – the easy, rippling sex-play – as the deeply rooted double dildo and the tight bondage continued to do their work on the captive couple.

'Quite beautiful, don't you think?'

Colin started guiltily. He had been so engrossed in the bizarre tableau that he had not heard Celia's approach, the thick piled carpeting in the corridor muffling the sound of even her spiked heels. He turned away from the bed and leaned towards Celia, lowering his voice.

'Are they okay like that?' he hissed. 'They haven't been like that since we went off earlier, surely?'

Celia smiled, a curiously lopsided expression. 'Yes they are and yes they have,' she replied. She stepped past Colin and stood over her two victims, who remained completely oblivious to her presence as they had been of Colin's. 'So sweet, don't you agree?' She turned and cast a sly look back at him. 'Or do you have anything against two women being able to satisfy themselves without the need of a man?'

'Er, no,' Colin muttered. 'No, whatever . . . I mean, well, it takes all sorts and well, we're all here anyway, aren't we?'

'Yes, we are,' Celia agreed. She looked back at the two girls, who had paused in their exertions and now lay inert, only the slow rise and fall of their tightly encased breasts betraying the fact that they were more than simply rubber statues.

'Which one would you like, then?' Celia asked. Colin swallowed and almost managed to keep the surprised look off his face. 'Millie being . . . well, otherwise involved, shall we say, perhaps I'll take her to my room and you can have Ingrid. I'd keep her in her rubber, though, if you want a really receptive reaction. It would appear she's a natural for all this.'

'Um, but what about Sassie?'

'You left her down in the stables, didn't you?'

'Yes, but I thought –'

'Then don't think,' Celia cut him short. 'I suppose I should have explained the rules here,' she went on.

30

'It's sort of taken for granted that the moment an outside girl comes in and goes into harness, she stays that way until you take her away again. Don't worry,' she grinned, seeing the alarm registering in Colin's eyes. 'She'll be quite safe and I think it will be quite an experience for her.'

'But the grooms –'

'Know what they're doing and yes, they'll probably make use of her, the same way they do all the pony-girls down there, unless you gave instructions to the contrary, that is?' Colin shook his head.

'No,' he admitted. 'I didn't think it was necessary.' He made as if to start for the door. 'Perhaps I should go back down there and –' Celia put out a hand and grasped his arm.

'How long were you out with that Jess girl?' she asked, raising one eyebrow. 'I think –' she continued, not waiting for the reply, '– it might just be a little too late for that now. But don't fret – I suspect young Sassie may well be having the time of her life right now. For a novice, she's quite something, you know. The way she just slips into role the moment she even smells a leather harness is quite remarkable.'

'But what if she isn't? Enjoying it, I mean.' Celia moved back to the entwined girls and reached down to begin the task of disengaging them.

'Don't kid yourself,' she said, hiding the grin on her face from him. 'You may be her master, but when a pony-girl like that gets the scent in her nostrils, one good cock is much the same as another. Maybe better, in some cases, but you probably wouldn't understand that just yet.'

The man known as Rekoli Maajuk to the Askarlarnis and as Richard Major to the rest of the world, stood before the full length mirror admiring his reflection

31

and the way in which the overhead lights shone on the tight-fitting black leather body suit he now wore. Behind him, Keith Lineker, known among their people as Ikothi Leenuk, looked far less approving.

'Why not just let me inseminate the creature artificially, Rekoli?' he urged. 'All this pantomime is so – so . . . well, so human. The worst of human, in fact.' Major's lips twitched slightly and he shifted his gaze so that he could see his long-time friend and colleague in the glass.

'Indulge me, Ikothi,' he said, quietly. 'Don't forget, I have been studying these people as long as you, but unlike you I have concentrated on the psyche rather than the physiology. Perhaps a little of it has rubbed off on me. Besides –' he added, smoothing back his dark hair and reaching for the black leather mask, '– the Tammy creature is a slightly different case, is she not?'

'Well, considering she was a male human and is now a female Jenny-Ann, most certainly she is different,' Lineker agreed. He grimaced slightly. 'And I know you only too well to know that's why you've selected her for breeding with.'

'But there are no biological reasons why she should not breed just as effectively and efficiently as any of the true females, is there? You said as much yourself.'

'No physical reasons at all, Rekoli,' the doctor agreed, nodding. 'Tammy's body is just as female as any of the others, just as fertile when allowed to be and just,' he added, pausing for the merest instant, '– as desirable, at least to those who have this whole human fascination with all this nonsense.'

'Perhaps you should give this nonsense, as you call it, a try, Ikothi.' Major paused, the mask held between his hands, and turned back into the room. 'It won't harm you, and we're keeping the pure female genetic line alive separately. A few more strapping boys and girls with your genes in them would be useful for the overall gene pool in any case, don't you think?'

'To produce anything that ends up as playthings for the debauched wretches who come here is something that I find abhorrent, as you know,' Lineker retorted, acidly. 'The purpose of my research is to find the solution to the genetic problems that affect our own females, but I can accept that the clone body programme has its benefits financially.'

'Our debauched human guests provide our main source of income here,' Major said. 'So yes, you could say it has benefits.'

'That I accept,' Lineker continued. 'However, I could not face the thought of siring any offspring that could end up in those stables, or pinned underneath a sweating, heaving human animal the way they do. When I finally sire children,' he added, 'it will be with a pure blooded Askarlarni girl and they will be pure blooded Askarlarnis, with all the attributes that honour brings.'

'Like dying in their twenties, unless you then find them a cloned host body to transfer to,' Major countered. 'Though of course –' he added, one side of his mouth twisting again, '– you would ensure that they breed first from their original pure bodies, wouldn't you?'

'You yourself just mentioned the pure line we must continue,' Lineker snapped back. 'Eventually I shall solve the mystery and there will be no further need for a production line of clones, not for our own people, nor to sate the base lusts of these damned humans.'

'But for now we need them, Ikothi, and we need also to produce the half-breed children in order to

33

extend our numbers and ultimate influence. We both know the half-breeds, cloned or naturally produced, are fitter and stronger even than we are, let alone a human counterpart.'

'Yes, of course they are!' Lineker sounded irritable. 'And the ones I am producing for our Latin friend will likely be stronger still.' He turned towards the door, pausing to look back as Major began raising the masking hood to his head. 'I just hope we don't live to regret our involvement with Señor Valerez, Rekoli. He may be human, but he is both cunning and vicious.'

'And we are Askarlarnis, Ikothi,' Major replied easily, 'which makes us more cunning, if maybe not more vicious. Return to your work, my old friend, and produce us the finest, strongest, fittest little band of Jenny-Anns you have yet produced. Let us whet the good Señor's appetite for him yet again and let him see that his efforts in bringing over those replacement girls were not wasted.'

'We are leaving these to their basic brains still?'

'The first ones, yes,' Major said. 'They function well enough for simple, uncomplicated tasks, after all. We'll leave the further modifications until after Valerez has satisfied himself that we are giving him what he wants. And then –' he said, smiling properly for the first time, '– we'll give him that little bit extra, something he neither wants nor expects, eh Ikothi?'

Had he been able to, Andrew Lachan would have screamed out loud at the horror of his situation, but a combination of tongue snaffle and one of the newly perfected vocal control units had ensured his silence throughout his ordeal, other than a few brief interludes when he had been permitted to talk with his beloved Jessie.

A brief attempt at resistance having brought swift retribution in the form of a terrible whipping that only his recently aquired and thoroughly unwanted Jenny-Ann body could have withstood, Andrew was now reduced to sulking in the far corner of the stable he now shared with Jess, hardly able to look at her now, only too well aware that he had been created in her image and that, apart from the few recent improvements to voice and eyes, they were as alike as two peas in a pod.

It was a cruel irony that was not wasted on Andrew and one that he knew, also, was not accidental. These people – how could he not have realised the truth behind their facade before? – were deliberately reminding him of the reason for his downfall and it was a reminder that would live with him every day of the rest of his now extended life, long after he was parted from Jess herself, as surely he must be eventually.

For the present it suited their spiteful purpose to leave Andrew with the pony-girl who had first stolen his heart and then led him, albeit unwittingly, into the foolhardy venture that had led to the deaths of the men he had hired to help him steal her away and to his own, even more hideous fate: his mind now locked forever inside this beautiful body that could no more allow him to satisfy his lusts than it could fail to raise the desires of any male who gazed upon it.

Bambi was the name they had given him, the only name by which he was to be addressed from now on. To his captors, Andrew Lachan was no more, as surely as the outside world had been led to believe that he had perished in an explosion aboard the luxury yacht he had named after his beloved pony-girl. No matter what he said, the grooms and Amaarini herself, who delighted in visiting him regularly, refused to acknowledge his original identity and personality, treating him exactly the same as he knew they must have treated Jess during all her time here. A time, he now realised, that extended many years beyond anything he would have previously believed credible.

'You'll believe it all right,' Amaarini had hissed at him, when Andrew had refused to give any credence to her claim. 'A hundred years from now, a hundred and fifty years from now, maybe even two or three hundred years – yes, you'll believe it, beautiful Bambi.'

'The nearest thing to immortality, that's what we've granted you,' she had added. 'That's something that all your money could never have bought you, the same as all your money could never have bought you Jessie. Well, Bambi, now you not only have Jessie, you could *be* Jessie!'

She had then taken the two of them, identically hoofed and harnessed, and paraded them before the big display mirror out in the stable's concourse, a performance which she had repeated on an almost daily basis ever since. The two of them were sometimes even worked together as a pair, a not uncommon practice in a place where there were several groups of identical clones, passed off to the visitors as twins, triplets or quads, who gladly paid extra for the novelty.

So far, however, Andrew/Bambi had been spared the ultimate degradation, though he/she knew that the moment would not be postponed indefinitely. The guests who had paid for the services of the delectable Bambi, with or without her 'twin', had been carefully selected from that element who, peculiarly, did not yearn for actual intercourse – contenting themselves instead with the ritual and the control, all the while with Bambi's virgin female sex locked safely beneath a protective leather gusset, a special trophy awaiting exactly the right claimant at exactly the right time. Even the dildo that she had worn during the race session had been specially chosen so that its girth and length were not sufficient to tear her.

'Why don't they just get it over and done with?' he had whined to Jess, during one of the interludes when he had been permitted the freedom to talk to her. Jess had stared at him with her big, soft eyes – the same big, soft eyes that now stared out from Bambi's own beautiful face – and shook her head, sadly.

'You need to understand the way they think,' she replied. 'Once it's done, it's done. Yes, they know you'll hate it, but then afterwards, once the initial shock wears off, it won't seem that bad after all and though you'll never enjoy it the way a genetic female would, you'll learn to tolerate it. Your body has been designed to respond, regardless of what happens up here.' She tapped her forehead with one permanently mitted hand.

'Oh yes,' she continued, seeing the disbelief in his expression. 'You'll have orgasms, the same way the rest of us do, whether you want them or not. Who knows – give it a few decades and you may really enjoy it and they know that, too. The longer they keep you waiting, the more you'll start to think and act like a pony-girl. But they won't wait that long to break you in, I don't think.

'No, your virginity will be sold for a good price, as all ours were once, mine included. My only regret is that I lost mine long before you first came to this place.' Her features softened and she held out her hand to his cheek.

'I know that you loved me when you were my master and I truly worshipped you, too. If only you could have accepted things as they were.' She lowered

37

her eyes and half turned away. 'I doubt I shall ever stop worshipping you,' she continued, huskily. 'Only now you can never be my master again and for that fact I would cry, were I able to.'

Andrew-now-Bambi understood that feeling only too well, for although his eyes could shed no tears, inside he was crying – crying for everything he had lost, crying for everything he could never have, nor ever do again. He stared down at the protective leather triangle, with its decorative studs, framed between the twin mounds of his formidable breasts and began to tremble, partly with rage, partly with frustration, partly now with a cold horror of realisation that he was now, physically at least, a woman and that soon men would pay to do to this body as he had paid to do to Jess's.

And, unless there was some miracle in the meantime, this beautiful epitome of feminine sexuality would not be treated with the same reverence that he had once given to its twin.

Anna swayed unsteadily as she walked ahead of Colin along the short length of passageway between Celia's quarters and his own. The fluorescent lighting panels above produced a curious rippling effect on the black latex that covered her from head to toe and he was reminded of a lizard in the sunlight, except that no lizard he had ever seen had had buttocks like this, nor legs as perfectly muscled, the high heels emphasising their length and sleekness.

Inside his room, he closed the door behind them and checked that the locking catch was in place. In the centre of the carpet, Anna had turned to face him, eyes glinting through the thin lenses that were part of the tightly-fitting hood, the only openings in it beneath her nostrils and over her mouth – though this latter was currently covered by the broad padded strap that Celia had used to retain the gag that now filled the tall Norwegian girl's mouth in place of the incredible penis gag arrangement she had previously been sharing with Millie.

Further down, two more rounded apertures in the latex allowed her nipples to protrude, the stretched fabric gripping them and thrusting them into even greater relief than normal. Between the tops of her thighs an ovaloid opening pushed her sex lips into an inviting pout, beneath which the smooth black surface showed glistening evidence of her continued arousal.

'Shall I take the gag off?' Anna's hands were not bound and Colin realised she could have removed it herself, but he knew she would not attempt that in his presence. She shrugged her shoulders and then gave a barely perceptible shake of her head.

'You'd rather I left it in, eh?' No, he realised, that wasn't how it was supposed to be done. He swiftly corrected his error. 'Well of course,' he said, 'it doesn't really matter what you want, but I think I'd prefer a silent slave, at least for the moment.' He paused and considered for a moment, whilst Anna stood passively, her eyes never leaving him.

'I want to see you play with yourself – there,' he added, pointing a finger at her exposed sex. Her eyes did not seem to flicker as she stretched down one hand, one latex-sheathed finger extended and carefully inserted it into herself. 'Slowly, Ingrid,' he said, using the name they had agreed Anna would go under whilst they were out here on the islands.

He heard her give a small gasp from behind her gag and felt himself beginning to stir as her labia suddenly gaped open, the finger producing a low slurping sound as her juices began to flow out and around it.

'Stop!' Anna obeyed instantly, remaining frozen, the finger still inside her. 'Take it out and come over here.' Colin began rapidly unfastening the clips that held the front of his tunic top together. 'Wait,' he instructed, as she drew close. He could smell her clearly now: sweat, latex, musk, arousal. She would, he knew, do anything he told her to.

'Take the damned gag off yourself,' he commanded, willing his fingers to stop trembling. With a superb grace, Anna reached up and behind her, her own fingers seeking the buckle at the back of her head. Colin returned his attention to his breeches, forgetting his boots in his haste.

'Allow me, master.' The gag was already out and the black-suited figure was bending before him, hands quickly busy, unfastening the heavy footwear and removing each boot in turn. His breeches fell about his ankles and he stepped out of them with some difficulty, managing only because he was able to use her shoulders to steady himself and because she helped by manouevring the tight leather over each foot as he raised it.

'Show me what you can do, slave,' he whispered. Anna needed no further urging. Still on her knees, she reached up, one hand encircling his stiffening penis, the other cupping his balls. He shivered at the rubberised touch and closed his eyes, his own fingers gripping her shoulders even more firmly. His shaft finished stiffening with amazing rapidity, the semi-translucent flesh stretching to reveal a web of blue veining, his entire groin throbbing as she began manipulating his genitalia with a gentle yet insistent expertise.

He opened his eyes again and looked down, just in time to see her red lips opening, her face moving forward, the purplish knob disappearing as she sucked him into her mouth, tilting her head slightly and raising her eyes as if seeking his approval. Colin groaned.

'Yes, that's good, Ingrid, very good.' He took a deep breath, willing himself back in control of his reflexes, but he knew it would be ultimately a losing battle. For a moment longer he wrestled with his thoughts – whether to try to establish his position again, or whether to yield to the inevitable.

Anna sucked again, the rough surface of her tongue running along the underside of his shaft and inevitability won. With a strangled cry, Colin yielded, grabbing at her head to pull it closer as he exploded into her willing throat, jerking uncontrollably as she continued to suck every last drop from him, her hands now around behind him, cupping and grasping his quivering buttocks.

He heard himself cry out, felt for a brief moment that his legs must surely collapse beneath him, and then he was back in control again, thrusting her face away from him, hauling her upright and pushing her back across the room until she stumbled and fell back across the wide bed, legs spread wide, her sex open and inviting. Colin stared down, first at her, then at himself. His erection was undiminished, his cock as stiff as ever it had been.

'Fuck you, you horny little bitch,' he hissed. Anna raised her legs, spiked heels pointing almost in opposite directions. He saw her tongue emerge to run along between her other lips, her hands now reaching up for him, grasping him, guiding him towards her and then he was inside her, entering easily, but then immediately finding himself gripped there as she flexed her vaginal muscles.

'Yes,' she whispered, as he leaned over her. 'Fuck me, master. You fuck your slave good.' She gave a

41

small gasp and then a shudder and Colin felt the grip
on his cock tighten as she rose to her first climax ...

SASSIE

I know I should have been scared and that's not
hindsight; I knew it even then and yet I felt strangely
calm. No, that's not right – I was far from calm, with
every nerve fibre seemingly stretched like a bowstring,
my stomach turning over and over as if some manic
hamster were using it as his exercise wheel.

No, what I was was utterly detached from anything
I might have once acknowledged as reality. If anyone
had called me by my real name, I doubt I would have
reacted to them, nor to it, for I had actually become
Sassie, become the epitome of most men's wildest
fantasies, bare-titted and belled, my fanny also bared
and available for anyone who desired it, my arms
useless and even my ability to speak intelligibly
removed by the tongue snaffle plate and thick rubber
bit.

Jonas obviously recognised the signs and knew
exactly what was happening to me, though he gave no
outward indication that he was treating me any
differently to the way in which he treated his regular
charges. His reaction, having fucked me until I all but
passed out, was non-existent, he simply withdrew
from me, wiped himself on a piece of rag and then led
me by my bridle rein down to the hosing and
showering area.

I expected him to strip me then, but he merely
wetted another piece of cloth and sponged my groin
area and neck, the first to at least partially clean away
the evidence of our coupling, the second – presumably, at least – to cool me down somewhat. After
that, he turned me away and took me back into the

42

stall I had been occupying before, hitched my rein over a hook and, closing the lower half of the door behind him, sauntered away whistling to himself.

He was not gone long, however, returning no more than five minutes later carrying a shallow steel tray in which I saw was some sort of oatmeal mixture. In his other hand he held a plastic water bottle, from the top of which extended a short length of plastic tubing.

Placing these burdens aside, he quickly removed my bit and the stubby snout part of my mask, but made no attempt to release the tongue snaffle within my mouth. Instead, he proferred the bottle, pushing the plastic tubing between my lips.

'Suck slowly, Sassie,' he instructed, raising it to assist the flow. I gulped the water gratefully, oblivious to the amount that splashed out of my unpractised mouth. 'Now, eat some,' he ordered, removing the bottle and replacing it with the tray. I eyed the unpromising mixture and then looked questioningly at him, wondering exactly how he expected me to eat.

'Eat the way any pony does,' he said, understanding the question I was unable to voice. 'Get your snout in there and suck it up. Don't worry about the mess – I'll clean you up again afterwards.'

The stiff rubbery plastic stuff from which my face mask was made did not help me, for where the fabric curled in over my lips, it desensitised them considerably and I made more than just a mess of trying to feed. However, the porridge-like stuff tasted surprisingly good and even though my stomach was still compressed within the tight girth corset, it felt empty and hollow and I knew I needed to get something sustaining into it.

Jonas laughed uproariously at my pathetic efforts, but he was patience personified, standing there with

43

the tray and occasionally using his fingers to scoop stray dollops of the mixture back between my lips, so that eventually I managed to consume a good three quarters of the meal, with less than a quarter of it smeared around my rubberised face or splashed about my feet.

'Good girl,' he murmured, when I swallowed the last mouthful, and even before it had started downwards he was fitting the snout back across my mouth, the bit following in short order. Holding me tightly by my bridle, he reached out and caressed the tips of each of my nipples in turn and immediately those awful, fantastically beautiful bolts of fire began shooting through me again.

'Whoa, what a randy little filly you are!' he exclaimed, gleefully. 'Up for another good tup, by the looks of it.' He turned me slightly and patted me on the left buttock. 'Not now though, girl, much as I'd like to. Been on duty all night, I have, and I'll be needed again just after lunchtime, so I'm off for a few hours' shut-eye.

'Don't you worry, though,' he said, in what was supposed to be a consoling tone, 'Higgy'll be back down here soon. He wanted first go with you anyway and he was a bit pissed off when he was needed for other duties. Still, that's the crack, as the Irish say.'

He led me to the very back of the stall area and pointed a finger downwards towards the straw, which had been piled thicker here than it was by the doorway.

'Settle yourself down now,' he advised. 'I'll not hook you to anything, so you can stretch yourself out. Just lay back against the wall and let yourself slide down, mind. Takes a while to get used to not having your arms to help, but it's better than sleeping standing up, which is what the four legged pony varieties do, of course.' He chuckled to himself and turned away for the door, without waiting to see whether I might need any help in carrying out his instructions.

'See you later, Sassie gal,' he said, banging the bottom section of the door closed once more. He grinned and tipped a mock salute at me. 'Good tight fuck you are, I'll give you that. Hope I'm around when you're next free, eh?'

And with that he was gone, leaving me standing there, back against the wall, totally bemused and feeling inexplicably frustrated by this latest turn of events. A good tight fuck, he'd said, and yet he was now more interested in sleeping than in repeating the experience. Despite the fact I knew deep down I should feel completely humiliated by this, my overriding thought was how long it would be before Higgy did make an appearance again.

My treacherous damned body, resplendent in its pony-girl finery, was already beginning to yearn yet again and, whilst Sara would have been horrified at the prospect, Sassie was already at the point where one cock was pretty much as satisfactory as another – the satisfaction was now the key concern, not who gave it to me!

Geordie sat back in the ancient rocking chair and eyed his host, as Frearson took down the heavy crystal decanter and proceeded to pour out two generous measures of a dark liquid. They had been ashore barely ten minutes and the *Essie* was already being refueled and checked over by two efficient-looking mechanics in overalls. Frearson had immediately led his passenger along the short pier and up some rough-hewn stone steps to his storm-weathered house.

'Brandy,' he said, passing one to Geordie. 'But don't you dare breathe a word of it. I may have spent half my life away, but I'm still supposed to be a true Scotsman.'

'My lips are sealed,' Geordie promised him, solemnly. 'Or at least, they will be when I've drunk this.' He sipped speculatively and rolled his eyes in appreciation. 'Excellent,' he said, gasping as the fiery liquid bit at the back of his throat.

'Well earned, I think,' Frearson said, raising his own glass. He eyed it briefly and then put it to his lips, savouring the first taste with exaggerated care.

'I can't say as how we earned anything much,' Geordie complained. 'All we did was chug up and down, waiting.'

'And watching,' Frearson said, detaching himself from his glass with a firm smack of his lips. 'And listening,' he added, with a wry grin. 'Oh yes, laddie, I wouldn't say we wasted our time entirely.'

'Well, what do we know now that we didn't know already?' Geordie demanded. Frearson waggled his bushy eyebrows.

'Well, we know for certain now that they're using a submarine to bring in whatever it is their trafficking. Up until now we only suspected it, but we just happened to be in the right place at the right time last night, so we can put a tick in one more box.

'And that also confirms what we suspected, that we're not dealing with a bunch of small-time muppets. To go to these lengths they're definitely running large and valuable cargoes, into the tens of millions each time, I should think, rather than the hundreds of thousands class.'

'So now your lot raid the island?' Geordie said, knowing the answer even as he asked the question. Frearson shook his head as firmly as ever.

'Not yet,' he confirmed. 'Our lot simply carries on watching and listening. Same as I said before, if we stamp down too early, all that'll happen is that they'll find another base to off-load to.'

'Not if we get their sub at the same time,' Geordie pointed out.

'Always assuming it *is* their sub,' Frearson countered. 'What if it is a bloody Russki doing a bit on the side that his lords and masters in the Kremlin know nothing about? For that matter, the way Moscow is these days the Russian navy could even be sanctioning the thing themselves. Lord knows they're strapped for cash all the time!'

'Would they make a fuss if our navy lads did round up a drug running sub, d'you think?' Geordie asked. 'Surely they'd want to keep something like that very quiet?'

'They'd make a fuss all right,' Frearson grinned. 'And they'd accuse us of planting whatever it was we found and no matter what proof we had it wouldn't do any good. No, we need more time and, assuming it is a private operation and the sub was sold on as surplus, then we'll bag the buggers, but not before we've finished tracing the lines in both directions.

'Wherever that sub is running from could make a difference, too. Most of the South American governments are anti-drugs, at least on the surface – no pun intended, by the way – but there are a few who still turn a blind eye and deny they have a problem, though the revenue props up their Mickey Mouse regimes for them, believe me.

'So, what we need to do is identify the beginning of the chain; the people doing the running, exactly who and what out on those islands is actually involved and how they distribute the stuff once they've got it this far. Then, and only then, we move in and scoop the whole bloody operation in one go.'

'Which could take months yet,' Geordie said, disconsolately. Frearson nodded.

'Or years,' he said, but the twinkle in his eye suggested he didn't believe that as a possibility. 'And meantime, Sergeant Walker, consider yourself permanently promoted and temporarily seconded to our little team.'

'One question?' Geordie said, trying to look impassive at this latest news. Frearson nodded.

'What's the official name of my new unit and what do I call you?' The older man laughed and gulped another mouthful of brandy.

'You can call me either Angus or Mister Frearson,' he replied, eventually. 'I don't mind either way, but as for the official title for our unit, I'm buggered if I could tell you what it is, or even whether we've actually got one!' He paused, apparently thinking.

'Probably something along the lines of drug enforcement, I guess,' he said at last. 'But we do a lot more than that, believe me. We're in a sort of grey area, where responsibilities and jurisdictions overlap all the time, so I suppose we're sort of like expert handymen. We just refer to ourselves as The Firm – hardly original, I know, but it does for us.'

He stopped again, squinted at his glass, evidently decided it still contained sufficient brandy for a toast and raised it high above his head.

'To you, laddie!' he cried. 'To you and to The Firm. Welcome aboard!'

Tammy leaned against the lower half of her stable door and stared miserably out into the now deserted concourse that ran between the two long rows of stalls. They had kept her with her voice inactivated for nearly three days now, the tongue snaffle and bit just there, she now knew, as a more physical reminder to her as to what she now was, the coiled whip hanging on the wall of her cramped quarters further emphasising how much her world had changed.

The days had now begun to blend into one another and time for Tammy was becoming little more than the periods between exercising and feeding and the periods of the exercising and feeding themselves. She knew she was becoming confused and had an idea that that was possibly something to do with the various medications they gave her from time to time, but she was beginning not to really care now.

There seemed little point in worrying about anything now, she thought, hazily. Once things had been so very different, but now they had changed and she accepted now there could be no going back; no returning to the old life, to the old body, to being Tommy MacIntyre, trawlerman, football fan, one of the lads with an eye for a pretty girl.

This body was now Tammy and Tammy had taken the place of Tommy, the way they had explained it. At first he had refused to accept that could be possible, but the full breasts, the pretty face, the warm little place between the tops of his thighs . . . yes, the old Tommy would have had an eye for Tammy, all right, but the old Tommy was dead, his body now either buried or cremated by the friends and relatives he had left behind, friends and relatives who would simply have assumed that he had drowned in the storm that had taken the lives of the other crewmen aboard the ill-fated trawler *Flora*.

Tammy struggled to focus her thoughts, a process which was becoming more difficult now. She tried to wriggle her shoulder muscles in an attempt to ease the cramped position of her arms in the leather pouch behind her back, but it had been tightened and raised to allow little freedom of movement. Frustrated, she stamped her foot, the metallic ring of her shod hoof boot on the stone floor beneath the thin covering of straw ringing out down the length of the cavern.

The stiff leather collar made it difficult for her to look down at herself, but the engorged nipples with their gold rings, thrust forward by the prominence of her breasts, were difficult not to see. The slightest movement caused the tiny bells that hung from the nipple rings to tinkle annoyingly and remind her of how the grooms seemed to take a special delight in fondling her breasts whenever they were handling her.

The bells reminded her too now that the touching of her sensitive flesh sent strange message sensations throughout the rest of this body, sensations and reactions over which she seemed to have absolutely no control. Once – was it long ago, or not? – the thought of a man touching any part of his body would have sent Tommy spiralling into a rage, but now, this Tammy creature he had become seemed not to mind it at all; in fact, Tammy's body seemed to enjoy such intimate contact and the little cleft between her legs could grow warm and moist even at the thought of it.

She shook her head, the heavy pendants that now adorned her earlobes flicking against her upper jawbone and cheeks, clicking against the buckles there that held the bit so firmly far back in her distended mouth.

No, a small voice was saying somewhere. *No, this isn't right at all. No, you don't really feel like this. This is not you. You're not Tammy at all.*

And then a different sound, the hollow reverberation of heavy boots against stone and she was Tammy again, lifting her eyes hopefully to look along the concourse towards the tunnel, ears pricked, eyes peering through the gloom towards the shadowy figure who appeared there, walking with a slow deliberation that she somehow sensed was bringing him ultimately to the door of her stall.

SASSIE

Higgy was plainly unimpressed with having had his regular routine disrupted and, I suspected, with having been usurped by one of the younger grooms in the pecking order when it came to me. He also looked as if he hadn't had much sleep, if any, and he banged around, in and out of the other stalls, shouting out instructions to another couple of younger men who appeared shortly afterwards. Finally, after what must have been about twenty minutes, but which seemed to me like hours, he appeared at the door of my stall, leaning over it and peering in at me.

I lay motionless in my straw initially, feigning sleep, waiting to see if he would disturb me, knowing as he must surely have done that I had been on my feet for several hours, even without the additional exertions associated with the usual pony-girl activities here. He disturbed me all right.

'On your feet, you idle fucking filly!' he roared, kicking against the door with his heavy boots. 'C'mon, let's have you up and make sure that little bastard has sorted you out properly!'

Tired as I was – I yawned as I struggled to get myself into a position from which I could rise unaided – I felt the little electric surges starting up anew. Vaguely I did hear that same little voice asking me just what I thought I was acting like, but I quickly thrust it back down where it had come from and, once I had regained a standing position, sashayed over to Higgy with what can only be described as complete arrogance. He seemed surprisingly pleased at this.

'Ah, I do love to see a properly proud pony,' he chuckled. 'Makes it all the more satisfying when I whip her hind quarters for her, you see?' I could see that, all right, for I was learning fast, but I continued to regard him impassively, chewing ever so slightly against my bit, blinking as seldom as I could possibly manage.

'Let's have you out here then,' he said, swinging the lower door aside. 'You need a damned good brush, get rid of all those bits of straw and then I reckon a good hosing down will do you no harm. Got a lovely new skin suit over there, jet black with just a white flash and blaze – reckon you'll make a fine sight in that, especially with a pretty silver harness set against it.' He reached in and caught hold of my short lead rein, tugging my head firmly, just in case I had forgotten who was in charge, it seemed to me, though there was little chance of that.

'Fucked you good and proper, did he?' he whispered, as I came out alongside him. 'Well, you ain't seen nothing yet, Sassie my girl, I can promise you that. And this time, old Higgy's going to make sure he gets his oats before he feeds you any more of yours and turns you out for the hoi polloi to have their fun with you!'

The newcomer's features were completely disguised by the close-fitting leather hood, but Tammy recognised Major's voice the moment he spoke.

'I'm going to tack you up myself today, Tammy,' he said, speaking with surprising gentleness. 'I know you'll be a good girl for me. I shouldn't like to have to get the grooms to deal with you, as they're such rough young tearaways, aren't they?' She saw his exposed lips curve into a smile.

'I did think of having you just stripped down and sent up to my quarters –' he continued, walking all around her, as if seeing her for the very first time, '– but then I thought why shouldn't I enjoy the facilities I provide for others, eh? It's another very pleasant day outside, so a drive across the island and then . . . well, you know what comes then, no doubt, even though I know you've never actually been put out for guests wanting that.'

He finally came back around in front of her and stood again, looking her up and down.

'You're very beautiful, Tammy,' he told her, nodding his approval. He reached out and placed one gloved hand carefully on her girth corset, immediately over her stomach. 'And you'll look even more beautiful before too long. The doctor tells me he's prepared your cycle properly, so you should conceive straight away.'

Tammy eyed him, her features set like stone, though inside her stomach gave a sharp lurch and her brain was threatening to go into a spin again. Despite the way in which her body seemed to have led and conditioned her mind and despite the fact that she had known that this was what Major intended for her, it still seemed a shock to hear him discuss the matter so bluntly and blandly.

Thank God my mother can't see me now! The little voice echoed around inside Tammy's skull as Major reached up to remove her bit and bridle. But as soon as his hands brushed against her thrusting nipples, the voice was banished in a rush of wind and her every thought was focused back on what was being done to her.

She suddenly felt as if she had woken up from a nightmare and found herself in a completely new time and place. Her inner turmoil seemed to subside and, in its place, descended a tranquillity that was like a mild stupor. She stood, barely moving and completely unresisting, as Major stripped off her bridle and harness, unfastened her nipple bells, unlaced and unbuckled her hoof boots and then carefully peeled off the latex-like pony skin she had worn for the past several days.

Then, selecting a new bit and bridle from the rack near the door, he slipped it over her head, adjusted it lightly and gave an experimental tug, nodding with approval when she bowed her head and immediately began to move towards him.

'That's very good, Tammy,' he smiled. 'I see they've been training you with their usual thoroughness. Come, let's get you washed down. We can forget about a skin suit, too, as it really is quite warm up there today. The air on your own skin will do it good.' He turned her round and loosened the arm pouch, pulling it down and tossing it aside; though Tammy's upper limbs were so stiff that she made no immediate attempt to lower them.

He hosed her with less direct enthusiasm than the grooms usually employed, turning the water from jet to a medium spray and letting it play over her flesh as she turned herself about to receive its cleansing touch, shaking herself, her breasts bobbing and swaying, the stiffness in her upper limbs easing until she was able to straighten them and use her mitted hands to massage the two firm globes and to rub her artfully shaped mane of hair until it was soaked through.

'That must feel so much better,' Major said, turning off the water finally. Gratefully, Tammy nodded and stepped towards him, her feet and steps feeling awkward now that she no longer had the elevated hoof boots to shape and guide them. Cautiously, she raised her right hand and pointed towards her mouth. Major smiled, but shook his head.

'No, Tammy,' he said, gently but firmly. 'Pony-girls don't talk, do they? Even *I* know that rule.' Tammy sighed and lowered her head slightly. 'Perhaps later, when we are not in the public eye, so to speak,' Major said. 'I must confess I am interested to hear certain things from your viewpoint, but not yet – afterwards will be much better, I think.'

He led her, unresisting, back to her stall, where he used the usual rough cloth to finish drying what the air had not already dried. He then selected a new pair of hoof boots from a small trolley that had seemingly miraculously appeared whilst he had been washing her. These were thigh high, as was the usual style, but a deep purple in colour, with gold relief and lacing.

'The colours of the Roman Caesars,' he said, as he finished fitting the second boot. 'You are a royal filly now, Tammy, and soon you will be a royal mare. Perhaps,' he said, pulling the first matching leather sleeve up her arm, '– we shall have to consider a new name for you, before you get too used to this one.' He laughed and began tightening laces once more.

Major was slower than any of the grooms, who regularly practised tacking and untacking their charges, but he was just as throrough and it was clear to Tammy that her master had watched the process several times before, even if he had never actually performed it personally. Very soon the girth corset was sitting snugly on her hips, her stomach being compressed to the dimensions expected of a pony-girl, the harnessing tightened about her breasts, pushing and compressing them outwards, the nipples hardening even further as the pressure was increased.

'It's a curious thing, Tammy,' Major said, conversationally, 'but I have never totally understood the human male's preoccupation with large breasts. They are, after all, designed to serve a specific purpose and I understand that many women hate the weight and inconvenience. And yet,' he said, shaking his head, 'other women go out and spend all their savings on having their natural breasts enlarged beyond anything nature might have given them anyway.'

He squeezed Tammy's right breast as if testing it, exerting only the slightest pressure, but spreading his fingers so that he held the globe in a very proprietorial way. Immediately, Tammy arched her spine, reacting instinctively and then trying to press her thighs together, aware of the sudden heat between them and of the fact that she might easily betray her body's excitement.

'Amazing,' Major muttered, speaking as if to himself now. 'I should have thought you would have hated these things, given your particular circumstances, and yet you react as directly and as basically as if you had had them all your life. Most interesting.' Tammy shivered slightly and felt as if she ought to be blushing, but of course, as she already knew, that was one function this body did not perform.

'We shall have your pretty bells back,' Major announced, flicking slyly at the right nipple ring. 'But this time they shall be real gold, not the cheap plated things you usually wear. See, my pretty filly girl, I have had these made especially for you.' From the trolley he now picked up a pair of miniature bells, shaking them before her face so that they gave off a mellow clinking sound. To Tammy, they appeared to be little different from her original decorations, but the moment Major clipped them to her rings and let them go, she felt the difference in their weight, which dragged at her nipples in a way that ought to have been painful and yet which she found even more stimulating than ever.

'Only the best for you, my dear,' Major whispered. He leaned forward and brushed her lips with his own, this time his right hand cupping and hefting her left breast. She heard him chuckle, deep down inside his throat, a curious rattling sound.

'Quite a little joke, isn't it, Tammy?' he said softly, drawing his head back slightly. 'Here you are, dressed like an animal, acting like an animal, and yet you are the one who is nearer to being human than I ever shall be. Though for today –' he added, pausing only to lick her ear lobe with the tip of his tongue, '– I think I shall enjoy playing the base human for a change, as I can see you are going to enjoy playing the pony.'

Colin was sitting, wrapped in a silky robe, propped up against a pile of pillows when Anna finally emerged from the bathroom. Completely naked now, her body still appeared as tautly defined as it had done within the firm embrace of the latex suit and she moved with the grace of a natural athlete, her weight on her toes, her head erect on her long, slender neck. Colin nodded appreciatively and was rewarded by the sight of some slight blushing in her cheeks.

'Feeling better for that?' he asked. Anna nodded. She was carrying a small towel in her left hand and it was obvious that it had taken some effort of will for her not to use it to cover herself.

'Much better, thank you . . . master,' she added, as an afterthought, as if only just remembering the possibility of listening devices in the room. Colin had checked by eye and found nothing, but he knew that meant nothing. They had decided against the risk of bringing an electronic sweeping device, in case there were scanners on the islands that could detect its presence. Instead, they had to rely on perpetual caution, keeping conversations to topics that would be considered normal here and remembering to use their pseudonyms at all times. For Anna, this was a simple matter of addressing Colin and Celia as master and mistress respectively, whilst they in turn addressed her as Ingrid, and Mel by her usual slave name of Millie.

'You were a long time in your bondage, Ingrid,' Colin remarked, casually, though he was intrigued by the Norwegian policewoman's apparently easy transition into this bizarre world. 'I trust it was suitably uncomfortable?' Anna's cheek colour deepened still further.

'It was not too bad, master,' she replied, carefully. 'I have endured similar before.' Was she deliberately giving him an opening, he wondered?

'How many former masters have you had?' he asked. He kept the tone light, conversational. Anna appeared to be considering this.

'Two masters, master,' she said, at length, 'and three mistresses. None were permanent arrangements though, master.'

'Ah.' Colin nodded. Yes, Anna had definitely not come to this situation as a total novice, but then that much had been obvious. Her reply also seemed to confirm that she was bisexual, something which Celia's much more experienced eye or "radar" had detected immediately.

'Do you prefer a master or a mistress?' It was a very direct question. Anna seemed puzzled by this, but he wondered if this was simply part of the act; there could be cameras as well as microphones, after all.

'I've never really thought about it, master,' she said, finally. 'It has always been a matter of ... serendipity? Is that the correct term?' Colin smiled up at her and then patted the bed alongside him, indicating that she should sit.

'Serendipity will do, Ingrid,' he said. She sat, placing the towel to one side and half turned so that she was facing him. Her breasts rose and fell gently, smaller than Sassie's or Millie's, but firm, and with very large and prominent nipples that were now puckered. With a deliberately slow movement, Colin raised his right hand and stretched it out, one finger extended to trace a small circle around the left nipple. He saw her stomach contract slightly, heard the small intake of breath.

'You are very pretty, Ingrid,' he said, softly. 'Very tall, too.'

'I am sorry if my height displeases my master.' She turned her face away and Colin silently applauded her. If anyone was monitoring this scene, it would be very convincing.

'Not at all,' Colin said. 'I like my slaves in all shapes and sizes.' He reflected on this observation momentarily. Using the plural had the right sound to it, conveying an attitude of experience he certainly did not have and it was a moot point as to whether Anna could truly be described as *his* slave. True she was now acting as though she were, but Colin knew that she would probably respond better under Celia's control, at least for the moment. And then, of course, there was Sassie . . .

Pushing thoughts of Sassie from the front of his mind, Colin decided to test Anna, to see how far he could push her – to push himself, even. Earlier, when she had been an anonymous rubber doll figure it had been easier for him and, he suspected, easier for her, too. This was much more intimate.

'Stand up, Ingrid,' he ordered her, quietly. Without turning back to look at him the tall girl did as she was

59

told, facing away from him, hands at her sides, apparently waiting for further instructions. 'Turn around.'

She obeyed, hands still by her sides.

'Legs apart,' he said. She slid her feet wider on the carpet and Colin felt a stirring at this immediate and unquestioning response. He looked up at her, but her eyes were downcast, looking at her feet. 'Use your fingers to open your pussy lips.'

With only the slightest hesitation, Anna moved her hands round, over her hairless mound, and gently prised her sex lips apart, displaying a pink mouth that deepened to dark red, her clitoris astonishingly visible, elongated and engorged.

'I want you to make yourself come, Ingrid.' It was potentially a stiff task, Colin knew. So far there had been plenty of stimuli in everything that had happened, with deliberately ritualistic build-up, intricate costumery and bondage. This was completely different and he wondered how he might feel if the tables were ever turned on him.

Anna, however, did not seem fazed by the instruction. One finger, already lubricated from her own fresh excitement, began to massage her clitoris and her breathing immediately began to deepen and accelerate. Then, as the already swollen nubbin began to grow even further, she suddenly looked up, fixing Colin with an unblinking gaze, her rhythm never faltering.

The message in her eyes was unmistakeably a challenge, not to his authority, but to his own acceptance of their situation. Colin nodded and carefully drew his robe aside, revealing the stiffness of his own erection. Slowly, he encircled his shaft with the fingers of his right hand and, his eyes never leaving hers, began to masturbate himself in time with her movements.

Three

SASSIE

My master for that morning appeared to be reasonably young, though the mask-hood that covered his head and face made it impossible to be sure. However, the tight white breeches and sleeveless top he wore displayed a well-muscled body and a healthy bulge between his legs. He stood watching, as Higgy harnessed me between the shafts of one of the lightweight gigs and although my blinkers prevented me from getting a good look at him – his eyes in any case were the only part of his features visible – I sensed his approval at what he saw.

'Sassie's not one of our regulars, Master Harvey,' Higgy explained. Harvey – was that his first or last name? Not that it mattered, for unless he decided otherwise, I wasn't going to be addressing him at all and even then it would be only as 'master', I knew.

'Apparently she's quite something, however,' the groom continued. He pulled harshly on the strap between my shoulder harness and the left side shaft – perhaps a trifle too harshly, I thought, wincing as I was tugged sideways. Higgy was annoyed, I knew, as the sudden arrival of Master Harvey put paid to any notion he was entertaining of having his own turn with me immediately.

'I watched her running last evening,' Harvey said, nodding. 'I was surprised her own master and mistress haven't placed her on the reserved list. If I owned such a fine creature, I doubt I'd be so keen to share her.' He spoke with a soft Midlands accent, his tone and pitch suggesting maturity without great age, much as his body did.

'Still,' he continued, and I saw him wave a hand airily. 'I've never been one to look a gift horse in the mouth, so why should I start with a gift pony, eh?' He chuckled at his own joke and I felt a shiver run up and down my spine, as the import of his words struck home. A 'gift pony' – yes, that was exactly what I had become, whether by the deliberate design of my own master, or by an oversight on his part, it mattered not.

I had been left here in these stables, dumb, defenceless, available and with no way of expressing my own wishes. Neither did I have any idea how long this state of affairs might continue. What if anything happened to Colin? What if the true purpose of our mission was discovered? I could become Sassie permanently, I now realised, but although the reality of that brought another shudder, I was not entirely sure whether it was of horror, fear, or simply just . . . anticipation?

No, surely not? A game was a game, but that . . .? And yet I truly felt no trepidation, only excitement and, as Master Harvey moved around to get a better view of my front, desire to please and satisfy. Two grey eyes regarded me through narrow slits in the leather.

'Nice tits,' I heard him murmur. Beside me, Higgy nodded – I couldn't see him, but I felt the slight movement transferring through his arms and marvelled at how sensitive I was becoming to these things.

'I think maybe a tit harness,' Harvey continued, stroking his masked chin thoughtfully. Higgy released his grip on my tack and walked around to stand beside him, adopting a suitably subservient pose.

'Yes, good choice, Master Harvey,' he agreed, after a few seconds in which he was apparently considering the suggestion. 'A harness makes a pony more aware of her tits, for sure.'

I soon realised the truth of this.

The tit harness was a thin tube – it looked like stainless steel – at each end of which was a small round spring clip, designed to snap to the nipple rings. There were different lengths of bar and Higgy brought a selection, holding each one up to my chest in turn, until Master Harvey selected his choice. It was then only a matter of seconds before it was attached and I was astonished by the effect.

The bar chosen was just long enough that it pushed each of my nipples about four inches wide of its natural position, at the same time distending my breasts slightly in an outward direction. This constant pressure immediately began to take its toll on me and my whole body began to respond in the only way it now seemed to know. Something in my demeanour must have betrayed this fact, especially to Higgy.

'Ah yes, sir,' he muttered, nodding eagerly. 'Yes, that's made all the difference. Want me to check and see how wet she is?' He moved forward, apparently not anticipating a negative response to this offer and probed between my legs with his fingers, immediately finding the evidence of my arousal.

'How about a crotch strap with a vibrating plug? Guaranteed she'll come and keep coming all the time you've got her out. I know some drivers really like that effect and I can fit her with a tail plug, too – very nice effect, the two together.'

Master Harvey nodded, slowly.

'Ye-es,' he said, eventually. 'Yes, do that, Higgy, if you're sure it won't tire her to the extent of making her useless?'

'Not if you handle her right, sir,' Higgy said. 'I'll fit a vibrator with a control – there's a thin wire and a handheld button for you to switch her on and off. Oh yes,' he added, as he started to move away, '– it don't hurt none to rest her up at least every twenty minutes or so.

'That might not seem very long, I know,' he grinned, 'but believe me, it'll seem like a week to her!'

Lachan seldom reacted to the arrival of the grooms now, but his entire body stiffened at the entry of Amaarini, for her presence usually meant trouble for him; she seemed intent on making him suffer as much as possible for the aborted raid on the island, not content with the fact that the punishment of being confined in a female body and treated like a pony-girl should be more than enough suffering for any one human being.

But then, as he had now discovered, Amaarini was not human at all, and although she might look and sound human enough, whatever motivated her psyche clearly lacked any element of compassion. She had made it clear to Lachan that his ultimate fate, whether he died or lived on for centuries in his helpless servitude, was of no real concern to her, beyond the fact that she was determined to exact the maximum revenge for what she considered his ultimate affront to their island hospitality.

'Up, Bambi.' On the other side of the inner stall room, Jessie lay on her side on her raised bed area, watching the pending confrontation with apparent disinterest, her eyes barely open, her entire body relaxed in its harness. Stiffly, Lachan got to his feet, swaying slightly as he adjusted his weight to compensate for the unnatural angle of the hoof boots.

'I've decided Jessie has earned a day off today, Bambi,' Amaarini announced. Lachan realised he hardly ever reacted when she used the name they had given him in his new identity. 'So far, you see, you've had it fairly easy, haven't you? Well, that all changes from today and I've thought of the ideal way to break you in.' She grinned and the malice in her face was like a wall of burning ice.

'One of our new guests seemed to take quite a shine to Jessie last night,' she continued, 'so I've invited him to have her for the rest of the day. He does seem to be something of a beginner, however, so the real Jessie may be somewhat wasted on him yet.

'Therefore, Bambi *dear*,' she said, 'I've decided that *you* shall take Jess's place for the day. You are completely identical, obviously, so there is no way a novice could tell you apart from any behaviour due to your own lack of experience. You won't be allowed to talk, of course, but then that can be explained by the snaffle and even if this fellow were to consider removing that, your lack of speech will be explained by your rigid pony-girl discipline.

'I shall simply tell Master Anderson, or whatever his name is, that whilst Jessie wasn't given instructions not to speak last night, she is now being punished for some earlier infraction. Of course, like any good pony-girl, she – or should I say you – will be allowed to whinney to show your appreciation when your master finally decides to fuck you!' She turned to Jess and smiled again.

'And he does fuck quite well for a beginner, doesn't he, Jessie?' she added, the sneer in her voice intended for Lachan. 'So then,' she said, turning back to him.

'Let's have you outside and we'll get you properly harnessed for your duties. Bare-arsed day today, too – fine weather outside and a nice gentle breeze to keep you on your toes. And stand up straight, you idle filly. You know what happens to ponies who slouch? Well, we'll start by adding a brace to your harness and maybe you'll remember your proper posture in future.'

She stepped closer, gripping Lachan's chin between finger and thumb in a grip of surprising strength.

'And I'm not even going to bother being there to watch you get your first proper fucking, either,' she grated. 'You'll just be another stupid pony-girl doing what she's been trained to do, won't you? I wonder how that makes you feel, Mister damned Lachan, eh? All the money in the world can't help you now – though enough of it can purchase your services for a few hours, the way you used to buy Jessie.

'I guess you never expected to be on the other side of that sort of arrangement, did you? Well, fate is a peculiar thing, isn't it, and now you're just Bambi.' She released her hold and stepped back. 'So, Bambi, let's move it. I've got my own schedule for today and I don't want to waste my precious time on a slut pony like you, do I?'

'We're arranging for that Indian girlie to be brought over,' Frearson said. Geordie nodded and waited for him to go on. The aging Scotsman had a habit of making a simple announcement and then following it up with a sometimes lengthy qualification or explanation, as Geordie had already learned.

'The Smorgersborgers interpreter isn't that brilliant, apparently,' Frearson continued. 'But then there are apparently dozens of different dialects where the girl comes from, so it needs a real expert.'

'And we just happen to have a real expert?' Geordie grinned and Frearson smiled in turn.

'Well, we just happen to know someone who knows one,' he chuckled. 'Fellow by the name of MacAndrew, apparently. Flying him up from Bristol today. Him and the girl should both be here by tonight, so we can start questioning her properly straight away. I want to know about this Alex person she apparently kept on about. No way it can be your sergeant, I suppose?'

'No, no way.' Geordie shook his head regretfully. 'I'm afraid I saw the body and it was definitely Alex Gregory. I wish there could be some doubt, but there isn't. Must be another Alex – just a coincidence, that's all.'

'Coincidence,' Frearson muttered. 'Funny word, that. Funny thing, too, coincidence.'

'You haven't actually seen the pony-girls yet, have you, Ingrid?' Colin breathed out a thin stream of smoke and swung his legs over the side of the bed. Anna, stretched out across the end of the bed, looked up at him and shook her head.

'Not yet, master,' she said. 'I was otherwise occupied last evening, if you remember?' Colin grinned, recalling the scene in Celia's room when he had returned from the race circuit.

'Of course,' he said. 'Well, I think today you shall see what all the fuss is about. Not as a pony-girl yourself,' he added, quickly, 'though I did consider it. No, I have a better idea. You shall be my groom and attendant for the day, I think, though I need to consider the appropriate costume.'

'Of course, master.' Anna was keeping rigidly in her role, all the time conscious of the possibility of other ears listening in on them. She sat up, stretched to ease the tension in her shoulders and watched as Colin padded barefoot towards the bathroom.

'Put a robe on and go along to Mistress Celia's room,' he called back, over his shoulder. 'Ask her if she can spare me a few minutes, assuming she's not otherwise engaged.'

Celia escorted Anna back to Colin's room a few minutes later and he explained what he wanted to her in a hushed voice that Anna could not quite hear. When he had finished speaking, Celia nodded and turned to look at Anna, a smile of amusement on her face.

'Yes,' she said, 'I think that would be most suitable. She has the height and the figure for it, certainly. I'll just pop along and see what might be available.'

She returned after about ten minutes, carrying a wicker basket in which she had piled an assortment of white garments and wearing an expression that Colin realised indicated that she had come up with an idea that she, at least, considered novel. He watched her as she began laying out the items, marvelling at how she had kept her figure and at how attractive her face still was, even though her best years were now well behind her.

Much of it, he knew, was due to skilful make-up and regular, stringent exercising, but some of it was also in the sheer force of her personality. He was reminded of those female film and television stars who seemed able to defy age, whose charisma included an ageless quality that enabled them to turn back the clock, seemingly at will.

'Right then,' she announced, turning back and pointing a finger at Anna. 'In the bathroom with you and let's get started.' Anna saw that she was holding a small collection of bottles in one hand and prepared herself to expect almost anything. Colin, too, recognised that Celia was looking very pleased with herself, but he was not prepared at all for the sight that greeted him when the two females eventually re-emerged from the bathroom.

One of the bottles had clearly contained bleach, for Anna's already pale-blonde hair was now snow white and had been backcombed so that it was now drying in a frothy cloud about her head. Her fair skin had been dyed a dark coffee colour and her blue eyes now startling against the darker complexion with the white halo of hair made even more stark in contrast.

'Behold my version of the Amazon Warrior princess,' Celia announced, laughing at Colin's stunned reaction. 'Of course, she'll soon be a captive warrior princess,' she added, smirking. 'So, what do you think?'

'Well, I –' Colin fought to find the appropriate words. 'Incredible, I guess,' he said, eventually. 'For a moment there, I thought you'd used another of those face masks. How long does that stuff last?'

'The body stain will last about a week or so,' Celia explained. 'It's pretty much waterproof and even sweat shouldn't fade it. It either needs a special solvent, which they have here too, or else we can leave it to nature. Normal exfoliation gets rid of it ultimately, as it doesn't go beyond the outer layer of skin, but it breaks down under light, too. I did explain all that to Ingrid, in case she thought she might have to walk around looking like this for the next six months.'

Anna gave a little smile, the white of her teeth flashing more noticeably than ever, the natural red of her lips less apparent than before.

'Well, I must say it's quite an effect,' Colin said. He sat back, reaching for his cigarettes. 'So, what comes next?' Celia smirked again.

'You just relax there and get yourself into the conquering hero frame of mind and leave Princess Pussy here to me,' she said. 'It's going to take quite a while to do her make-up before I do anything else, so maybe I'll take her back along to my room for that bit. I doubt either of you have anything quite suitable here.' She turned back to Anna.

'Hands behind your back, slave,' she chuckled, and produced a pair of leather cuffs from the things that she had left in the wicker basket. 'Can't have prisoners of war wandering about the place with their hands free, can we?'

Sol's day had begun much earlier and already, it seemed to him, had gone on far too long, even though he knew that his sufferings for that day had probably barely started.

Fiona had harnessed him before first light, removing the rigid prosthesis from his erect organ, strapping it back tightly to the triangular leather harness and then adding a single strap about his balls instead of separating them with their individual restraints. It was marginally less uncomfortable like this, but Fiona was not yet finished.

To a small ring set in this strap she added a pair of pendulous leather weights, joined together by another ring and hook arrangement that allowed them to swing freely between his legs, one beneath the other, so that every step set them in motion and the increase in pace which Fiona and her whip demanded made them flail about madly.

The resultant strain on his trapped testicles was therefore both terrible and unpredictable and Sol was forced to bite deeply into his gag in order to prevent himself from crying out. Behind him, as if oblivious to his torture – which he knew she wasn't – Fiona

70

bounced up and down on her seat, urging him to even greater efforts.

Finally, after what seemed an eternity of stumbling headlong over the uneven network of narrow tracks, they had emerged into a small clearing and Sol had all but collapsed with relief when she reined him in. Behind him, he felt and heard her dismounting and for a few all too brief seconds entertained the hope that she might allow him to rest for a while. It was a vain hope, however.

'Got to go back and find you a little playmate,' she announced, in a light voice that he knew was hiding her true intentions. 'I could just leave you like this for a while, of course, but you might just take it into your silly head to go wandering off and that just wouldn't do, would it?' She looked down to where the weights were slowly swinging to a halt.

'Put a bit of spice into your step, didn't they?' she laughed. Sol eyed her balefully, trying to shut out the deep throbbing in his groin. It was an impossible task. 'So, I think maybe we ought to let you out of the shafts and stretch a few muscles,' Fiona continued, grinning maniacally. She reached past him and began unbuckling the first of the straps that held him to the shafts.

Ten minutes later, Sol found himself beneath the overhanging branch of a tree on the edge of the clearing, leather cuffs around each sleeved wrist attached to ropes that Fiona had thrown up over the branch and used to haul him up, until even the tiptoed stance enforced by his hoof boots was not enough and only the very tips of his hooves now remained in contact with the ground.

Not satisfied even with this, she had added a spreader bar between his ankles, so that only one foot at a time could now touch the earth, and if he allowed his legs to hang straight as gravity required, neither of them quite made contact and all his weight was forced onto his shoulders. As a final touch, Fiona tied a thin strap to the top of his bridle and dropped it behind him, reaching around to draw it forward between his legs and tie it around his testicles over the strap that was already there to take the ball weights.

She pulled it tightly before knotting it, forcing his head back as far as the high collar would allow, so that now Sol was forced to stare almost straight upwards into the leaves above. Then, with a casual stripe of her crop across his taut buttocks, she stepped away.

'I'll try to be as quick as I can, Solly boy,' she laughed, 'but you know how these things are and they're so-o busy in the stables today, or so they tell me, so I'm not sure what sort of slut they'll have allocated me today.' The sound of her laughter as she walked away down the track was soon replaced by a high and tuneless whistle.

Sol groaned into his bit and shut his eyes, trying to shut out the pain, but it was a losing battle and he knew that it would be some time before he could expect any relief. Fiona would not be in a hurry to get back to him and no one else would come to his assistance, even if they did stumble across his plight. There was a simple rule of non-interference on the island – if you came across a slave in whatever situation, it was taken for granted that he or she had done something to deserve it and would have to remain as they were until the master or mistress responsible returned to release them.

In Sol's case, as he hung suspended in the early morning sun, it was, he knew only too unlikely that even Fiona's return would mark an end to his sufferings. In fact, he was sure it was likely to mark only the next chapter in whatever invidious revenge she had planned for him . . .

Alex was less than pleased to see that she had been given to Fiona Charles for the day. Even though she had had little first-hand experience of the woman's spiteful attitude, during her time in the stables she had heard plenty of stories concerning the television star and her treatment of anyone unfortunate enough to fall into her hands.

Her own time as a pony-girl had done nothing to improve her demeanour; in fact, it had made it even worse if that were possible, and Alex had been given a brief glimpse of the manner in which she was now avenging her treatment by Sol, staring out of her stable in horror as she had watched Fiona whipping him up and down the length of the concourse, forcing him to prance with his knees rising to almost impossible heights. And now here she was, dressed in a crisp white blouse and a tight black leather skirt that was slit to the thigh on one side to reveal the tops of her fishnet stockings, the spiked heels on her ankle boots tipped with steel that glinted menacingly at every step.

'Ah, quite a pretty pony,' she said, prodding at Alex with the tip of her crop and then using it to flick each of her nipple bells. 'You look familiar, pony-girl. Have I had you before, or are you another of the twins around this place?' Alex, of course, could not reply, for which she was grateful, though she did have to suppress a wry smile at the thought of what Fiona's journalistic reaction would have been had she even suspected the truth.

Today, Alex was naked under her harnessing, Amaarini having decided that the weather was warm enough and that the fresh air would be healthy for her. The leather fittings the grooms had fitted to her after Amaarini had returned her to the stables were all in a deep red, with bright gold rings, buckles and studs, all designed to reflect the light, both natural and artificial.

They had rouged her lips and nipples too, adding dark blue shadow above and below her eyes, apparently to Fiona's specifications, and then, apparently also at Fiona's request, inserted a tapered rubber plug into her anus, from which now bobbed a creamy coloured tail.

'Yes, very pretty indeed, pony-girl,' Fiona said, completing her inspection. 'What did they say you were called – Jangles?' She flicked at a nipple bell again and snickered, nastily. 'Yes, jingle-jangle,' she said. 'And your ears and cunt the same, too!' She leaned closer.

'I know exactly how that all feels, pony slut!' she hissed. 'They even pierced my clit, did they tell you that? That's something they don't usually do even to you sluts, but I bet they made sure all you whores knew they'd done it to me, eh?'

There was a madness in her eyes, Alex saw, and she realised that the way in which Fiona had been made to honour her lost wager and the extremes to which some of the stable staff had gone had badly affected an already unstable personality. Fiona Charles was a walking ego and that ego had been damaged; therefore, not only would she do her damnedest to make Sol suffer, she was clearly going out of her way to inflict as much retribution on anyone and everyone she suspected might have taken any sort of satisfaction from her plight. In the next few weeks, Alex suspected, Fiona would go through every inhabitant of the stables and make sure they were reminded that she had now been returned to a position of power

74

over them; that hers had been a temporary condition, whereas theirs was permanent.

Fiona had money whilst they, the pony-girls and assorted other island slaves, only had money sufficient to place themselves in their lowly positions, or that was how the woman saw it. How she would have reacted if she realised that they were nearly all real slaves and not just being paid to pretend, Alex could only imagine. Meantime, she hoped fervently that the fact that Fiona believed them all to be employees of the island might at least instil some sense of restraint in her, but how far Amaarini and the rest of them would allow her to go before they reined in her excesses was open to question.

'Let's get you between the shafts then, shall we?' Fiona said, straightening up again and regaining some sort of composure. 'We have a whole beautiful day ahead of us and I don't want to waste any of it, do I?' She grasped Alex's bridle rein and gave it a sharp tug, causing the bells on her ears to jangle as her head jerked to the side.

'Jingle-jangle, jingle-jangle,' Fiona chanted, child-like, turning her back and striding towards the line of waiting gigs and sulkies. Alex clattered in her wake and strived to retain her balance against the insistent pulling, so that she was quite relieved when she was finally backed between the shafts of a lightweight sulkie, its red upholstery and trimmings matching her own tack.

To either side, other girls were being harnessed, mostly by grooms, but occasionally by their drivers, and Alex realised that Amaarini had not been exaggerating when she had said that this was going to be a busy few days. She was not absolutely sure just how many pony-girls there were in the stables in total, but already it seemed that their numbers were stretched and some of the part-timers from the upper levels would like as not be conscripted in for the duration.

'Right then, Jangles,' Fiona said, completing her final check of all the straps and clips. 'That seems to be everything, but I'll explain a few rules before we go, seeing as I've probably not driven you before.

'For a start,' she said, 'I like my ponies to trot smartly at all times, head up, chest out and show off those titties and their pretty bells.' Not that the strict harnessing arrangement made it possible to do much else, Alex reflected to herself, ruefully. 'I like to see those knees high – this isn't a race, after all, though we may have a few informal contests later, depending upon who's about this afternoon.

'Smartness, girl – smartness and pride, or I'll stripe that pert little arse of yours 'til you look like a tigress, understand? And pay attention to my signals, or I'll use the whip instead of the reins.' She patted Alex sharply on her left breast and wheeled away; a moment later Alex felt the weight shift as she pulled herself up into the driving seat, and then the whip cracked loudly alongside her right ear, something which Alex knew was totally against the usual protocol until they were out in the open.

'Hey-hup!' Fiona cried, apparently not caring what anyone else thought. She shook the reins vigorously, giving another hard tug that drove the bit hard back into Alex's mouth and Alex leaned forward, taking up the strain. Again the whip cracked.

'I said giddup, you lazy slut!' Fiona cried. Alex flinched. The rules were that ponies trotted or walked slowly up the tunnel to the exit doorway, but her new driver apparently was having none of this. With a sigh and a grunt, Alex threw herself forward even harder and, bells clinking and jangling, hooves ringing on the hard stone floor, set off across the remaining space towards the tunnel at a pace that would have done justice to a race itself.

Desperately, she found herself hoping that they would not meet a returning team, consoling herself with the fact that it was still very early for that anyway. On the other hand, she thought to herself, as they raced into the tunnel and towards the U-shape of light that marked the outside world, it paid never to rely on anything in this crazy place.

Millie was feeling rather frustrated and neglected. Things were not turning out the way she had anticipated and the entire trip was in danger of becoming an anti-climax, despite the vibrating dildo upon which Celia had left her impaled for the past few hours.

The stool upon which both she and the quivering phallus were now mounted had been specially constructed mostly, she knew, as a form of punishment device, but what she had done to deserve being abandoned to it she had no idea at all. When Celia had finally separated her from Anna she had accompanied the older woman back here and, despite her exhausted state, had managed to do everything the mistress had expected of her; not falling asleep until she was certain that Celia herself had done so first.

She had been awoken some time later to be confronted with the punishment stool and, without ceremony and without even being allowed to change out of the tight fitting latex which she had been enduring for so many hours, had been installed on it, the phallus deep inside her, ankles cuffed to either side of the support stand and wrists shackled together behind her back.

Celia had then inserted a simple ball gag, though the harness which held it in place was complex

77

enough to ensure that it could not be pushed out with her tongue, and then left her to it, pausing only to explain that the vibrator would turn on and off at random intervals and run for random periods.

Now, a lonely, doll-like figure, her back aching, she sat brooding in her enforced silence, looking at her reflection in the long mirror on the opposite wall and waiting for the next burst of activity from the only diversion that had been left to her.

It really was not fair, she fumed to herself. All the rest of them were out there somewhere, flaunting about and enjoying themselves, so why had she been left here to suffer in solitude like this? If her ankles had not been so securely fixed, Millie would have stamped her foot in sheer frustration . . .

Tammy, like Alex, could not fail to notice how busy the island seemed, with gigs and sulkies along most of the wider pathways and even, she noticed as they trotted past the race circuit, several enthusiasts engaged in impromptu competitions on the track.

The forecast of unusually clement weather had, it seemed, encouraged a higher than usual number of visitors, but the clear skies also brought with them a disadvantage. Tammy noticed the presence of an unusually high number of guard patrols, the men walking about in twos, one of each couple carrying a small back pack and clutching a handheld microphone unit.

No cloud meant the possibility of low flying aircraft, and low flying aircraft would offer unobstructed views of the island to their occupants. It was rare for any pilots to venture this far out, for the two islands were both well away from the regular routes, but it had been known to happen and the security wing here would be on full alert.

Radar would give several minutes' warning of any unidentified approaches and the electronic systems were supplemented by lookouts posted on the top of the crag. Radio alerts would then be broadcast to the patrols, who in turn would use their portable speaker systems to alert the various drivers. The procedure then was for every driver to head for cover beneath the trees, if possible using designated areas where the natural foliage had been supplemented by camouflage netting. Woe betide any visitor who failed to make cover within the prescribed three minutes. Even though there was a safety margin of a further three minutes built into the system, stragglers would find their future status on the island severely compromised and repeated offences would lead ultimately to a complete ban on further attendance.

So far, according to Jessie – Tammy's main source of information on Ailsa and its strange occupants – no one had ever risked that final sanction and the procedure was practised with regular drills.

Major was an undemanding driver, allowing Tammy to trot gently, keeping his whip sheathed and his use of the reins to guide her to a minimum. Compared to some of her peers, she realised, hers was an easy lot, especially when she saw two pony-girls being driven together, clad not just in their harnesses but in heavy rubber skin suits and full face masks. As Major steered her to one side to allow the oncoming pair to pass, Tammy could hear their laboured breathing, but the overweight woman who drove them was either oblivious to their condition, or else, had set out deliberately to cause it.

She herself wore only a pair of white leather shorts and a halter top of the same, from which her huge breasts threatened to explode with every rut over which her wheels bounced. Tammy cringed at the sight and wondered just how she viewed herself; few women of her experience who looked like that would have flaunted themselves so brazenly, she thought.

Perhaps, however, she mused, as the sound of the two pairs of hooves faded behind them, perhaps this was the woman's way of getting back at a world that had been so cruel to her physically: to be able to hold such total power over two such beautiful creatures – and the Jenny-Anns, if they were nothing else, were all such perfect specimens of sexually desirable womanhood – was her way of convincing herself that wealth was preferable to beauty every time.

After half an hour or so of trotting along the paths, they came to a small clearing that Tammy calculated was not far from the sea itself and there, sitting on an isolated rock, she saw a familiar figure. He appeared to be reading from a small notebook, but he looked up at the sound of their approach.

'Good morning, Rekoli,' Lineker hailed Major, as Major reined Tammy to a halt. 'I see you are determined to go through with your scheme?' He nodded towards Tammy. Major jumped down from his seat and Tammy heard him laugh as he stepped forward.

'And why not, Ikothi?' he parried. 'After all, she's a beautiful creature and this is a fine day, though this thing is rather hot and uncomfortable.' He reached up and a moment later pulled the hood mask from his head. 'I'll have to put it on again if we hear anyone else coming,' he said. 'I thought it best to remain anonymous for all this.' He laughed again and patted Tammy lightly on her shoulder.

'In fact,' he said, 'I'm enjoying this so much, I think I might just make it a regular habit, at least until her belly gets too large.' He paused, thoughtful for a few seconds. 'Perhaps we could have her harnesses specially adapted for her, eh?'

'Though keeping the royal purple, I presume?' Lineker remarked, drily. 'Ah well, Rekoli, it's not for me to stop you making a fool of yourself. Just keep the mask on, eh?'

'Of course,' Major said, agreeably. He smiled. 'You think the purple is a bit too much?' he asked, seriously. 'I hadn't really thought about it, but I suppose it might cause a few tongues to wag.'

'And if it did, would that worry you too much, my friend? I think not.'

'Maybe not,' Major said. 'But tell me, what brings you out here today? I thought you would be hard at it, deep in your innermost sanctum.'

'Indeed.' Lineker nodded. 'I have been hard at work, it is true,' he said. 'But now everything is set and we must simply wait a few days. My people are quite capable of monitoring the systems, so I thought I would permit myself a little relaxation and, as you so rightly say, we have the perfect day for it.'

'I sense there is more to it than that, Ikothi,' Major countered. 'I've known you too long.'

'True,' Lineker replied, sighing. 'True on both counts, as it happens.' He paused and glanced down at his notebook. 'It's our South American friend,' he continued, at last. 'He worries me.'

'He worries me, too,' Major said, 'but then that is a good thing. Complacency is a weakness and worrying prevents complacency. That is why I worry all the time and not just about Señor Valerez.'

'But Valerez is a real danger,' Lineker insisted. 'He is not just rich and powerful; he is totally ruthless, a psychopath. There is no predicting what he might do.'

'So we predict that he might do everything and anything,' Major replied, easily. 'And we make our own plans to counter anything and everything and in that way we shall not be caught by the unexpected when it happens, as surely it will. Meanwhile, access to his fortunes would do our ultimate cause no harm at all, Ikothi.'

'And our destruction would do that cause every harm,' Lineker said, harshly. 'Which is why I cannot comprehend why you are agreeing to let some of us go right into this lion's den. If we are on his territory then he will hold all the advantages.'

'That I know,' Major agreed. 'And I have known it from the very beginning, but it suits me to allow him to think his silver tongue and seemingly bottomless wallet has won me over.' He regarded Lineker. 'There are some things I have not discussed fully, even with you, I am afraid. I thought it better if I kept them to myself, but I think now might be the time to talk openly.'

'You know I have never betrayed your confidence,' Lineker protested. Tammy could see that he was offended, though he was being careful not to display his ire too openly. Major nodded and laid a hand on his arm.

'I know, Ikothi,' he said, consolingly. 'But I thought it better not to burden you with my thoughts, at least not whilst you have been so preoccupied with your own work.'

'And now?'

'And now, I think,' Major said, 'we both have a little time to spare. Your first batch of the new clones will not be ready for some time yet, so everything – Señor Valerez included – is on hold, no? Therefore, we must use this enforced interlude to consider our options.'

Tammy, standing patiently between the shafts, deliberately kept looking straight ahead. The two Askarlarnis, she realised, had either forgotten she was there or else regarded her as little more than an unthinking beast; certainly a lower life form who was never going to be in a position to repeat anything she overheard.

However, though Tammy knew this latter assumption to be undeniably true, she found the conversation which followed both utterly horrifying and, at the same time, totally fascinating. And whatever her new masters and mistresses thought of her, however easily they had somehow managed to bring her into near acceptance of her new gender and role, she was still, beneath the veneer of harnesses, hooves and bridles, an intelligent and inquisitive human being . . .

Four

SASSIE

I had almost forgotten about Colin, my real master, as I had forgotten largely the original reason for our coming here to these curious islands. I gave it little enough thought at the time, it's true, but now I think I understand what happened to me, though I know I should not take any pride in the way I let things just take me over.

The dildo Higgy had inserted inside me felt snug and fat, filling me completely, yet not stretching me. The same was true of the butt plug that held my tail: it had been carefully sculpted so that there was a thinner part just before the flanged base that prevented it going completely inside me and my sphincter muscles settled around this quite happily. However, as soon as I began to trot and Master Harvey activated the vibrator for the first time, the combination of the two intruders all but sent me into a delirium.

I climaxed within only a few steps and I wanted to stop, to squeeze with my muscles and savour the feeling, but this was clearly not part of Harvey's plan.

'Trot on!' he commanded, flicking the whip over my head as I made to halt, and I remember biting hard into the rubber of my bit in order to force myself to obey him. Then, as I gathered speed again, everything became a complete blur as the multiple orgasms blended together in one long and shattering surrender to the inevitable.

When I next regained my senses I realised, to my astonishment, that I was still running – loping slowly now, rather than trotting as I had been before. The vibrator had stopped, but I could feel its presence down there, along with that of the rear plug: the swish of my tail against the backs of my thighs above the tops of my boots added another layer of stimulation.

'Good girl,' I heard from behind me, followed by a low chuckle. Clearly my unconscious performance had met with Master's approval. I tossed my head and this brought another laugh.

'Atta gal!' he cried. 'Show everyone what a proud pony you are!' At this, I suddenly realised just how many other people there were out there. Other ponies trotted by every few minutes, singly and in pairs, pulling a variety of vehicles and driven by an even greater variety of handlers. Some, ponies and drivers alike, had their identities hidden behind masks and I found myself wondering if any of them were my friends.

Anna would make a fine pony, I thought, with her height and those seemingly endless legs of hers. Millie was slightly shorter than the average pony-girl, but even she, especially in the high boots, would not look out of place. And which of these drivers might be my own master, I wondered? Would he be thinking of me as he drove? Would he be comparing me with whatever proud lovely was currently in his charge? I found myself hoping fervently that any comparison would be a favourable one.

The vibrator started up again, but this time only for a matter of seconds, and then it became still again. However, even that short burst had proved sufficient to stir my juices again, and all thoughts of anything or anybody beyond my current position and current master were banished as I lurched towards orgasm once again.

'Steady, Sassie.' I felt the slow drag on my reins which signalled me to slow down and I did so with reluctance. Only a few days earlier the mere presence of a dildo inside me – the mere fact that I was helpless in my pony regalia, the feel of the bit pressing back into my mouth and the breeze blowing gently against my naked flesh – all those things combined would have kept me in a state of permanent orgasm, but now I knew I needed more still. Permanent arousal I had, yes, but now I was an experienced pony-girl and an experienced pony-girl needed driving to her climax.

Trying to smile around my bit, I slowed as required and snorted as a sudden gust of wind blew directly into my face. No hurry, I told myself, peering sideways to where the sun was less than halfway up the eastern sky. The day had really barely begun yet and I had the feeling I was in the hands of a master who knew only too well what a pony-girl needed.

I dropped to a walk as we entered one of the clearer spaces that appeared to be everywhere among the tracks here and wondered how long it would be before the mechanical beast in my vagina would be replaced by a real, throbbing, flesh and blood one. Not too long, I hoped . . .

Lack of proper sleep was beginning to take its toll and Colin only realised that he had dozed off when the return of Celia and Anna brought him back to wakefulness with a guilty start. He opened his eyes, rubbing them first from tiredness and then in amazement, as he stared at the exotic creature now standing before him.

'Beautiful, isn't she?' Celia said, clearly very proud of her handiwork. Colin sat upright and stared. Yes, he thought, but then Anna had already been beautiful and what she had become was something even more than that.

Her lips were now as white as her hair and outlined with a thin red line, which also had been used to define the perimeters of her eye make-up. False eyelashes had been carefully placed above and below each eye, white as Anna's hair and lips now were and made all the more stark by the black eyeshadow and the silvery highlights beneath her eyebrows – now also white – and along the tops of her cheekbones. Minuscule glitter particles had been added, too, and white and gold pendant ear rings, producing an overall effect that was at once completely alien and yet at the same time calculated to raise the most base male desires. Colin felt himself stirring and shifted his position so that his robe hid the evidence of his arousal.

As his gaze travelled downwards, Colin saw that Anna's nipples had been painted white, a thin red line circling them and their aureolae, and thin gold pins inserted through each one were set off by a slender gold chain connecting the two in a graceful loop. A further white and gold jewel shimmered in Anna's navel and broad white and gold bands encircled her upper arms.

'You've got some creative imagination, I'll give you that!' Colin exclaimed. Celia shrugged.

'I got the basic idea from a painting or two I've bought prints of,' she replied, modestly. 'Remind me to show you my collection some day.'

* * *

Millie lay in the bath, luxuriating in the hot water and playing idly with the soap bubbles. She sighed. At least, she consoled herself, she was off that damned stool and free of the bodysuit which Celia had despatched for a much needed cleaning. But why was she still not being included in whatever was going on out there?

She had been forced to sit and watch as Celia had prepared Anna and it was obvious that something really interesting was being planned, so why wasn't there a role for her to play?

'Just stay here and enjoy a bath,' Celia had ordered, when she finally released her. 'If I'm gone for any length of time, try to have a nap – I expect you need one.'

'This is a waste of time for me,' Millie sulked, blowing her nose on a tissue. 'I thought I came here for –' She managed to stop herself, just in time, catching Celia's warning glare.

'Sorry, mistress,' she said, adjusting quickly. 'It's just that I thought you really wanted me with you and yet I've been virtually ignored.'

'I'll find something to amuse you later, hussie,' Celia promised. 'Meantime, you stink to high heaven, so get yourself cleaned up and into a nice lacy basque and some stockings. You can give my poor back a massage when I return later.'

'You can give my poor back a massage later!' Millie mimicked, when the door closed behind Celia again. 'I'll give you a massage. What the fuck am I, a bloody nursemaid?'

Now she washed the soap from her hair and stepped from the bath, heading for the shower unit in the corner to complete the rinsing process.

'Bloody unfair,' she muttered, wincing as the cool spray hit her shoulders and back. 'I'd rather play at being a pony-girl than have all this hanging around. At least there's usually a damned good screwing at the end of it all!'

'Valerez thinks of himself as a very clever man,' Major said, 'and by human standards he most certainly is. However, like most very clever men, he makes the mistake of believing that no one else could possibly be as clever as he is. Valerez, don't forget, still believes that we are human in origin, Ikothi, and we must take care to ensure that nothing occurs to make him doubt that belief. He is a dangerous enough adversary as it is – you have said so yourself – so we must take care not to let him think we are in any way superior, nor that we even consider ourselves so.'

'I understand that, Rekoli,' Lineker conceded. Tammy shifted her weight from her right foot to her left, trying not to draw attention to herself. She already knew quite a lot about the people responsible for her situation, but now they were obviously moving into new territory, discussing something of which she had previously been in complete ignorance.

'However –' Lineker was saying now, '– I cannot conceive how you could possibly even consider allowing our technology to fall into his hands, and that will surely happen if we take ourselves over to his country and allow a laboratory to be set up there. Once Valerez learns what we know, he would have no further use for us and I am certain his wealth would be enough for him to bring in human experts to continue the programme.'

'Ah yes,' Major said, nodding sagely. 'The programme.' Tammy shifted her weight back again and tried to moisten her lips with the tip of her tongue – a task that was all but impossible with the bit in her mouth.

'This programme of which our friend talks so much –' Major continued, after a short pause, '– is quite something, would you not agree? He offers us almost unbelievable sums in return for which we will ensure that he gets a steady supply of his human mules, which will both haul his filthy produce over the mountains and also act as willing sexual diversions for his men. An interesting concept.'

'And a concept which I can turn into reality,' Lineker reminded him. 'We know the process works, just that the clones for which we do not have ready human brains will require a little more time in order that their own brains may develop far enough in order for their bodies to function at the basic level.'

'More than just a little time, Ikothi,' Major said. 'You yourself estimate between eighteen months and two years, do you not? That may not be a lifetime, even in human terms, but it is a long time for someone like Ramon Valerez to wait, just so that he can have alternatives to four-legged mules.'

'I don't understand the point you are trying to make, Rekoli,' Lineker said, looking puzzled. Tammy narrowed her eyes. Human she might be, humble pony-girl they had made her, but perhaps, she thought, there was something of the human needed in order to understand human thinking. Lineker, the archetypical scientist, had clearly not absorbed as much of human nature as Major appeared to have done.

'My point, Ikothi,' Major continued, 'is this. Why would Valerez be prepared to offer such huge inducements for us to provide something which he can already acquire himself? True, any humans he uses would be less strong, less durable than the clones we can provide for him, but so what if they all end up dying of exhaustion, or falling into chasms and breaking their legs? A man like Valerez would simply go out and abduct himself as many replacements as he wants or needs, would he not?'

'You are saying that he has lied to us, is that it?' Lineker still did not seem to be getting the point, but Tammy thought she knew where Major was going with his argument. The next minute or so proved her guess to be remarkably accurate.

'Of course he has lied to us,' Major retorted. 'A man like Valerez lies through force of habit. If his lips move, he must be lying – there's a human joke that makes fun of such a trait, Ikothi.' Major continued, patiently. 'Yes, he has lied and he continues to lie. He tells us he wants human mules and will pay a large fortune for us to produce them for him. He also says that it will be easier if we move a production centre to his country, which makes logical sense, but only if he needs thousands of these clones.'

'He talks in such numbers, yes,' Lineker said.

'But why?' Major demanded, spreading his hands. 'Why would he need thousands? A hundred, two hundred, even three hundred – *five* hundred even, but not thousands. How much does he need to transport in any one year and where would he stable all these creatures, eh?' He paused. 'No, if Valerez needs thousands, then he doesn't need them as pack horses. But an army now, that's a different equation, I think.'

Cannon fodder, Tammy thought, grimly. Thousands of near mindless Jenny-Anns, their brains probably incapable of cognisant thought, but trainable in basic skills; like holding a rifle; marching, getting shot and falling down whilst their surviving fellows simply ignored them and marched ever onwards into the mouths of whatever weapons were aimed at them. The pictures that this prospect conjured up in her mind were too awful to dwell on. She shook her head, the tinkling bells causing Major to look back at her.

'I think,' he said, his eyes narrowing, 'that even my little pony-girl has got the idea, Ikothi. Yes, I see it in those beautiful eyes. A horrible thought, is it not?'

'Then we cannot allow this to continue any further!' Lineker exclaimed. 'Let our security deal with Valerez and his gorillas. They are only men after all, and we will be doing humanity a favour in killing them.'

'Indeed we would,' Major agreed. 'Until the next Valerez comes along and then his successor and his in turn. No, my friend, I have given this problem much thought and I believe the real solution lies in the problem itself. The project will continue, but perhaps not quite in the way friend Valerez envisages.' He paused, marshalling his thoughts.

'It is a dangerous game we enter, Ikothi, but then we have been playing a dangerous game for so many years anyway that, if we are successful, not only will we advance our own cause much faster, we may well play a part in removing one of humanity's worst scourges. And I think,' he concluded, 'that we owe our unwitting hosts of these past two centuries or so at least that much to demonstrate our gratitude for their hospitality, don't you?'

If Fiona Charles was not actually insane, Alex thought, as she plunged headlong through an overgrown section of one of the least-used island tracks, she was at the very least possessed of the sort of cruel streak that was normally only ever found in genuine psychopaths.

The side of her which she showed here on the island was a far cry from the happy-go-lucky, slightly daredevil, and admittedly raunchy television image that had made her so popular with the watching millions, but then that alone would ensure that she never betrayed the islands' secrets. Without doubt, her hosts would by now have collected enough video footage of her in action to ensure the death of a hundred media careers, let alone just one, and she would never dare risk them exposing her.

That was why, Alex realised, as they emerged back on to a clearer section of trail, Major had been able to insist on her honouring her wager and why she had been forced to accept the indignities heaped upon her by the grooms and other visitors alike. It would also ensure that the woman would never risk another such bet.

'Watch yourself, you stupid, brainless shit!' Fiona screamed. The whip cracked again, this time against Alex's unprotected right shoulder. She whinnied into her bit at the searing pain, knowing that the skin had been broken and that the enraged creature behind her was capable of inflicting even worse without caring. A low branch – fortunately little more than a long twig – slashed across Alex's forehead, blinding her for a split second so that she almost failed to notice the way the track veered sharply to the left.

Stumbling, she managed to shift her weight in the nick of time, whilst behind her the cart slewed wildly, its left side wheel bouncing over some surface tree roots.

'Bitch!' The whip slashed over Alex's other shoulder. 'Bitch, you did that deliberately! I'll make you so sorry for that!' Another crack, but this time the whip just failed to make contact, though Alex knew that was not by design. In her fury, Fiona was losing control completely and that did not bode well for the next few hours.

As the trail straightened out again, Alex found herself praying that someone, somewhere, was monitoring the various cameras she knew were secreted throughout the island and that whoever that someone was would see that action was taken before this deranged harpy damaged her permanently, or even worse.

Anna appeared to be in an almost trance-like state, Colin observed, as Celia set about organising the rest of her costume. There was a detached air about her, a nearly ethereal quality, as if the way in which her outward appearance had been transformed had somehow affected her entire personality.

She stepped gracefully into the high-heeled white sandals that Celia placed on the floor in front of her and stood motionless as the older woman laced them, the thongs criss-crossing up to her knees. Colin blinked, realising for the first time that her toenails were now white and that her fingernails had been covered with long white nail extensions. His heart thumped heavily against his ribs and his erect penis throbbed in time with it.

'We must get some pictures of this,' Celia enthused, straightening up again. 'They'll produce some here for us, if we ask.' Cameras, the rules stated, were strictly forbidden on the islands, at least in the hands of visitors. He stared at Anna and nodded in agreement – this was one vision of which he wanted to have a permanent reminder, though he did fleetingly wonder at how Sassie would react to that.

Guiltily, he realised that he had not thought about her for several hours now and wondered how she was faring in the stables, but just as quickly he pushed that thought from his mind, forcing himself to concentrate instead on the tableau that was unfolding before him.

Celia was now buckling a white leather belt about Anna's hips; it was studded with silver and there were silver rings set in it at intervals. From this, at the front, descended two narrower straps, each one set a few inches wide of centre to either side. These were now pulled down and through Anna's thighs, Celia adjusting them carefully so that they sat to either side of the younger woman's sex, before running them through buckles at the rear and drawing them in tightly, so that the labia were forced into further prominence. They looked extremely tight and uncomfortable, but Anna merely fluttered her extraordinary eyelashes as Celia fastened them.

A further leather harness followed, a parody of a brassiere; without cups and only two narrow leather platforms to support and lift Anna's pert breasts. Two straps ran up either side to her neck, where they joined a collar. The whole thing was set with studs and rings to match the belt about her hips. Finally, two wide leather wrist cuffs were buckled in place, from which, on the insides, dangled stainless steel clips. Celia lifted each wrist in turn, snapping its clip to the side of the belt, using strategically positioned rings to make the connection, and then stood back.

'There!' she exclaimed. 'One captive princess warrior, for the use of. Mind you –' she added, turning to Colin, '– we really ought to do something about the way you look, too.' She winked and grinned. 'I'll go see what I can find, okay?' she said, turning towards the door.

'I might be a little while,' she said, looking back over her shoulder. 'Say half an hour, at least? Maybe you'd like to use the time to aquaint yourself with your new hostage, my lord.' She laughed again and reached for the door handle. 'I think you might find her new tongue stud quite a novel experience,' she added. Before Colin could think of a reply, she was gone, the door closing almost noiselessly in her wake.

SASSIE

We came eventually into yet another clearing, at the edge of which, beneath the overhanging branches, was a crude shelter, comprising four poles driven into the ground which supported a roughly lashed framework over which a lightweight plastic tarpaulin had been draped.

The whole thing was open-sided and, as we approached it, I saw that it housed another piece of timber construction, though this had been made with considerably more care and had the appearance of something intended to withstand a lot of punishment. Overall, my impression was that of a vaulting horse, or pommel horse, similar to ones we had been expected to force ourselves over in my school days, but I surmised, quickly and correctly, that the purpose of this horse was quite different.

Four sturdy legs, one on each corner, held up a shallow, box-like structure, into the longer sides of which had been cut two semi-circular depressions of differing sizes, each of which had been padded with a layer of leather. As we came closer still, I saw that a similar box lay on the ground beyond the main construction and immediately realised the purpose of the whole thing. A minute or so later I was experiencing that purpose first hand.

Freeing me from the shafts, Master Harvey led me forward to stand next to the 'horse', the depression on the side nearest me just below the height of my waist. This close, I saw that the further depression had a much narrower diameter than even I had first thought; just large enough to cradle my neck whilst the larger hollow accepted my girthed waist.

'Bend over,' Master Harvey instructed. 'I'm sure you've worked out what this is for, haven't you?' I could not answer, of course, but I obeyed, settling my stomach first and then extending my collared neck to the furthest semi-circle. Immediately, Master Harvey lifted up the second half of the box and lowered it – pinning me – my trussed arms fitting within the space remaining above my back. I heard a series of snaps as locks or catches were engaged and realised that I was now even more helpless than I had been before.

I could not raise my head now and the blinkers further restricted my field of vision to the few square metres immediately ahead of me. Into this now came the lower half of my master. I could not help but notice that he had opened the fly of his breeches and that his cock, a sizeable weapon was already erect.

Hands sought and found the clips that released my bit, but he made no attempt to remove the snaffle and I wondered whether he was aware that it was there. He would soon realise, I thought, somewhat grimly.

'You know what is expected?' I heard him say. His voice was a trifle more gruff than before, but otherwise quite dispassionate. I tried to nod.

'Unghkk!' I managed and was rewarded by the sound of a deep chuckle.

'Want me to take that out for you?'

'Unghkk eeeffff ussster!' He obviously understood my attempt at speech, but he simply laughed again.

'Sorry, little filly,' he said, '– but no can do. Haven't got the key tool with me, so you'll have to go nice and careful, understand?'

'Efffff ussster!'

'And then, if you do a good job,' he continued, 'I might just take your tail out and plug you there as well.' I stared at the thick shaft before my face and tried not to wince at the thought of having that where he was talking about putting it, but almost immediately I had more urgent matters to deal with.

Stooping slightly, he presented the burgeoning tip of his cock to my lips and pushed it into my mouth.

I strained to keep my teeth clear of his flesh and hoped he had not suddenly forgotten about the snaffle, but I need not have worried. Master Harvey, it seemed, had his own special preferences and right now one of those was for me to bring him to his climax using just my lips.

'Good girl,' I heard him grunt and felt his hands gripping my bridle at either side of my head. 'That's it, just nice and easy. My, but those lips feel so soft, Sassie. So soft you don't need to spoil things with a tongue now, do you?'

I guessed, quite correctly, that he was very near. His voice had suddenly become very unsteady, his breathing quite ragged, and a few seconds later he came, exploding into my throat with a ferocity that almost choked me. At that same instant he must have triggered the remote control, for, as he withdrew, the vibrator inside me sprang back into life.

I groaned, his semen dribbling from my lips and I quickly surrendered to the inevitable. My hooves kicking wildly in the air behind me, not caring at all about the spectacle I must be presenting, I was greedy for my own release again as I had been for it that very first time I had donned a harness and bit.

'Aye, it's amazing what takes different people's fancies,' Angus Frearson said sagely, when Geordie had finished giving him a carefully edited version of events at Celia's farm and her description of the kind of activities that took place on Ailsa Ness. 'Even more amazing that they'll pay so much good money for it, too. Mind you, laddie, we all have to have our little hobbies and diversions, don't we?'

'You don't think it's all . . . well, a bit perverted?' Geordie asked. Frearson spread his hands.

'Who am I to judge, son?' he said. 'There'll be those who'd condemn it, certainly, but I've always been a live and let live man meself. Doesn't sound like they do anyone any harm – certainly not at this Butler woman's place – so let the buggers get on with it, I say.' He shrugged. 'No, stuff like that doesn't worry me one bit, laddie, and if you've found yourself getting drawn to it, that's your business and not mine. However,' he said, leaning back in his chair and entwining his fingers, 'when it comes to other things – drugs and murder for a start – now that's when I do get interested, same as you. We're both policemen, after all, and sworn to uphold the law and all that verbal bollocks. 'So, if that crowd out there want to mix harmless fun with things that ruin thousands or millions of innocent lives, then it's our job to make sure they rue the day, eh?'

'The sooner the better, I'd say,' Geordie retorted. Frearson nodded again.

'Aye, I know how you feel at the moment,' he agreed. 'And our time will come, as surely as night follows day.'

'Nothing on that sub, I suppose?' Geordie asked, changing the immediate subject.

'Nothing we don't already know,' Frearson replied. 'The navy lads have put a coastal defence plane up and they're shadowing it for a while. It's currently making a long slow sweep around, heading for the North Atlantic, but any fool could have worked out that's what they'd do, assuming they weren't actually Russian and wanting to head back that way. Going the other way means the Channel and it'd be a bloody hard job hiding a sub down there. Besides, running submerged through the Channel is asking to have their conning tower lopped off by some idiot merchant skipper. He paused, and continued thoughtfully. 'No, they'll head for the North Atlantic and they won't turn south, if south is where they're intending to head, until they're well out and away from land. Mind you, if they think that means they're safe, they've got another think coming. The good old *Andrew* will be on their tail all the way to wherever it is they call home.'

'And meantime, we just sit and wait,' Geordie sighed, resignedly. Frearson smiled.

'Well, we can do more than just wait,' he suggested. 'For a start, I know a lovely little pub that does a spectacular roast lunch. And they won't tell on me for drinking brandy, either,' he added, with a wry chuckle.

Colin lay back across the bed, staring up into Anna's dark features, watching her as she pursed her lips and then ran her tongue along them, her eyes closed as she slowly ground herself deeper on to him. She was quietly lost in her own little private world, Colin knew, and there was nothing for him to do that did not risk invading that privacy. All Anna needed from him now was the erect phallus on to which she had so eagerly lowered herself; she could not touch him with her hands, which fluttered uselessly in their cuffs at her sides; she did not need his hands, nor even his lips, as her nipples were thrustingly erect of their own volition.

At last she slowed her gyrations to a complete stop, sighed, and opened her heavily-painted eyes.

'Beautiful!' she breathed. 'Thank you, master.' She spoke with a slight lisp, thanks to the tongue stud, he knew, but Colin did not know how to respond to this, so decided silence was the best policy. Apparently Anna expected nothing more.

'I hope that my master enjoyed that as much as I did?' she said. The white, red-lined lips twitched slightly. She was doing very well with her role, Colin thought, very well indeed. Now he did know what to say.

'Your master is fairly pleased with you, slave,' he said. 'For a princess warrior you are certainly one horny little bitch!' Make what you will of that, he silently told any eavesdroppers. And then: 'Perhaps we should get a stud put in your clit, slave? The one through your tongue was certainly as interesting as Mistress Celia suggested it might be.'

'Whatever you wish, master.' He could see she actually meant that, for her eyes had begun to glaze over again and he knew that she was imagining it for real. Whatever else she was back home in Norway, Colin told himself, she was no innocent that was sure, and he was equally certain that this was far from her first experience of extreme erotic sex practices. No one, no matter how broad minded, could throw themselves into this from scratch with so much enthusaism and conviction.

'I wish,' he said, slowly, 'for you to remove yourself from me, clean me carefully with that wicked little tongue of yours, and then we'll go and find Mistress Celia. First, however, I shall release one of your hands for two minutes, so that you can go over and pour me a glass of wine. I really don't have the energy to do that for myself right now!'

If Alex needed any further confirmation as to Fiona Charles's vindictive nature, the sight of Sol, dangling helplessly from the tree, would have been more than enough. Just how long he had been left like this she could not be sure but it had to be considerably more than two hours, even from the time since Alex had first seen her, for the woman had not been out of her sight ever since.

'Recognise him, Jangles?' Fiona sneered, as Alex trotted to an obedient halt a few feet from the hanging figure. 'Doesn't seem half so much a man now, does he, though he does have a nice big cock, you have to say that much for him. It'll grow even bigger if I take those restraining straps off it, but that's for later on and only if you're a good pony bitch.' She laughed harshly.

'Before he fucks you, Jangles, you're going to fuck him and fuck him good, or I'll thrash the skin off your lazy fat arse!' She jumped down and strode across to stand in front of Sol, who had finally managed to open his eyes and was staring balefully back at her. 'Miserable little shit!' she hissed at him.

'He used to fuck my arse every night I was in the stables, did you know that?' Fiona snarled. 'Yes, of course you know that, don't you, Jangles? I expect everyone in the stables, everyone on this fucking island even, all know all about Solly fucking the television star in her pony stall!

'Gave you an extra special buzz, that did, didn't it Solly, eh? Yeah, I'll bet it did.' She swung her arm suddenly, her gloved palm exploding across his cheek and rocking his head back violently. 'That give you the same buzz, does it, Solly? Well, don't worry, I'll find you something that does.' She paused, panting. 'Look at the pretty pony I've brought you for a start. Isn't that just too kind of me, eh? Bet you've had her arse a few times, same as you did mine, so now it's going to be her turn. I might even fuck you myself, depending on how she does with you. Yes, maybe I'll fuck you whilst you're fucking her, just like a little daisy chain.'

Alex heaved a sigh of relief for Sol's tortured arms and shoulders when Fiona finally loosened the ropes and lowered him back to the ground. She wondered whether he might not have taken advantage of having his hands free, if only for the few seconds it took for her to resecure them in the back pouch, but concluded that he probably had little strength left in them and just as probably knew that he could face even worse punishment for striking or resisting a guest, even one as malicious as Fiona Charles.

Having satisfied herself that Sol was once again quite harmless, Fiona stooped to release the leg spreader and then strolled casually back to the sulkie. Alex heard her rummaging about with something and then she reappeared before her, holding a double dildo, complete with harness.

'For you, pretty Jangles,' she announced. 'This end goes up inside your fanny and this –' she said, indicating the longer end, '– is for lover boy over there. I usually reserve this for nice slack pussies, but a bit of effort from you and he'll be slack soon enough.' Behind her, Alex saw Sol's eyes had grown wide at the sight of the huge cock and she shuddered in sympathy with him. The end intended for her was impressive enough and would fill her completely – the thought of the even larger shaft going anywhere, let alone where she was expected to put it, would have brought tears to her original eyes.

'Now then,' Fiona was saying, 'I wonder how best we should do this? Perhaps if we put Solly over the back of the cart and strap him down? Yes, that should be best, I think, then we can fix his knees to the wheels and keep him nice and open for you. Not a bad position for a quick warm-up whipping, either,' she added, her eyes narrowing.

Beneath the tree, Sol sobbed through his gag, but all three of them knew that any chance of sympathy from Fiona was about as likely as lead turning to gold.

* * *

When Colin finally walked into the stables concourse with Anna teetering behind him on a long chain leash attached to her collar, he saw what he expected to see and what he *was* expected to see. Jessica was in full harness, between the shafts of one of the standard lightweight sulkies, sucking quietly on her bit, her hooves moving slightly at regular intervals as she shifted her weight and sought to keep herself from stiffening up.

Colin's expression softened at the sight of the dark-haired pony-girl, memories of the previous evening flooding back, expectations for the coming few hours riding very high. Yet again he managed to force all thoughts of Sassie into a back compartment of his mind and concentrated instead on what he had to look forward to; the beautiful slave princess creature that Celia had created from Anna, and the erotically docile Jess.

He could not know, of course, of the switch that had been made and that the girl he took for granted as being the same one from the night before was actually her former lover and master, Andrew Lachan. And Lachan, held silent by electronic means and snaffle plate and bit, could do nothing to enlighten Colin. Whatever had happened to Jessie only hours earlier was almost certainly going to happen to Lachan in the imminent future, and there was nothing he could do to stop it.

Angrily, he tossed his head, a very un-Jess like action that he hoped might prompt some degree of suspicion, but before Colin could react, Higgy appeared from inside the nearest stall, striding purposefully towards them.

'Don't mind Jessie, sir,' he said, casually. 'She's usually so docile, I know, but when she finds a master she particularly likes, well, she gets all excited and just can't help herself. Whatever you did to her last night, sir, I reckon it must have made quite an impression on her. Ain't seen her this worked up for ages.

'Take my tip, sir,' he added, leaning closer in what appeared to be a conspiratorial gesture, but still speaking in a voice carefully calculated to be loud and clear enough for Lachan to hear, '– you give her an extra taste or two of the whip. She really likes that when she's in one of these moods and it'll make her a little less – well, you know what I mean, sir, I'm sure you do.'

Colin wasn't sure that he did know, but he nodded all the same, striving to affect a knowing air. Higgy meantime had turned his attention to Anna and was visibly impressed.

'Very nice, sir!' he exclaimed. 'Very nice indeed.' He scratched his chin and gave Colin a sideways look. 'Don't suppose you'll be needing us to put her up down here in the stables tonight, by any chance?' Colin smiled and shook his head.

'I don't think so,' he said. 'This particular slave looks much nicer draped across my bed, I can tell you.'

'Ah, that she does, I'm sure, sir,' Higgy agreed, but he could not quite hide the disappointment in his eyes. 'Going to hitch her to the back of the sulkie, are you, sir? Give her a nice brisk bit of exercise that will.'

'Well, there's just the one seat,' Colin replied, with a hint of sarcasm in his tone, 'so I guess she'll have to run, won't she? Unless there's a pony she can ride, that is?' Higgy grinned and touched his forehead.

'I can arrange even that, if you like, sir,' he replied, willingly enough. 'Though you'd have to give me a bit more notice, or else leave it for a quiet day. It's a bit hectic here today, as I expect you can see for yourself.'

'Maybe for the future, then?' Colin said. He passed Anna's leash to Higgy, who guided her around behind the sulkie and fastened the free end to the rail at the rear of the seat.

'Watch her with these shoes,' the groom called, as Colin began to climb aboard. 'The heels don't look too solid, not if you go over any uneven ground. What with no rain for a few days, there's a few ruts on the tracks now.'

'Thanks,' Colin said, gathering up the reins in his hands. 'I didn't intend going at any great rate anyway. Just a nice gentle walk.' Ahead of him, the pony-girl tossed her head and stamped her foot. 'Assuming Jess behaves herself, that is,' Colin laughed.

'Same as I said, sir,' Higgy said, coming up alongside him. 'You give her a good dose of the whip if she acts up. She'll be fine once you sort her out with a good tuppin', anyway.' He winked and moved further forward to pat 'Jess's' rump. The girl tried to shy away from him, dragging the shafts of the cart sideways and Higgy leant in to her, whispering something in her ear that Colin could not hear. Whatever he said, however, seemed to have the desired effect, for the girl immediately resumed a static position, eyes straight ahead.

'She'll be okay now, sir,' Higgy grinned. 'You let me know if she gets too frisky, though. We've got our own ways of dealing with disobedient ponies here.'

A few moments later, as the bizarre little caravan headed up the tunnel, the groom turned away and strolled casually over to the stall from which he had earlier taken Lachan. He opened the top half of the door and swung it back, peering at the remaining occupant inside.

'Well, they're away now, Jess,' he said. 'Shame you couldn't see that lovely bit of slave flesh he had with

107

him though, but never mind.' Jessie looked up from the pile of straw on which she was lying. She wore no bit and Higgy had, as usual, seen no need to fit her with a snaffle plate.

'Poor Andrew,' she sighed. 'This is destroying his mind, I think.' Higgy snorted, derisively.

'Then he shouldn't have played where he oughtn't, gal,' he said. 'And enough of this "Andrew" malarky, Jessie – there's no more Andrew. That didn't look like no Andrew to me. That looked like Bambi.' He snickered and shook his head. 'Shame she looked like you as far as our friend there was concerned, though . . .'

Perhaps, Tammy thought to herself, as she trotted slowly away from the clearing, perhaps things weren't so bad after all. When all was said and done, at least she was alive and, although this body and persona were far from what she would have chosen for herself, apparently it would last a lot longer than her original one.

She had never given much thought to death and dying, at least not until the storm and the wreck of the poor little *Flora*. She could so easily have suffered the same fate as her shipmates, but now she could look forward to a lifespan several times that which she could have hoped for before and, for all the weirdness of her situation and the weirdness of the people here, Major himself at least seemed intent on giving her an easy life.

What am I saying? The man, or whatever he is, wants me to bear him children and any minute now he's going to fuck me! He can't do that – I'm not a woman!

Tammy shook her head again, trying to banish the voice from her head. It was no good thinking like that, she told herself, fiercely. What's done is done and this body was very definitely female. Forget the past, forget Tommy. That way lay madness.

You're already mad, even thinking that you can accept all this! You're not a woman, Tommy, you're a man!

No. No, she was a woman now! This was a woman's body and her mind was a woman's mind now. No man looked or thought like she did, no man even possibly could.

You're letting them win, letting them brainwash you!

Let them, Tammy thought, placidly. Let them wash away the past; it would make the future so much easier, so much safer. If she bore children for Major, he would keep her safe, keep her comfortable. She wore his purple harness, which made her special – he had told her she was special, hadn't he?

She breathed in deeper, tossed her head and gripped the bit even more firmly between her teeth. Yes, she was special. Very special . . .

'We're going for a walk shortly, Millie,' Celia announced. 'So you can get yourself dressed in this.' She indicated the red pile she had deposited on the end of the bed. 'I'm too tired for anything extravagant, but it's such a nice day it would be a shame to waste it stuck in here.'

'Yes, mistress,' Millie agreed, sullenly. She was still feeling annoyed at the way she had been left out of everything so far, and the promise of a walk, whilst at least better than being left stuck on that damned stool, was hardly very exciting. The idea of coming to this place, she thought, was to carry out some sort of investigation and that had sounded quite thrilling at the time; the reality, at least so far, had been quite different.

'We'll go over and see if there are any races worth watching,' Celia said. 'Maybe we can find someone with a pony you can drive yourself. Would you like that, Millie?'

'Yes, mistress.' Millie began sorting through the rubbery clothing.

'Maybe you'd rather spend some time as a pony yourself, instead? I hear they're a bit short in the stables at the moment.'

'Whatever you say, mistress.'

'Sulking doesn't suit that pretty face, Millie,' Celia said. 'So get that mask on and cover it up. Snap to it now, or I'll take the strap to your backside.'

'Yes, mistress.' Millie picked out the mask and held it up. It was a fairly standard helmet design; red latex, intended to cover everything but the eyes, nostrils and in this case, she was glad to see, the mouth. Sometimes these masks had integral gags and that would have meant immediate silence. At least for the moment, it seemed, Celia was happy to leave her able to talk.

Millie pulled the mask slowly over the top of her head; there was no back zip, so obviously that was how it was intended to be put on, which was quite unusual, but the rubber seemed much stretchier than was usual and it drew down into place without too much difficulty. Carefully, she adjusted the fabric so that everything aligned properly and tested it by breathing through her nose: she had once made the mistake of not doing that and immediately upon having a gag thrust into her mouth had found it hard work getting sufficient air into her lungs through the tiny gaps that were then all that were left to her.

The rest of her costume was all fairly standard stuff, too. First came the rubber stockings, red again, as was everything Celia had selected for her this morning. They were very long, reaching right to her crotch, and the rubber suspender belt had specially

110

abbreviated straps to accommodate this. The panties were brief, tight and crotchless, pressing firmly against either side of her labia and forcing them out into a firm-lipped pout.

There was no brassière, but the brief little dress had been moulded to support her breasts: snuggling her like an extra skin so that her nipples popped out through the two appropriate circular openings like two little peaks. The sleeves were long and ended in gloves, which required a great deal of patience and no little skill to put on, but eventually Millie managed it and then engaged in a brief contortionary exercise in order to close the back zip that in turn drew the mandarin-style collar tightly about the collar of her mask.

'There are no shoes, mistress,' Millie observed. She gave a quick twirl, letting the short, flared skirt billow out to reveal the tops of her stockings, as she knew was the intention. Celia looked up from where she was wriggling herself into a black leather dress that looked as if it were two sizes too small for her ample bosom.

'Bottom of the closet,' she said. Millie nodded silently and padded across the room, drawing back the door and stooping to reach inside. She found two pairs of boots, both mid-calf in length, one pair in black, the other in red. Taking an educated guess, she selected the latter and walked back to sit on the edge of the bed.

The heels, she saw, were as extreme as they could be without actually being 'ballet style', for which at least she was grateful. Walking on absolute tiptoe was a skill which required a lot of practice and very strong leg muscles and whilst Millie could manage after a fashion, she had never actually been required to move far whilst wearing a pair. These at least allowed her toes to bend, so that there was sufficient area in contact with the ground to affect a sufficient amount of balance.

'That's good, Millie,' Celia observed, when Millie finally rose to her feet again and tottered across the room. 'Now get the cuffs and collar from the top drawer and put them on yourself. They're all self-locking, so just snap them on.'

The leather collar and cuffs were all in black, Millie saw, forming a good contrast to the colour of her outfit. The collar was wide, but not so wide as a posture collar; the wrist and ankle cuffs were also broad and all five pieces were studded and set with D-rings to enable chains or ropes to be attached when desired. For the moment, however, it seemed that Celia was content to leave her slave with full freedom of movement of her limbs.

'You can carry this, Millie,' Celia instructed, handing her a small, leather sack-like bag. 'And in case you're wondering, yes, it contains a couple of suitable gags, a blindfold and various restraining clips and chains. Whether they're used or not is up to you, to an extent.'

'Thank you, mistress.' Millie gripped the sack, testing its weight. It wasn't that heavy, she found, but it was heavy enough. 'I shall try my hardest to please you,' she said, almost automatically.

'And I –' Celia said, stepping forward and stroking Millie's rubber-covered cheek, '– shall endeavour to make sure that you do. Now, look sharp and let's get out into the fresh air.'

It was Colin's intention to spend the next few hours exploring the island in daylight, but as the sulkie rolled slowly along behind 'Jess', he realised that this was not going to be quite as simple a matter as he had hoped. The original plan had been to meander about, moving up and down the various tracks, perhaps getting to the shore at different places and trying to identify anything that might give a clue as to any activities here that would justify applying for an eventual warrant.

However, there were not just a lot of guests about, but also a number of patrolling security personnel, presumably he thought, judging from the way in which they kept looking skywards at regular intervals, in readiness to get everyone and everything under cover at the first sign of any approaching air traffic. This good weather, he thought, irritably, was going to make things harder for them.

'Harder,' he murmured, half out loud, '– but not impossible.' He guided 'Jess' to one side of the track to allow an oncoming gig to pass, nodding to the female occupant, who smiled back at him from beneath a half mask that left her mouth and chin exposed. She was also wearing a brief tunic with cut-outs that left her generous breasts on full view.

'Nice,' she called across, nodding towards Anna. 'Is she available at all?'

'Maybe later,' Colin said. 'Depends how she behaves herself.'

'Of course.' The woman laughed and raised a hand in salute. 'Maybe see you this evening, then,' she said, as she went by. 'I'm in one six one. Just call me Sally.'

Smiling to himself, Colin shook his head. They all made it sound so matter-of-fact, he thought. Borrow my slave, drive my pony, fuck my whatever.

'Funny old world this, Jess,' he said, louder this time. The pony-girl snorted and her mane of hair swayed from side to side. She seemed so different from the way she had been the previous night, Colin thought, regardless of what Higgy had said. Perhaps

113

she was just tired and feeling a bit tetchy. He yawned, automatically.

'Don't worry, gal,' he called. 'We'll find somewhere to rest up before too much longer. I could do with a rest myself, I think.' He turned and looked back over his shoulder, to where Anna was dutifully teetering along in their wake. No doubt she would be relieved to get her weight off those heels, though she had offered not a word of complaint as yet.

'You too, princess,' he said. Her lips twitched into a half smile. 'Yes,' he said, '– and that, too.'

What a life, he said to himself. What a choice. The beautiful Jess and the gorgeous warrior princess. It was going to be hard to keep his mind focused on the job he was really here to do. But then, he thought, he was duty bound to preserve his cover story, wasn't he?

It felt strange to be standing there, with what looked like an erect penis thrusting out from between her legs. Alex could feel its twin inside her, stretching her, rubbing against her clit, and her muscles kept contracting around it without any conscious effort from her, it seemed. Fiona finished tightening the crotch strap at the rear and walked back around to stand in front of her.

'You look so good like that,' she said, breathily. 'I may even have to fuck you myself later. But first, pony slut, you're going to fuck my other pony slut.' She turned Alex to face the other cart, the one Alex presumed Sol had pulled here much earlier. Now though, he was not between the shafts, but stretched, face down, over the rail behind the seat. A rope from his collar was tied to the seat itself, whilst two shorter ropes secured his knees, wide apart, to the wheels.

Fiona took a secure grip on Alex's protruding shaft and gave a sharp tug. The inner dildo jerked in unison and Alex let out a sharp gasp.

'Come on,' Fiona snapped, and led Alex by the stiff rubber cock until she was standing just behind her intended victim. Peering down, she could see the tightly puckered target and could not believe that the enormous phallus could possible enter there. Fiona seemed to be considering this, too.

'Maybe some lubrication,' she said, voicing her thoughts out loud. 'Lucky I brought a little goody bag, isn't it?'

Five

SASSIE

By the time Master Harvey released me from what he told me was called a 'crush' I could barely stand properly. My knees felt like jelly and my head was reeling; I had lost count of how many times I had come as he fucked me, all the orgasms seemingly merging into one long climax. I swayed uncertainly and he had to support me as he led me back between the shafts.

'You can have a few minutes' rest before we go on,' he said, working on the first buckle. Rest? I needed to collapse on the ground, shut my eyes and let my entire body recover for an hour or more at least! This damned fool seemed to think I was some sort of super being if he expected me to go straight back to hauling him around this damned island again. I tried to turn my head to look at him and gave a sort of pleading whicker through my bit, but either he did not understand, or else he was choosing not to understand.

'They tell me you're a real champion little racer too,' he said. 'I missed a lot of last night, but from what I did see you're quite something.' I heard him chuckle, deep in his throat. 'I was lucky to get you today, I reckon. There was quite a lot of competition, I can tell you.'

A while ago, I realised, that would have made me throw my head back with pride, but now I was beginning to see things differently. To be a pony-girl was ... well, it had reached levels in me I had never even suspected existed; but was this what I really wanted? On the track I had proved myself worthy, had been the centre of adulation and admiration, but here, here in this little clearing, I had become ... what?

I closed my eyes and blinked back the tears that had started to form there. I prayed that my real master would come back for me soon, or even Mistress Celia, who understood how a pony-girl's mind really worked: unlike this brutish, uncaring creature, to whom I was little more than a means of gratification. This was not how it was supposed to be, surely? I would not have offered myself up so willingly had I known any of this side of it, would I?

Would I?

Higgy watched the final pony and cart disappearing up the tunnel and turned to where the younger grooms were gathering in the middle of the concourse. It had been a hectic few hours and now the silence in the stables, broken only by the fractured conversation of the lads, seemed almost unnatural.

'A good job well done, boys,' he said. 'You can all go up and get yourselves something to eat. I'll hang on down here, just in case any of 'em come back unexpected like, though I doubt we'll be troubled for a few hours yet.' There were a few appreciative mutterings and the lads turned to troop away.

The silence was now complete and Higgy was left alone at last. He sighed, stretched his arms and turned to look across to the closed door of Jess's stall. She alone of the girls had not gone out today: the swapping of Bambi necessitated that she be kept hidden from view, in case the subterfuge was discovered. Not that Jess and Bambi were the only lookalikes among the stable girls, but his instructions had been to make sure that the Anderson fellow was given no reason to suspect that he was not driving Jess again.

Higgy grinned to himself. The former billionaire Lachan would shortly be discovering not just how it felt to be in a pony-girl's body, but what it felt like to be treated like a pony-girl for real. So far as Bambi, he had been spared the ultimate conclusion, but today would be the day and not before time, in Higgy's opinion.

'Thought yourself so special, didn't you?' he whispered out loud. 'No one else ever allowed to touch your precious Jessie, not even me. Well, now you've got the same tits and the same face and I can do things for Jessie you'll never be able to do again. Just a pity they wouldn't agree to let me be the one to break you, but then I suppose they're right. I know the truth about you after all and better to have the other fella shag you the way he would shag Jess.'

'Talking to yourself again, Higgy?' The unexpected sound of Amaarini's voice made the groom start, guiltily. He swung round, wondering just how she had managed to come down the upper tunnel and cross halfway over the concourse without him hearing her, but then she was quite capable of moving like a ghost when she wanted to, even in those heels she habitually wore. If they clicked when she walked, Higgy knew, it was because Amaarini desired the effect that produced.

'Just thinking out loud, ma'am,' Higgy replied. He made a vague motion that covered the deserted stables from end to end. 'Everyone else is gone now and I always enjoy a bit of peace and quiet by myself, as you know.'

'Especially when you can share that peace and quiet with Jess, eh Higgy?' Amaarini gave him her peculiarly lopsided smile and Higgy knew it was a waste of time trying to deny what she had doubtless known for a long time.

'Jess is a bit special, ma'am,' he said, simply. 'I've got a bit of a soft spot for her, it's true.'

'More a hard spot, I think,' Amaarini retorted, but the smile remained in place. 'And you didn't care too much for Bambi in her previous existence, I know.'

'Ah well, that's all past now,' Higgy said. 'And I like to make sure Jess don't get too lonely, if you know what I mean.'

'Of course.' Amaarini moved closer, her smile changing into something of a puzzled expression. 'So, there's just you and Jess down here at the moment?' she asked. Higgy nodded. 'Then I can speak freely with you and you can speak freely with me?'

'You can always speak freely with me, ma'am,' Higgy replied, seriously. 'I'd have thought you'd know that, after all this time.'

'Yes,' she sighed, 'I do know that. So come, Higgy, let's walk – up into the open, perhaps. Let's not waste the lovely weather – we get little enough of it up here.' She moved past him, heading towards the outer tunnel.

'Tell me, Higgy,' she said. 'What is it with this human passion for girls to act like ponies?' Higgy fell into step alongside her. 'You must have some explanation. After all, you are half human yourself and not exactly averse to the sport are you?'

'You're also half human, ma'am, if you don't mind me pointing that out?'

'Slightly different, Higgy,' Amaarini replied. 'My body is mostly human, but my mind is Askarlarni, don't forget. Whereas you are half human in both body and mind.'

'Well, ma'am, it's difficult for me to explain to you,' Higgy said, after another short pause. 'With me, well, I've worked in these stables since I was old enough to harness a girl and they're near enough all I know. I treat 'em all well, discipline 'em when needed and give them what we both enjoy at other times.'

'And that's enough for you, is it? What about other women?'

'Other women? Slaves, you mean? Well, that new fella, Anderson, he's got a tasty slave with him, especially the way she's done up today. I wouldn't say no, if you know what I mean.'

'I've never known you be anything but blunt, Higgy,' Amaarini laughed. 'But what of the girls themselves? Are they mostly happy down here, once they get over their initial settling in problems, of course?'

'Oh yes,' Higgy assured her. 'Some do take a bit longer than others, of course, only natural, but eventually they all seem to realise when they're well off. At first, well, perhaps they don't like the idea of what they've become, but then it sort of gradually becomes a matter of pride. Even the part-time girls who come down from up top get caught up in it all, as you know, ma'am.'

'Yes, I do know.' Amaarini's forehead creased slightly. 'What I don't understand is why? Do you?'

'Never really thought about it that much,' Higgy admitted. 'You'd maybe better try asking them that, not me.'

'I did, once,' Amaarini said. 'I asked Jess and I asked that young Welsh filly who ended up going down to the Suffolk farm last year. Jess just acted her usual vague self and muttered about how proud she was to serve her master, and Megan – that was the name she was given, if I recall – she just said she couldn't explain it. Told me I'd have to experience it myself to know.'

'Cheeky little mare!' Higgy exclaimed, genuinely shocked. 'You should have told me and I'd have had her jumping hurdles for a couple of hours for that!'

'Maybe she was right, though,' Amaarini said. 'I mean, how can anyone possibly understand what's going through another's mind? There are so many different pressures, so many different influences. Maybe we think we understand, but how can we really, eh?'

'I suppose,' Higgy conceded. 'I've never really bothered about that sort of thing. Just as long as I turn my girls out well, that's all I ever worry about.'

'Well, you certainly do know how to turn a girl out well,' Amaarini said. They had reached the entrance and she stopped, just short of the sunlit grass beyond. At the far side of the wide expanse of grass that separated the hillside from the nearest trees, two pony-girls were trotting side by side, their drivers apparently in conversation with each other.

'I've noticed,' she said, 'that some of the guests prefer it when the girls wear those curious snout masks, but some prefer them without?'

'Matter of taste, I reckon,' Higgy said. He looked sideways at Amaarini, trying not to appear to concerned, but there was something about her tone, her whole demeanour, that was just not like her.

'What about the girls themselves? They prefer being without those masks, I presume?'

'Not all, no,' Higgy said. 'Some actually prefer the masks and the new ones almost always perform better in them. Something to do with being able to hide behind themselves, I suppose, same way some of the visitors and their slaves like to keep their masks on.'

'With the visitors, that's sometimes to protect their identities,' Amaarini countered, '– just in case they run into someone here who knows them.'

'You reckon?' Higgy let out a harsh little laugh. 'Well, maybe, but I reckon no one who comes here would be likely to try to hold anything over anyone else who came here. There's a saying about pots and kettles I seem to recall. It's not just about protecting identities, I don't think – more to do with *changing* identities.'

'That's the conclusion I came to,' Amaarini said, quietly. 'They use their masks as a way of submerging their real selves, to help them to become something they know they're not, but something they wish they could be.'

'Yes,' Higgy agreed. He paused, sucking contemplatively on his lower lip. 'Don't mind me asking,' he continued, at last, 'but is there a point to this conversation?' Amaarini did not answer immediately; her gaze was still apparently fixed on the trotting ponies by the woods, but there was a look in her eyes that made Higgy think her thoughts were even further away than that. Eventually, after what seemed an interminable silence, she turned and looked at him.

'It's about experience, I think,' she replied and her voice sounded as if it had somehow lost most of its usual authority. 'You see, Higgy, I've been thinking about asking you to help me with something, but if I do, I must have your word that it remains entirely between the two of us.'

'You have my word on it, ma'am,' Higgy replied, sombrely. Amaarini nodded, her expression now dark.

'I'll have more than that, Higgy,' she said, her voice little more than a whisper. 'If you ever breathe a word to anyone, I'll have your damned life on it!'

SASSIE

Harvey's totally unfeeling treatment of me had brought me back to some sort of sense of reality, if only temporarily. All I wished for now was to be returned to Colin or Celia, and if possible to get off this awful island and find some space and time for myself, to reconsider just what it was I thought I was doing. After a short while however, when we were once again trotting through the woods, I remembered that there was another purpose to our visit here and that, as leaving in the near future was obviously only a remote possibility, then perhaps there was something more I could do to play my part, other than to serve as a combination of camouflage and diversion.

I began to look around and take proper stock of my surroundings for the first time, to consider the paths and clearings not just as a background in which I could act out my fantasies, but as enemy territory, a stronghold whose weaknesses I could help determine. Striving to shut out everything that had gone before and to ignore as far as possible the almost extreme ridiculousness of my personal situation, I started trying to spot surveillance cameras and to form a map inside my head.

The first part of this quest was not too difficult: the cameras were small, but little if any effort had been made to conceal them. Trying to memorise their positions and the layout of all the paths was a different matter entirely. The tracks wound back and forth with no discernible pattern and, if there was any man-made influence to them, I guessed it was only to help what nature herself had originally started.

I knew the approximate size of Ailsa and also, from the photographs Colin and Geordie had obtained, its rough shape and main features: the tor dominated one end, and the lower hill formed most of the eastern end, beneath which lay the stables themselves, of course. It was not a large piece of land by any standards, but the wildness of its flora and the density of the trees and undergrowth made it seem much bigger, especially when I was being forced to travel about it on tiptoe, pulling a cart and man which together had to weigh close to three hundred pounds.

It was not long before fatigue began to effect the clarity of my thinking and I was mightily relieved when Master Harvey reined me to a halt, though naturally very apprehensive as to his intentions towards me. To my relief, he seemed interested only in resting for a while.

'I need to rest, Sassie,' he said, flopping down on a small grassy embankment, 'and so do you. I had very little sleep last night and I reckon the same applies in your case – and if we're going to pit you against any other girls this afternoon, you need an hour or so to get your strength back.' He sat for several seconds and then stood up again.

'Maybe it'd be better if you lie down,' he said, stepping towards me and starting to unfasten the shaft straps from my harness. 'I know it's not the usual form, but I like to win. The money isn't important, but I just don't like to be beaten, you see.'

I did see. It was exactly the same trait that had made Andrew Lachan such a huge success in business. The money – and he certainly made plenty of it – wasn't the real reason behind his determination to succeed; it was merely a trophy to prove his success in the game. That success and the power and influence it created were what counted: the fact that others had to look up to him, were controlled by him and depended on him. The way, I supposed, that Jess had depended upon him and been so totally in his power. The way I now was so totally in Harvey's power. Was I now seeing in Harvey a side of Lachan that I had only really seen in glimpses before? Had he been so absolutely unfeeling in his treatment of his Jess? I found myself hoping not . . .

'As far as I've been able to see,' Celia said, speaking in a loud whisper, '– there are only two cameras in this area and they're both a good hundred yards from where we're standing. One's in that rather straggly-looking tree back where the trail enters the clearing we just left and the other – no, don't even think about looking back – is over to our left, covering a fork in the next trail, where that little spring comes to the surface.'

Millie, walking dutifully alongside Celia, nodded. They had spent half an hour so far wandering about as if Celia were exercising her, a light chain leash leading from Millie's collar to Celia's wrist. A mistress with her slave, a scenario hardly likely to attract any undue interest.

'What about microphones?' Colin had warned them about the possibility of audio pick-ups and Millie had worked hard to stay in character and say nothing that might arouse suspicion ever since their arrival. Her eyes flicked nervously from side to side, but the bushes and trees could have hidden a small army, let alone a miniature electronic bug.

'I'm not sure they bother much out here,' Celia replied. 'In my opinion it would be a waste of time anyway. Fair enough, it's calm out here today, but as often as not there's quite a wind, even when it's reasonably fine and that would make picking up speech from a distance all but impossible. I'm no expert, of course, but we've tried something similar at my place and the results were worse than useless.

'No, I reckon they rely on visual surveillance out of doors, so as long as we just walk about naturally, we shan't interest them. Besides, judging from the number of security patrols they have out today, they can't have that many people to do the monitoring. Walk straight, slave!' She snapped out the order in a loud voice and Millie started in alarm at the sudden change of tone. A second or so later, two uniformed guards came into view around the bend ahead of them.

'Get over to that tree, you lazy whore!' Celia commanded, pointing her crop to where a gnarled-looking specimen had gradually been surrendering to the prevailing winds over the years and was now growing at an angle of approximately forty-five degrees to the ground. Understanding what was required of her, Millie tottered across the few feet of rutted ground and stretched herself, face down, along the trunk.

'I ought to string you up by your ankles and leave you for an hour,' Celia rasped. 'You're getting lazier and lazier, Millie, and I think you need a severe lesson. This is just a warning, but next time . . .'

The crop whistled through the air, landing across Millie's upturned buttocks, mercifully where the brief, flared skirt still covered them, so that the resulting 'thwack' sounded far worse than the actual result. Millie, however, squealed and kicked one booted foot in the air behind her.

'Please, mistress!' she cried. 'Please, I'll try harder, honestly!' One of the guards let out a gruff laugh as they sauntered by and Celia swished a second blow that landed within a millimetre of the first. Millie yelped again, but this time there was less play-acting and far more pain involved.

'Ow! Oooh!' She grasped the trunk tightly and screwed her eyes shut, waiting for the third blow and knowing that Celia would not be overly bothered by her suffering, especially if it convinced the guards that they posed no potential threat.

'Shut up and get up!' Celia ordered. 'And hand me that bag.' Millie winced and straightened herself, stooping again to retrieve the leather sack she had dropped before adopting her punishment position. 'I can't stand your noise, slave,' Celia said, taking it from her. 'I should have gagged you earlier, I suppose.'

Millie glanced towards the backs of the retreating men and groaned.

'Is it really necessary?' she hissed. 'They're gone now, aren't they?' Celia sniffed and shook her head.

'But they've got ears, stupid,' she said, derisively. 'They'll expect to hear a few more whacks and a lot more noise from you, won't they? Open your silly mouth and I'll put this on you until they're completely out of sight and then I'll just crack the tree trunk a few times. Or would you rather we did a proper job of whipping you instead?'

Colin heard the excited voices well before they emerged into the next clearing. There were about a dozen of them; two masters, three mistresses and five pony-girls, who were standing patiently between the shafts of their respective vehicles. Two female slaves were both dressed, in as far as they could be described as being dressed, in white rubber high boots and mitten-ended gloves that stretched up to their shoulders. They also wore masks that covered the top

128

halves of their heads, from the tops of which bobbed different coloured plumes of feathers – whether real or artificial, Colin could not tell. One plume was red and black, the other pale blue and yellow. They had been laced tightly into leather cinchers about their waists and from behind them rose tails whose colours matched their plumage.

As Colin reined in Jess – as he still thought her – to a halt, one of the men turned to greet him, his eyes going immediately from the pony-girl to Anna, and staying there long enough to show that he was most impressed by what he saw.

'Morning, friend,' he said, finally forcing his attention back to Colin. 'Fine looking bitch you've got there, I must say.' There was a general murmur of approval from his companions, who had all shifted their attention towards the newcomers.

'I'm rather proud of her, I must say,' Colin agreed, amicably. He half rose in his seat and looked towards the two slave girls. 'You seem to have a couple of little beauties yourselves,' he observed, drily. The first man nodded.

'One's mine,' he said, jerking a finger towards the black and red plumed girl. 'That's Lolly. The other one's called Babs and she belongs to Georgia over there.' He indicated a tall blonde woman, who was dressed in a simple leather skirt, halter top and knee boots.

'We're organising a hen fight,' he continued, smirking. 'Mind you, it's as much a cock fight, really, as you'll see. I take it you'd like to stay and watch? You're more than welcome, friend.' Colin nodded and began to dismount.

'Very kind of you, I'm sure,' he said. He strode towards the speaker, extending his hand. 'I'm Jason, by the way,' he added, using the alias with which he had entered the island.

'Boz,' said the man, gripping his hand firmly. 'It's not my real name, obviously, but someone once said I was the Dickens of a good fuck and somehow it just sort of stuck!' He laughed uproariously and several of the others joined in. 'But enough of me, let's get back to the real business. Who's got the kit?'

The 'kit' comprised an intricate double gag arrangement and two complicated double dildo harnesses. Boz picked up one of the latter and brought it across to show Colin how it worked.

'The usual thing is for the inner dildo to extend out into the outer one,' Boz explained, '– but if you look at this, you'll see that they're staggered.' He tilted the device so that Colin was able to see that the inner dildo was actually hollow and the outer half, because it was set slightly higher, left that hollow opening unimpeded.

'Intriguing,' he said. 'And does the outer one fit inside the inner – the outer bit of the other one, that is,' he added, nodding to where another of the men was beginning to fit the other harness to the blue and yellow plumed girl.

'That's the idea,' Boz said. 'The bit that goes inside holds her open and then the other girl tries to put her cock inside her. You'll see the sheath is cut away here,' he added, showing it to Colin. 'That's so her clit isn't covered up, otherwise there'd be no stimulation worth talking about, whereas with this the nub gets pressed out quite nicely.

'Of course,' he continued, 'she's trying to do exactly the same to the other girl at the same time. First one to achieve a full penetration wins the round. Then it's either the best of three, best of five, or whatever.

'Mind you, if either of the bitches comes, she loses by default and gets a good whipping on her arse, unless her master is satisfied she's put up a good show in the meantime. Thumbs up, thumbs down, very gladiatorial and all that.'

'Fascinating concept,' Colin said. He looked sideways towards the sun, trying to gauge the time; ideally, he wanted to get on with investigating the island, but he also knew the importance of acting as casually as possible, of blending in among the other visitors without drawing unwanted attention to himself. Staying to watch these proceedings could certainly do his cover no harm.

The black and red plumed girl seemed reluctant to have her harness fitted and Boz and the other man had to hold her arms, whilst the blonde female attended to the details. The slave girl shrieked and screamed, but none of the others seemed to take any notice of that.

'She likes to play the reluctant one,' said one of the other females. She was wearing a green cat mask and green leotard, with green and white ankle boots. Her hair was hidden completely from view, but her dark skin tone suggested she ought to be a brunette. 'She's a strange one is Lolly,' the woman continued. 'Makes like she hates every minute of everything, but she loves it really. She's been with Boz since she dropped out of university, apparently.'

Despite Lolly's struggles and protestations, it did not take the trio long to finish preparing her and Colin observed that when they released her, although her hands were practically unimpeded, she made no effort to try to remove the harness. Instead, she stood there defiantly, one hand on her hip, the other grasping the rearing dildo shaft.

'Hope the bitch knows I'm gonna fuck her brains out!' she shrilled. The other girl, who had accepted her harness without resistance, eyed her from a safe distance.

131

'We'll see about that, won't we?' she replied, evenly. She seemed slightly shorter and more lightly built than her adversary, but Colin noticed that she moved with an easy grace, carrying her weight on her toes, the steepling heels of her boots barely touching the ground.

'Gag strap,' Boz ordered. 'Better do Lolly first, otherwise we'll have to put up with even more of her wailing.' This time, however, Lolly seemed less inclined to put up more than a passing show and very quickly Boz fastened on the intricate harness, that held a stubby penis inside her mouth. From this extended about three feet of pliable rubber tubing, at the other end of which was another head harness and gag, identical to the one she now wore.

'Your turn now, Babs,' the second man said, and the blue and yellow plumed girl stepped obediently forward. The second harness was quickly fitted to her and the two girls stood eye to eye, prevented from moving more than a pace apart by the interconnecting strip. It was a simple but cunning variation on a traditional Basque form of knife fighting, except that the weapons used in this contest were far blunter and they were not intended to pierce the heart, either.

The spectators, Colin included, fanned out to form a rough circle whilst the two combatants now settled into a half crouch, mitted hands on their knees, their rampant phalluses seemingly mere inches apart. From screaming harpy, Lolly had now become deadly serious and very intent, whilst her opponent looked hardly less earnest.

'Best of five first, I reckon,' Boz said. The second man nodded and Colin realised that he was probably Babs's master. 'Hundred quid a fall, just to make things interesting?'

'Make it five hundred,' the other replied, grinning. Boz nodded his agreement.

'Fair enough. And Simone to be the judge if either of them comes?' He nodded towards the blonde woman who had helped in the girls' preparation. The second man also nodded.

'Fine by me,' he said. 'Want to call the whole thing then, Simone?' The blonde stepped forward and positioned herself alongside the girls, about two paces from them.

'Ready then, bitches?' She raised her right arm in the air and the two white helmeted heads nodded, their plumes bobbing back and forth in unison. 'Right then, on my count. One . . . two . . . *three!*' She dropped her arm and stepped back another pace and immediately there was a flurry of arms and legs which ended in both girls sprawling in an ungainly kicking, flailing heap.

For about a minute they rolled back and forth, first one seeming to gain an advantage and then the other, rolling her opponent and straddling her, but then, when she was forced to shift her weight in order to get her rubber cock between her thighs, finding herself thrust aside and again in turn on the bottom of the struggle.

'Stop!' Simone held up her hand and the two fighting slave girls stopped as if by magic. 'This is no good like this,' Simone said, shaking her head. 'Help me get them up again. I have an idea to make this more interesting.'

A few minutes later and Simone's suggested changes had been effected. Now each girl had her left leg doubled up behind her and secured there by leather straps, with her left arm secured behind her back. When Simone once more gave the command, they fell to the ground in an even more ungainly way, so that Colin, wincing, was astonished they did not damage themselves.

However, he could now see the reasoning behind Simone's changes. With only one leg and one arm each, neither girl could exert as much leverage and now it became a battle that required flexibility, upper body strength and timing. Lolly apparently had the greater body strength and both girls appeared equally flexible, but Babs, Colin saw, had the natural timing of a dancer or athlete.

At one moment it seemed that Lolly must take the first point, for she lay across the shorter girl, manoeuvring herself around for the final thrust, her one free arm pressed across her, gripping her left breast spitefully, but then, in a move that was so fast Colin could not afterwards describe it properly, Babs seemed to slide out from under her and flipped her with her unfettered leg. A split second later she had rolled over herself and, not bothering to try to pin her opponent's upper body, landed firmly between her thighs, her phallus in her hand, guiding it towards its yawning target.

There was a muffled shriek of annoyance from behind Lolly's gag, but it was too late. The white phallus slid fully into her and she relaxed, accepting the point against her. Babs, raising herself on her one arm, withdrew slightly and then thrust into her again, repeating the process a few times. Behind her mask, Lolly's eyes were screwed tightly shut, whilst Simone mouthed a silent count.

'Time out!' the blonde called, after perhaps a full minute. Slowly, Babs withdrew completely and Lolly opened her eyes again. 'One point, no climax!' Simone announced, as the other two women moved in to get the slaves back on to their feet. Boz turned to Babs's master and laughed.

'She's very good, your girl,' he said, nodding appreciatively. 'Want to make it best of seven? I've never seen Lolly come in one of these contests before and I reckon your little Babs might just be the one to do it to her!'

'You're sure you want to do this, ma'am?' Higgy stood in the vacant stall, with Amaarini just outside the doorway. 'I mean, Jess is safely out the back and she can't hear a thing through that door, but what if anyone comes down here?'

'Then you simply make sure that nobody enters here if I can be recognised,' Amaarini replied. 'You still think you can disguise me sufficiently, I suppose? My height, for instance?'

'The boots make all the girls seem tall,' Higgy said, 'and if I'm to drive you, well, no one will take much notice. Besides, we have some tall fillies here and then there are the ones who come with the guests. If any of the lads come back, well, they'll probably go up in the sun 'til they're needed, so they won't be interested in anything that might mean work. There's nothing much to do down here until they start bringing the gals back again and that won't be for hours as long as this weather holds, as they'll want to make the most of that.

'Anyone asks, I'll just give 'em some story about one of the guests wanting me to trot his girl for him. That often happens, especially if a fella finds himself a little diversion up top, if you get my meaning.'

'Yes,' Amaarini said. 'Yes, I do know what you mean. Well then . . .' She shrugged and stepped inside the stall, but Higgy looked less sure than he had previously sounded and now he hesitated.

'Are you sure about this, ma'am?' he asked. 'Only it doesn't feel quite right.'

'No, I'm not sure at all, Higgy,' she replied, smiling at him. 'That's the point – I'm trying to discover something I don't understand, so how *can* I be sure? Now, we shall start, otherwise the day will be over and these stables will be full of people again.'

'Well . . .' Higgy still hesitated. 'Maybe you could just try on . . .' He stopped, looking to the side, as if examining the contents of the tack rack.

'No, Higgy,' Amaarini said, firmly. 'No, I want you – us – to do this properly. I want you to treat me exactly as you would any pony-girl coming here for the first time.'

'*Exactly* the same?'

'Exactly,' Amaarini repeated. 'And I will not resist anything. I will obey everything. I will be a pony-girl and you will be my groom and master – for exactly three hours,' she added.

'Three hours?'

'Three hours should be enough for you to show me the full experience?'

'I reckon so.' Higgy bit his lip. 'The *full* experience?'

'Short of one thing,' Amaarini said. She gave him her crooked smile again. 'Do I have to spell that out for you?'

'There are other . . . intimacies,' Higgy said. Amaarini nodded.

'I know,' she said, quietly. 'Anything but actual . . . damn you, man, get on with it. Just keep your cock in your trousers, that's all.' She straightened her shoulders and moved stiffly into the centre of the stall.

'As of this moment,' she said, 'I am a pony-girl. You may name me yourself, if you wish.'

'Diamond,' Higgy said, quietly. 'You are now Diamond.' Another pause, then, 'Remove your clothes, pony-girl Diamond. Everything. You must be naked. Now!'

* * *

136

The hen/cock fight was reaching an interesting and intriguingly balanced point. Lolly, furious at losing the first point and plainly worried that she had come so close to losing the contest by default of climaxing at the same time, threw herself back into the fray after the two-minute break insisted upon by Simone and for a few seconds it looked as if her onslaught would overwhelm Babs. But the lighter girl had managed to absorb the attack far better than it had seemed to the onlookers and suddenly countered, just when it appeared that Lolly must force the equalising point.

From a prone position and looking exhausted, she timed her move to perfection and, just as Lolly was on the point of penetrating her, she rolled sideways, driving her free knee into the other girl's side with such venom that Lolly shrieked. Lolly was sent sprawling, grabbing at herself with her one available hand, momentarily forgetting any thoughts of defence. It was all Babs had been waiting for.

Continuing her roll, she managed to use her bound leg as a lever and flopped straight over on to her opponent, perfectly positioned between her splayed thighs to drive her phallus home. A long, wailing moan came from behind Lolly's gag, followed by a stifled grunt as she fought to control her body's response to the quickly pistoning thrusts that Babs immediately began to inflict on her. Simone, moving in closer, stooped to peer intently at Lolly's face, counting silently once again.

'Stop!' she cried, at last, kicking at Babs's upraised bottom. 'Time out! One point again, but still no climax.' It had been a close run thing though, Colin saw, and Lolly's features, where they were not obscured by the straps of the gag harness, clearly showed the signs of her struggle to remain in control.

Babs hopped backwards when she was helped to her feet and stood balanced on one leg, chest heaving, her artificial cock bobbing, glistening with Lolly's juices. A sudden thought occurred to Colin and he posed the question to Boz when the big man wandered back across to him during the break.

'What happens,' he asked, '– if the girl doing the fucking comes herself?' Boz laughed.

'That doesn't matter, not for scoring purposes,' he replied. 'And it does happen, though not as often as you think. The girls know that if they come it drains valuable energy from them, so the one on top – assuming she is on top, of course – will blank her mind against any such thoughts and concentrate on trying to get her opponent to come instead.'

'You say "assuming she is on top"?' Colin asked, puzzled. 'Surely she'd have to be?' Boz laughed again and shook his head.

'Not always. It's rare, of course, but it's possible for a girl to score a point from underneath, if the other one gets careless.'

'But if that happened, surely the girl on top could just lift herself off, so she'd be in no danger of defaulting?'

'Against the rules,' Boz said. 'Whether underneath or on top, once a girl is penetrated, she can't try to wriggle off the cock until the referee calls time. Hadn't you noticed how Lolly has had to just lay there and take it each time Babs has caught her? Of course, if the fucked girl is on top, it's harder work for the girl underneath to work her up properly, but I've seen it done.'

As if to illustrate his explanation, Lolly took the next point in almost exactly the way he had described. Realising that she was trailing badly and could afford no more errors, she fought cagily now and it was Babs, after a prolongued cat-and-mouse struggle, who made the next mistake. Trying to regain stability at the end of a roll, she allowed herself to straddle Lolly, who instantly seized her belt and drove upwards.

Babs's howl of anguish told the onlookers that the point had been made, even before Lolly started using her back and leg muscles to begin bouncing her victim up and down. The lighter girl rose and fell steadily and Colin saw the grimace on her already distorted features as she now took her turn to struggle against the stimulation. And possible it might have been, but forcing an orgasm on to an opponent from that position was clearly a far greater challenge.

'Time out!' Simone moved in and separated the girls. 'Two points to one,' she announced. 'Five minute break this time, I think,' she added, looking at the sweating, gasping contestants. Their bodies were streaked with perspiration and dust and their plumes and tails looked far less impressive than before they had started. 'Take their gags out and give them some water, will you, lads?' Simone suggested, grinning. 'It's a warm day today and this looks like it could go the full distance.'

When the contest eventually resumed, Colin realised that the way in which Babs had been suckered into losing the last point had affected her confidence, for although she continued to manoeuvre cautiously and concentrate on defence, she also missed two excellent attacking opportunities and nearly fell for the same trick yet again – only throwing herself sideways at the very last second. It therefore came as no surprise when the heavier Lolly eventually made her weight advantage pay and pinned and entered her at the end of a session that had lasted more than ten minutes.

'Time out,' Simone called and Lolly withdrew, after a fairly half-hearted attempt at securing the default orgasm, due, Colin realised, to the fact that she was as exhausted as Babs. The men helped their respective girls to their feet again and they prepared to engage again, but Simone was not happy.

'Let them rest again,' she said. 'That was far too long a round in this heat and they're losing too much body fluid. Give them another drink and sponge them down, and for Pete's sake, one of you give me a cigarette, will you?'

'Now this is very interesting.' Angus Frearson placed several print-out sheets on the desk and beckoned Geordie over to examine them.

'Satellite photos?' Geordie asked.

'Close,' Frearson said. 'RAF surveillance plane, high altitude. These are a bit grainy, but the originals will be a lot clearer when they get here.'

'That our submarine there?' Geordie jabbed a finger at the dark outline that was clearly visible against the background of ocean.

'That's our boy,' Frearson confirmed. 'And those –' he continued, pointing to two smaller dark shapes nearby, '– are buoyant, waterproof containers, probably fitted with radio beacons. The plane picked up some local signals that were probably coming from them, but they couldn't pinpoint it with absolute certainty.'

'So, they were dropping something to be picked up later,' Geordie mused. He moved the top sheet and stared at the one beneath it. 'Ah, and this was the pick-up, I suppose?'

'Yep. Ocean-going yacht, privately owned by one Eric Peabody.'

'Eh? You're having me on – no one's really called Peabody, are they?'

'Well, friend Eric certainly is,' Frearson chuckled. 'He's a financier, working out of London, Amsterdam, Berlin and also Moscow. Worth a tidy pile.'

'And so's that yacht of his, if it's as big as it looks here,' Geordie said.

'It is and it is,' Frearson said. 'She's called the *Estelle,* apparently after his mother.'

'Wonder what mummy would say if she knew her son was into smuggling?' Geordie said. 'Assuming that has to be contraband of some kind, which I think we can.'

'Almost certainly it is,' Frearson replied. 'Those canisters are all the rage at the moment. They can be dropped overboard and then there are chambers that can be flooded remotely, so they sink to a depth of about ten feet or so, leaving a little antenna on a float right above them. Impossible to spot with the naked eye, but anyone who knows the frequency can home right in on them, bring them up and bingo.'

'If these times are accurate, then *Estelle* collected barely an hour after the drop was made,' Geordie observed. 'They weren't wasting time, then. And where's she bound?'

'Not certain.' Frearson admitted. 'But that plane is keeping an eye on her now. The navy have a sub in the area which has taken over the shadowing of our sub. They won't even know they're being followed, not with the outdated gear they're bound to have.'

'So, will you have *Estelle* stopped and boarded?'

'Maybe, but not yet. We need to see what her next move is. My guess is that she'll offload again, probably in two separate drops, so that when she does steam into harbour she'll be clean as a whistle. This is a big operation, laddie, so they won't be taking any chances, not with Peabody's name at stake.'

'They're certainly trying to complicate matters as far as possible,' Geordie admitted. 'But why all this high seas stuff? I thought that was what they went to the island for, to drop off whatever they were carrying.'

'Me too,' Frearson said. 'And maybe they did drop some of their cargo. But the more I think of it, the less likely it seems that it would have been drugs of any kind, otherwise it would have been easier to redistribute again from there anyway.'

'So, they had something else to deliver to Ailsa?'

'That's my call, yes,' Frearson agreed. 'But that, old son, begs the question "what?", doesn't it?'

'And whether it was actually anything illegal,' Geordie muttered. Frearson gave a grunt of amusement.

'Oh, I think we can safely say it was that all right,' he said. 'If not, why not just use the Royal Mail? It may be a bit slow, but it'd be a fuck sight cheaper than sending that sub on a hundred mile detour, I'd say.'

Taking a deep breath, Amaarini quickly began to strip off her clothing, knowing that if she did not plunge straight in, her resolve might easily weaken. And yet, when she did hesitate before removing her panties, some inner motivation seemed to take control and, head held high, she stooped to slide the flimsy garment down her legs and stepped out of them.

Higgy, meanwhile, had affected to busy himself selecting items from the tack rack; keeping his back to her so that he did not have to watch her preparations. He was, Amaarini thought, far more used to having girls delivered to him already naked, and seeing her actually taking her own clothes off would possibly have unnerved him. She could see that he was already uncertain and disturbed at what she had asked him to do and half expected him to change his mind at the last minute.

However, when he did finally turn back round to confront her, she detected only the slightest flicker of hesitation and then the professional in him took over. He stepped towards her and she saw that he was holding a tongue snaffle; well, she thought, she had asked him to let her experience everything a new pony-girl experienced and the snaffle plate was standard for novices, as well as for the older girls whose voices could not be cancelled.

Staring straight ahead and avoiding his gaze, she opened her mouth. The plate felt cold and hard and there was an air of finality about the way it first snapped down over her back teeth and then was clamped there by the two adjusting screws. As Higgy withdrew his fingers, she tried to move her tongue: it was actually possible to slide it backwards and out from beneath the plate, she discovered, but then it was held uncomfortably to the roof of her mouth and she would still be unable to utter anything coherent, she realised. Quickly, she slipped her tongue back beneath the smooth steel and waited to see what Higgy would do next.

He decided to mask her before anything else, presumably, she thought, in case they were interrupted. The mask he had chosen was white, made from what the guests thought was latex but which was actually a substitute developed by their own laboratory that allowed the skin to breathe, enabling it to be worn for much longer periods without as much discomfort as would have been the case with natural rubber. It covered everything above her top lip, leaving the usual two nostril apertures and two almond-shaped eye openings only. There was also an opening at the back, just below the crown, through which he carefully drew her hair as he stretched the mask down over her head. She was impressed at how quickly he completed what was, after all, a quite complicated task.

The mask felt tight, moulding itself to the sides of her nose, but it also felt somehow comforting, reminding her of how she had enjoyed being wrapped in blankets by her nursemaid as a small child. The sound of her own breathing, magnified inside her head now that her covered ears were less sensitive to outside sounds, felt strangely exciting.

'Hold out your arm,' Higgy instructed, tapping her right wrist. She did so and he began sliding the leather mitt sleeve up it, adjusting it so that the laces ran directly up the outside in a straight line and then tightening them until the soft hide was stretched taut from wrist to shoulder. The other arm was treated in the same fashion and then Higgy began on her harness proper.

The girth felt far tighter than Amaarini had imagined it would, crushing her stomach and lower chest until she found breathing difficult, but she refused to allow her discomfort to show. She knew that pony-girls, like other slaves when corsetted, had to learn to breathe from the top of their lungs, using shallower, quicker breaths and, as Higgy drew the laces and straps inexorably tighter, she forced herself to practise this.

The upper harness came next but as Higgy began to push her breasts through the circular strapping, Amaarini automatically tried to shy away from him, his touch making her cringe.

'Stand, Diamond!' he snapped at her. 'We've got to show your tits to their best advantage, you stupid filly!' Amaarini's nostrils flared and her eyes burned with indignation, but then she realised that he was doing nothing more than she had asked of him. A pony-girl had to learn that her breasts could be handled at will – and were certainly handled by the grooms as a matter of course throughout their daily routines.

She forced herself to remain calm and was surprised at how curiously arousing it became as Higgy carefully tightened the straps, forcing her already impressive breasts into two elongated melon shapes. Idly, as she saw how her nipples were hardening and lengthening, she found herself wishing that they were pierced and that she could experience what it felt like to have them hung with the usual pony bells.

Higgy had finished tightening the upper straps now and it was time to finish dealing with her arms. There were several methods employed, depending upon the personal choice of whichever master was driving a girl on a particular day and what sort of tasks he had in mind for her. Higgy selected the standard method preferred by the grooms now; the soft pouch that was drawn up over the arms, with the two forearms resting parallel with each other behind her back. It was simple but effective, Amaarini knew, but she had never before realised just how effective and, as Higgy secured the shoulder straps that prevented the pouch from slipping down, she understood that she had now been rendered totally helpless and completely unable to fend for herself. In addition, the way her shoulders were now pressed backwards, her breasts were being thrust even further forward, seemingly inviting attention. Higgy was quick to oblige.

Although her nipples were not pierced, Amaarini had not reckoned on the circular clamps and now, as the first one was tightened about her left nipple, she let out an involuntary gasp. If Higgy heard her – which he most certainly must have – he simply ignored her and proceeded to treat the second nipple the same, before stepping back to admire the effect.

'Big teats you've got there, pony-girl,' he said, forcing a chuckle in an obvious attempt to disguise the nervousness in his voice. He looked straight into Amaarini's eyes, but she in turn stared straight over his shoulder. Would he, she wondered, be tempted to do what she had seen grooms do to other pony-girls: sucking on their nipples to arouse them even further? She felt a slight shiver at the thought, but the shiver faded when she realised that Higgy was still not yet sure enough of his ground to go that far. Instead, he produced two small bells and attached one to the bottom of each clamp.

'Shake your tits, Diamond,' he said, huskily. 'Let's hear what they sound like.' Amaarini hesitated, but only for a second, and then another cold shiver ran up her spine as her bells tinkled in time to her gyrations. 'That'll do for now, pony-girl,' Higgy said, suddenly sounding much more confident and authoritative.

Amaarini was well accustomed to walking in high heels, for it was almost expected by the guests that all the female staff would dress to enforce the image of domination. But the hoof boots were a totally different proposition. They were not just a lot higher, but the heels were angled forward to blend in with the thick soles, forming the impression of a real hoof. The weight had to be kept well forward, over the toes, or else she knew she would simply topple backwards. Once secured properly between the shafts of a vehicle, it was almost impossible for this to happen, Amaarini knew, but until that moment came all pony-girls quickly learned to walk as if on tiptoe in bare feet and now she would quickly have to master that art.

The boots were of the longer variety preferred by most guests; a curiosity to Amaarini, when she considered the usual human male preoccupation with long, bare, suntanned legs daily on show in the tabloid newspapers. Why was it, she wondered, that encasing perfectly beautiful legs in leather, rubber, or even plastic seemed to give them an even greater appeal in so many men's – and women's – eyes?

Her own legs, she knew, would stand comparison with any female legs anywhere on the planet, for her body, like the bodies of the Jenny-Anns, had been produced for her using exactly the same techniques perfected by Lineker over so many years. And although some of her Askarlarni peers had expressed a preference for something less than the perceived human male view of perfection, she had decided that generous breasts, long, well muscled legs and a perfectly sculpted face were not choices to be scorned. Looking as she now did, Amaarini knew that she could exercise a considerable power over the majority of the opposite sex, and even over a section of her own.

The boots, once they had been properly fitted on her, made her legs feel totally different from what she had expected. She had worn thigh-length boots before, of course, but the hoof boots clung to every contour, giving support to every joint and muscle, and holding her ankles so that it was almost impossible to alter the elevated angle of her insteps. She felt like a puppet somehow, but then that, she realised, was how all slaves, pony-girls or not, were supposed to feel: totally helpless and completely under the control of their masters and mistresses.

In this case, of course, Amaarini knew that she was not really under Higgy's control in any real sense – this was, after all, an experience limited to only a few hours – and yet she could still appreciate the feelings that must go through a pony-girl's head, especially the first time she was ever harnessed. Without arms, perched precariously on her hooves and unable to communicate other than by a series of grunts and groans, she was already beginning not to think of herself as having any choices, perhaps even of being ever again regarded as an intelligent being.

So why, Amaarini asked herself, did so many of them apparently come so quickly not just to acceptance, but even to actually enjoying the experience? Why did they seem to relish being reduced to the level of an attractive and helpless plaything? Jangles, for instance – Amaarini had seen the file they now held on her previous life and as Alex Gregory she had been an individualistic, intelligent achiever with high ambition and fierce determination, who was also both quick-witted and incisive. A far cry indeed from what she now was and yet her initial anger and resentment seemed to have melted away in an impossibly short space of time. Was it a purely human trait, a weakness that no Askarlarni mind could ever quite understand, let alone fall prey to?

Deep in these thoughts, Amaarini failed to notice Higgy preparing a dildo by lubricating it with a light grease, and the first touch on her sex made her jump and yelp in protest. The groom seemed intent on carrying out the instructions she had given him to treat her just the way he treated any other girl in his charge, and she had forgotten that it was quite commonplace to exercise the ponies with something in place to keep them stimulated and alert. He was also, it seemed, quite unaware that she was physically still a virgin in this body, but by the time he realised that, if indeed he noticed it at all, the deed was done.

Amaarini groaned, her stomach lurching, but her horror was more from the effect the rubber phallus was already having on her than at losing a maiden-head that she had never really considered, let alone considered important. She gritted her teeth as far as the tongue snaffle would allow and tried to fight back the sensations that were spreading through her body. She had had sex in her original Askarlarni body, but it had been a sterile experience – sterile in more ways than one, as it transpired – an act performed merely as a ritual for procreation that had left her wishing afterwards that she had settled instead for the prefer-red modern approach of artificial insemination. This was something totally unexpected, the way in which this human-based body was reacting to the most crude of stimuli. It was distasteful, disgraceful and yet . . .

She shook her head, willing such base thoughts from her mind, but Higgy apparently mistook her efforts for something else.

'Steady there, Diamond,' he cooed, encouragingly. 'Let's get your bridle on first. Then you wait 'til I get you between the shafts and you start trotting proper-ly.' He stooped down again and began fastening the broad crotch strap that was used to keep the dildo in place, apparently unconcerned now with his proxim-ity to her sex; handling her as dispassionately and expertly as he must have handled more than a hundred excited pony-girls before, and the way he would probably still be handling them in another hundred years . . .

Six

Simone finally decided that the two girls were ready to resume their contest again and they were once more set opposite each other, the connecting strap between their gags stretched to its limit.

They both started cautiously, wriggling their bodies when they hit the ground to ensure that they kept their open target areas well clear of their opponent's phallus and scorning possible opportunities to attack on several occasions. For two or three minutes it appeared that the fight was going to degenerate into a defensive stalemate.

Then, without warning, Lolly brought her free knee around in a scything arc, catching Babs in the middle of her thigh and delivering the perfect 'dead leg'. The leg itself was the one that was already bent double, but the pain was none the less distracting, so that Babs was caught completely by Lolly's next move. Using her one free arm and leg, she launched herself upwards and dropped with all her weight on to the unfortunate girl's solar plexus, winding her and paralysing her completely.

Babs was now totally at her mercy, unable to move with anything approaching control and, with a gurgle of triumph and with a slow deliberation that was almost surgical, Lolly settled between her thighs and slowly took her for the third point. Her efforts to produce an orgasm, however, were doomed to failure; the pain she had inflicted was overriding any other sensations she could hope to inflict and Simone, realising this, completed the count in record time, anxious to check that the smaller girl was not too badly or permanently hurt.

Fortunately, once they had been separated, Babs quickly recovered both her wind and her composure and, after only a few minutes' respite, nodded that she was prepared to continue.

'Three two to black and gold,' Simone reminded the small audience. 'And . . . *go*!' She dropped her hand and the two girls were almost immediately on the floor.

This time, however, Babs adopted an entirely different tactic. Worming her way over her opponent, she contrived to get behind her, wedging her doubled up leg beneath her and using her free leg to form a figure four lock about her waist. There was no way she could hope to gain the equalising point from that position, but it quickly became apparent she was not aiming for an immediate score.

Instead, she wrapped her arm about Lolly's upper body and managed, despite the mitted glove, to grasp her breast, massaging the nipple in the palm of the hand, the friction having an immediate and unexpected effect. To the astonishment of all, Lolly immediately began to gasp and tremble, forgetting all about everything except trying to fight what was obviously an imminent climax. She should, Colin realised, have simply tried to roll herself free, or at least pull Babs's hand away from its target, but for some reason she seemed unable to grasp this concept – let alone the offending limb.

'She's losing it!' one of the women cried. 'Sheesh! Touch her tit and she goes to pieces. God how I wish I had nipples that sensitive.'

152

'No good if she comes before the point's made!' another female voice shouted. Babs, however, obviously knew the rules, for just as Lolly appeared on the point of succumbing, she released her leg lock and without breaking the contact her hand was exploiting so drastically, rolled easily over Lolly's unresisting body and thrust her phallus into its helpless target.

A keening wail came from behind Lolly's gag, but this time, instead of trying to hold out as before, she simply wrapped her arm about Babs's buttocks and appeared to be trying to pull her deeper into her. Babs needed no such urging. Once, twice, three times she withdrew and thrust again and on the fourth stroke Lolly's back arched as if she had been electrocuted and an even higher pitched scream indicated her final surrender.

'Yellow and blue, default win!' Simone shrieked, but it was far from the end of the spectacle. As the two masters approached each other with outstretched hands to shake, their two slaves continued on, oblivious to anything else but each other and after only a few seconds more, another strangled groan indicated that the victor had joined the vanquished in a shared orgasm that showed no immediate signs of abating.

Colin, conscious of the pressure building in his own groin, turned away, checked that Anna's leash was still securely attached to the back of the sulkie and climbed aboard and shook the reins as a signal for Jess to start walking. She leaned forward and the cart began to move forward, none of the original group seemingly interested in the departure of their new friend and his companions.

It was only after they had moved on down the trail a hundred yards or more and were safely out of sight and earshot of the continuing commotion behind them, that Anna spoke.

'Master Jason,' she said, softly. 'I think it is safe for us to talk freely here.' Colin turned his head, surprised at the sound of her voice and of the urgency in her tone.

'Whoa, Jess,' he called softly and then, to Anna, 'What is it?' The tall would-be warrior princess nodded to indicate the pony-girl.

'It's her,' she said. 'The pony-girl. Back there . . . she was using her hoof to try to write something in the dust.'

'She was?' Colin looked suspiciously at the pony-girl's back. 'I didn't see anything myself,' he admitted. 'I don't suppose you could see what she was trying to write, could you?'

'Not so well as to be completely certain,' Anna replied. 'But I think it was one word – Lachan – though the last letter was a bit of a mess as she couldn't stretch her foot far enough to her right to complete it properly.'

'Lachan?' Colin repeated. 'Well, she was special to him, though she refused to talk about him when I asked about previous masters before.'

'Perhaps she realised it wasn't safe to talk where you were?' Anna suggested. 'But she knows this island as well as anyone, I suspect, so perhaps she has just been waiting until you took her to an area where there was no chance of being observed or overheard.'

'Yes, you could be right,' Colin agreed. 'Is that how it is, Jess?' he asked, addressing himself to the pony-girl. There was a pause and then she nodded her head. Another pause, whilst Colin considered their options, only to realise that there was really only one.

'Right,' he said, looping the reins over the driving rail and climbing down from his seat, 'I reckon we get your bit off you and see what it is you want to tell us.'

* * *

The moment was close now; Major loosed the final trace strap and reached out for Tammy's bridle rein. Tammy, chest rising and falling slowly, stepped slowly from between the shafts.

'You should be proud, Tammy,' Major whispered. He smiled and reached out a hand to caress her left breast, massaging the firm flesh gently. 'You are a beautiful girl now, with a long and fruitful life ahead of you.'

Yes, Tammy thought, she should be proud and why not? Nothing that had happened had been her fault, after all: the storm, the wreck, becoming what she now was . . .

'You are a very desireable female now.' Desireable, yes. Yes, that was the word. Her stomach felt tight, warm, her legs shaky. She wished he would free her arms and remove the bit and snaffle to give her back the use of her voice; she wanted to tell Major how proud she did feel, how lucky to be the one he had chosen, how she would try so hard to love him and to be a good mother to his children, to hold him, return his caresses, kiss him and . . .

She felt him unbuckling the crotch strap and drawing out the rubber phallus that had been her constant companion and reminder, then touching her, fingers seeking that special spot. She closed her eyes, breathing slowly, pressing herself forward, pushing her breasts against his chest, trying to nuzzle against his cheek with her face. Softly, his lips brushed her nose.

'You shall have a new stall, Tammy,' he said. 'You shall have a stall like Jess's, with your own private place – and I shall visit you most days from now on, I think. It will be good for me to have somewhere special and some*one* special, too. My own people just do not realise how much I need . . . the pressures, the responsibilities . . . the loneliness . . .'

Tammy felt something warm probing between her thighs, something hard, warm, alive, and she shifted her feet wider, opening herself to him, trying to show him that she was ready, pushing her hips forward to demonstrate her eagerness. She closed her eyes as his fingers traced lines down her shoulder blades, his lips kissed hers, ignoring the bit between them. She groaned, wanting to be able to return his kiss properly, wanting to return the love, the . . .

And then he was inside her, solid, pulsing, his heat mingling with her own. She opened her eyes again, looking into his face.

'That feels so nice, Tammy,' he sighed. She lifted herself as far as she was able and then let her weight fall back again. He grunted and smiled at her. 'Yes,' he said. 'So nice. Perhaps I am beginning to understand something of so-called humanity after all, though I cannot afford to allow myself too many of your weaknesses.' He sighed and thrust himself deeply into her, lifting her completely off her feet, supporting her balance with his hands about her waist. Tammy felt her hooved feet waving helplessly in the air and the sensation was incredible. She was his, completely his, and totally in his power.

'Yes, this is a very agreeable sensation,' he said and then, without another word, she felt him coming within her, spraying into her the hot seed that she knew would be eagerly received by the fruitful womb she now had. She heard a low whimpering sound, a tremorous thing from somewhere deep in her throat and her head fell forward on to his shoulder as she cried without tears, sobbing her ultimate joy and acceptance.

Amaarini could feel her heart beating furiously against her ribs, and the rubbery mask covering her ears made the sound of her blood pulsing in her temples seem unnaturally loud, but Higgy's voice still came to her, firm and clear; the voice of control, the voice of her master for the next two hours or so. She shivered, feeling suddenly cold, naked and very vulnerable. This, she thought, was how every pony-girl must feel the first time she was between the shafts, blinkers and the stiff posture collar of the bridle keeping her field of vision to this one narrow strip dead ahead of her as she waited for the command to walk on and to go out into the world for the first time in her new role.

The dildo felt huge inside her, felt as if it was alive and throbbing. She knew this was just an illusion and that the sensations had to be from her own vaginal muscles responding to the unaccustomed invasion. It was not, however, at all an unpleasant feeling, though there was something about it that was also vaguely disturbing, as if her body was somehow trying to detach itself from the proper control of her mind.

'Walk!' She felt a gentle tap on her shoulder from Higgy's whip – he would usually use a little more force than that, surely? – and she leaned her weight forward, the way she had seen so many of the girls do. Behind her, the cart creaked and the wheels began slowly to turn, and she was surprised that the load did not feel too heavy, certainly not as heavy as she had anticipated. Without being told, she started to turn to her left, heading towards the exit tunnel, but a sharp tug on the right hand side of her mouth startled her into returning to the straight.

'Wait for my command, pony-girl Diamond,' she heard Higgy call out, and she smiled grimly around the gagging bit. A novice pony was not expected to use her own initiative and she would certainly not be expected to know her way round the island. Now came the tug on the left side of the bit and she responded instantly, correcting again when the short right tug was repeated.

'Very good,' Higgy said. 'Now on.' He shook the reins slightly and Amaarini felt the leather traces flicking over her naked shoulders. Ahead the tunnel loomed, the small spot of light at its end marking the world that was waiting for her – a world full of pony-girls just like her – trotting proudly with their bouncing, belled breasts and their flashing hooves. She felt a mild sense of excitement, of daring. Safely anonymous behind her mask, this was actually quite fun – almost funny in a way, she thought.

No one but the two of them knew who she really was, so she could just relax, let herself go completely into this new role and surrender her usual self a little to this tide of new emotions and experiences. It would not last long, she knew, but for two hours now she could forget about everything else and concentrate on the game. Of course, unlike her human counterparts, she would not be able to surrender her real identity completely and let herself – her real self – be submerged by the experience, but then, unlike the other pony-girls – who by now would be realising that this new life was their only life and that they would return just to their stall at the end of their day – this was only a pretext, a complete sham. Long before sundown she would be back as her usual self, either behind her desk, or striding along the corridors, or else sauntering free to enjoy the evening air in whatever way *she* decided.

Her various bells sounded louder still inside the confines of the tunnel as they echoed off its smooth walls, and a curious knot began to form in Amaarini's stomach as she realised it was the bouncing of her own naked breasts that was causing one pair to ring so merrily. As her nipples throbbed, tingled and ached she shook her head, willing them to stop, wishing she had her hands free, and wondering suddenly if this had been such a good idea after all . . .

'That's better,' Colin said, drawing the snaffle plate from Lachan's mouth and folding away the tiny utility knife that had been his constant companion since his boyhood. The ordinary screwdriver attachment had been useless, but the crosshead attachment, after a little careful fiddling and a good deal of patience, had finally turned the clamp screws sufficiently to loosen them.

'Now,' he said, standing squarely in front of the pony-girl. 'You wanted to tell me something about Andrew Lachan?' The girl nodded her head and opened her mouth, but made no sound.

'Well?' Colin tried to look encouraging, but her eyes were troubled, her features twisting into a grimace. 'You know Andrew Lachan?' She started to nod again, but then changed that to a quick, impatient shake of the head, followed by a shrug and a low grunt that seemed to come from her stomach.

'Well, you either know him, or you don't know him, so make up your mind.' Colin sighed. 'Look, Jess,' he said, as patiently as he could manage. 'We know Lachan had a thing with you. Quite what the relationship – arrangement, call it what you will – quite how things were between you, well, we don't know, but the man named a damned boat after you, so you weren't just casual acquaintances, were you?'

Again she shook her head.

'Well?' Colin stood with hands on hips. 'Look, we don't have all day. I'm assuming this is a safe place to talk –' a brief nod '– but someone could come along this way at any moment and I get the feeling you could be in as much trouble for talking to me as I could be for asking questions, right?' Another nod. The girl shuffled her feet and backed away slightly, the sulkie creaking behind her. Then, extending the tip of one boot, she carefully began to trace out a shape on the hard ground. Her efforts barely affected a mark on the baked earth, but Colin thought he recognised what she was trying to indicate.

'Letter P?' She nodded, eagerly. Again she began to trace. 'E, I think?' She nodded yes and began again.

'N,' Anna volunteered. 'P – E – N, pen. She wants a pen?' The pony-girl nodded quickly.

'Why not just tell me?' Colin demanded, his eyes narrowing and immediately sweeping around the trees. Had he been mistaken about microphones here? Had Jess been mistaken? And yet she had confirmed that it was safe to talk here.

'Maybe she can't,' Anna suggested. She stepped around to join Colin in front of the girl. 'Can you speak?' A shake of the head. 'They've done something to your voice?' A nod. 'Some sort of injection, maybe? A paralysing agent, local anaesthetic?' A shake of the head this time.

'Doesn't matter how they've done it,' Colin interrupted. 'But if she can't speak, she can't speak, so where can we find ourselves a pen and something to write on? This ground is rock hard and we'll be here all day at this rate.'

'Well, don't look at me,' Anna retorted, snickering. 'I'm not hiding any writing materials in this outfit.'

'Maybe Celia,' Colin said, thinking out loud. 'That little pouch thing she keeps on her belt has all manner of funny things in it, just like a woman's handbag.'

'We'd better try to find her then,' Anna said. 'She should be out here by now. She told me she was going

160

to take Millie out for some exercise and try to snoop around a bit, though where to start looking . . .'

'We'll try back around by the race track,' Colin decided. 'Might even find someone else we can borrow a pen and paper from.'

'Oh yes?' Anna sounded amused at the suggestion. 'And what are you going to give as a reason – you want to send a postcard home to your mother?'

'Well, have you got a better idea? I can't go back to my room and leave you two unattended, can I? That sort of thing would look extremely suspicious here, I think.'

'Well,' Anna retorted, 'as it happens, I think I do have an idea. Bring Jess over here to the side of the track. There's a bare patch of earth there, see? And then we need a bit of twig for her to write with – we can fix it to her hand with one of the straps, to save taking the entire sleeve and glove off, just in case someone comes along suddenly. If they ask, just say she was getting cramp in her elbows and you freed her arms to get the circulation going again.'

'A twig?' Colin nodded, but then began to frown as he turned to look at the patch of ground Anna had indicated. 'More like a steel chisel needed to make much of an impression there, I think. There's been no rain for days.'

'Yes, well, you get Jess over there and get her arms free and I'll find the wood. As for the ground being too hard, I think I have a solution to that little problem, too.'

SASSIE

My 'rest period' lasted no more than half an hour and in truth was hardly much of a rest. Master Harvey helped me down on to the grass and stretched out beside me. I closed my eyes and would have easily surrendered myself to sleep – even with the discomfort of having to lie on my bound hands and arms – for I was more tired than I could ever remember having been in my entire life, and not just physically but mentally exhausted, and now totally confused.

However, within a minute or two, Harvey apparently had a change of heart, for I felt his hand creep across my breast, his fingers seeking my nipple, which he held and began to roll gently between finger and thumb. The bell gave a quiet 'chink' as it moved and I opened my eyes again.

Harvey had propped himself up on one elbow and was lying sideways, looking at my face as he sought to stimulate me. I sighed, wishing he would realise that I needed rest so badly, but the nipple refused to support that claim and was already standing up stiffly.

'You look so beautiful, just lying there with your eyes closed,' he told me. Luckily for both of us, I was unable to reply, but even if I had been able to speak it would have made no difference. I was a pony-girl – his pony-girl for the duration, bought and paid for – and I was expected to do whatever my master required of me. He lifted himself higher and peered down between my thighs.

'Wet again, Sassie,' he murmured. Idiot, I thought. I wasn't wet *again*, I was *still* wet from earlier as my damned body was seemingly intent on reminding me of how it had surrendered and accepted its humiliating treatment. Master Harvey, however, obviously thought no further than his own needs and accepted as a fact that I was simply there to gratify him.

'And see what you're doing to me,' he said, fumbling with his breeches and opening the front to reveal that he was hard again. I sighed, wriggled to try to ease the weight on my arms, and slowly opened my legs. If it was inevitable, which it was, then there was little point in delaying it, but why was it that as he rolled over between my thighs and began to push into me again, the juices which eased his entry were no longer just the residue of our previous coupling?

A while later, back between the shafts again, I was plodding gamely along the track, fighting to keep my eyes open whilst my legs worked independently of my brain. I failed to see the oncoming cart and was almost too slow in responding to Master Harvey's signals and shouted instruction. I looked up and managed to step to the side only in the nick of time.

'Sorry!' Harvey called out. I heard the swishing sound from behind me and yelped as his whip cut across my shoulder. 'Stupid bitch!' Again he spoke to the other driver.

'She's still a bit of a novice,' he explained, by way of excuse. 'Not one of your regular girls, so your lads told me before I brought her out.' I turned my head and saw Higgy sitting just a few feet from me. He grinned and then returned his attention to my driver.

'No harm done, sir,' he said, pleasantly, 'and you're right, she's not one of ours, so I'd suggest you go easy with the whip. Her owner might not be too pleased if you break her skin.'

'Well, if he wanted to leave her for stable duties, surely he knows what to expect,' Harvey retorted. 'But you're right and it's probably my fault. Probably still thinking about the good seeing-to she's had.' He laughed raucously, and I felt myself blushing, even though it was fatigue and not his masculine susceptibilities that had been responsible for the near collision.

'Doesn't pay to overdo things with a new pony,' Higgy cautioned. 'It takes a good while to train one properly.'

'That what you're doing today, Higgy? Don't usually see you out here unless it's a training session. Must say, your filly looks very handsome. Don't fancy swapping places for an hour or so, do you?'

'I don't think so, sir,' Higgy replied, levelly. 'This is the first time outside for this one and I'm still getting the feel of her.'

'Hah!' Harvey exclaimed, amused. 'Yes, bet you are, Higgy, you rogue. Wouldn't mind a feel of her myself. Fabulous tits and the length of those legs, well . . .'

'She's a fine specimen, it's true enough,' Higgy said.

'Make a good racer, too, I reckon.'

'Quite likely she will, Master Harvey,' Higgy agreed.

'Fancy giving her a run out round the track against Sassie here?'

'Hardly a contest,' Higgy replied. 'Sassie there may not be one of ours, but she's got top potential. Didn't you see her last night?'

'Towards the end, yes,' Harvey said. 'But you can see for yourself that she's not exactly on top of her game today, and your girl looks strong enough. Tell you what, be a sport and I'll slip you a nice little bonus before I go and nothing need be said, eh?'

'Well, I don't want your money, sir,' Higgy said, 'but maybe a couple of laps would get her used to the track. And as you say, Sassie's looking a bit tired.'

'Well then, let's do it,' Harvey said. 'Maybe a quick gallop will help get Sassie's blood flowing again, too.'

'There is an English saying, I believe,' Anna said. She looked down at the ground at her feet, made a final examination and then carefully squatted, feet well apart. 'I believe it goes along the lines of, "When the going gets tough, the tough get going"? Well, now is the time for me to go.'

A moment later a stream of warm urine splattered down on to the hard ground. Colin made to turn his back, but Anna glared up at him.

'Don't just stand there getting all modest,' she snapped. 'Give me your hand so I can move a little and use your boot to spread it as far as you can. That's a stick she's got to write with, not a fine nibbed pen!'

A minute later, Anna was back on her feet and the pair of them inspected the results of her efforts. A dark patch, uneven in shape but about a foot square, lay between them. Colin wrinkled his nose and Anna smiled.

'Crude, but effective,' she said. 'I believe that is another English saying?'

'Yes, and never more appropriately used, I think.'

'Well, if you'd remembered to bring a water bottle with us, maybe we could have used that. So stop being so damned sniffily English and let's get on with it, shall we? This sun is warm and that'll dry out before long, and if you think there's any more where that came from, forget it. Mind you,' she added, casting a look at Lachan, '– she's probably got a bit in reserve if we get really stuck!'

'You reckon they'll get that Indian girl here today still, do you?' Geordie was becoming rapidly frustrated by the lack of activity, and the news that they would not be putting out again that day had done nothing to ease that frustration.

'That's what they told me,' Frearson confirmed. 'And I've heard nothing to the contrary since. Look, why don't you get your head down for a few hours? You must be shattered after last night and there's a spare couple of rooms up top.'

'Maybe later,' Geordie said. 'Right now, though I know I'm tired, I know I just wouldn't be able to sleep properly. Too many things on my mind.'

'Of course,' Frearson sympathised. 'Colin Turner and you go back a long way, don't you? And isn't there something between you and one of those girls?'

Geordie shrugged. 'Depends on your definition of "something", really,' he said. 'It's a bit complicated,' he added, seeing Frearson's intrigued expression. 'Maybe another time, eh?'

'When you know more yourself, you mean?'

'Something like that,' Geordie agreed. 'Probably just me and women in general,' he added, as an afterthought. 'Never had any problem pulling,' he said, 'but I'm getting to the stage when I'm starting to think it ought to be more than just a case of getting your leg over.'

'Galloping maturity,' Frearson nodded. 'Happens to a lot of us, that does. So, you haven't found your ideal woman and, unless I'm no judge, you suspect this latest one might not fit that bill either?'

'To be honest, Angus, I hardly know her,' Geordie said. 'Matter of a few days, though it seems a lot longer, I suppose.'

'Well, give it time, laddie. These things do take time, you know.' Frearson hesitated and said, 'Something about all this kinky stuff you don't get on with, is there? I take it that's how you met this young lady?'

'Yes, you could say our meeting was just a bit unconventional,' Geordie said. 'But it's not just that. There's one female I can't seem to get out of my mind, which is stupid, because there was never anything between us, and certainly not in a personal way. Maybe there might have been, if there'd been more time, but as things turned out . . . well, no use wondering, I suppose.'

'Ah, I see.' Frearson considered for a moment. 'Would this possible unrequited love have anything to do with your unfortunate late colleague?' Geordie looked away, staring out the window.

'Well, like I said, it's stupid. I only worked with her a short time and she was my superior anyway. Besides, I never really even looked at her in that way, not until after she died and then, almost ever since, it seems I start comparing every other female I meet with Alex Gregory.'

'Interesting,' Frearson said. 'A shrink would make a month's fees out of explaining that, but I reckon it's quite simple. We always want what we can't have and it's easy to attribute virtues to someone we don't really know, especially when events mean we're *never* going to get to know the truth, whatever that might be.

'She was quite a girl, from what I hear. Young for a sergeant and tipped to go a lot further, though she had a bit of an individualistic streak – some might say rebellious, I suppose.'

'She knew her own mind all right,' Geordie said. 'Very bright, very dry humour, and very determined and strong willed.'

'And also a bit foolhardy,' Frearson added. 'Jumping out of a plane in the dead of night the way she did was damned stupid, however you look at it.'

'But she was an experienced sky diver,' Geordie pointed out. 'And she was convinced there was something out on that island that needed looking at closer. Turns out she was right and the rest of us were all wrong. I just wish she was still around to know that – and to know that *we* know that now, too.'

'Yes,' Frearson said. 'I do understand.' He tried to suppress a gruff chuckle, without much success. 'Mind you,' he said, 'I'd bet a month's money she'd have been shocked to find out just what it was she was heading into. Didn't you say she was a bit straight-laced as far as that sort of thing was concerned?'

'Only a guess on my part,' Geordie said, 'but I reckon so. And the way this investigation is going, well, I'd have liked to have seen her face. Can't imagine her parading round that island in a pony harness, not in a million years!'

Thankfully for Alex, Fiona appeared to have lost interest in having her play a continued part in her ongoing revenge on Sol and, apart from using her as a means of transport, had all but forgotten she was there. Instead, she now delighted in humiliating him before every other visitor they encountered and was currently offering him to three female slaves and their master, all of whom were clearly old acquaintances.

The man's name was Vaughan and he looked as if he was in his early sixties, although his body was still lean and athletic looking and did not look at all out of place in a skin tight, black spandex body suit. His three girls were dressed in the same material, though their suits had been drastically cut away to leave their breasts, buttocks, vulvas and shoulders exposed. The colours of their outfits were also far more lurid in fluorescent shades of yellow, turquoise and pink. Their names, or at least the names he had given them, were Daisy, Maisy and Lou.

From what Alex could see of their faces, Daisy and Maisy were probably twins and certainly sisters, though they were far two short and petite to have been Jenny-Anns so she presumed Vaughan had brought them with him. The third girl, the one dressed in yellow, was about the same size, but black, very black and it was she whom Fiona and her master had singled out for Sol's latest torture, although the sisters were also involved in what Fiona laughingly described as 'supporting roles'.

On a clear piece of embankment alongside the trail – it was not large enough to deserve being classed as another of the numerous clearings – Sol was now staked out, arms and legs stretched wide, visibly plugged with a dildo, a penis gag projecting from his mouth. On either side of him crouched Daisy and Maisy, each with their lips glued to a nipple, whilst Lou began by crouching between his splayed thighs and applying her tongue to his balls.

'He'll stay hard anyway,' Alex heard Fiona explaining to Vaughan, 'but your girls should be able to get him up to a real inner pitch to match his erection.'

'Oh, they'll do that all right,' Vaughan chuckled, in his deep baritone. 'Better than a kilo of Viagra, those three.' As if to prove his point, Sol's head began to roll from side to side.

'Steady!' Fiona called out and Vaughan clapped his hands.

'Low gear, girls!' he commanded. 'Keep him on the brink now, don't push him over. Just say when, my lovely,' he added, turning to Fiona. 'Even if he does come, these three minxes would have him ready again in a matter of minutes, whether the medication was in him or not.'

'Splendid,' Fiona grinned. 'I want him to feel like a wrung-out dish rag before he goes back in his stall tonight. The bastard had me so exhausted I didn't know where I was half the time I was in those damned stables, so now I want him to know just how that feels!'

'Well, I'll swap you the girls for your filly here, if you like?' Vaughan suggested, half turning to Alex and nodding. 'Keep them for the rest of the day and I'll swap you back this evening?'

'No, I'll keep her for the moment,' Fiona said. 'These heels are all very well, but too much walking in them is crippling. Much easier to ride. Mind you, why don't you all stay with us? I'm making my way down to the track eventually to see if there's any action to be had there.

'Come to think of it, I left Solly's gig back down the track a little way. You probably passed it in one of the clearings. You can send a couple of your girls back for it, once they've finished with him.'

'Okay, you're on,' Vaughan agreed. He turned his attention back to the four figures on the bank. 'I assume you want Lou to fuck that face cock in a minute?' he said. Fiona nodded, enthusiastically.

'I thought she might do that and suck him off properly at the same time,' she suggested. 'Those lips of hers are certainly made for sucking cock.'

'Lovely and soft,' Vaughan agreed, 'but then they're all good. They've had a good teacher,' he added, laughing again. 'Lou-Lou!' he called, clapping his hands again. 'Get yourself ready to do a reverse on him, as soon as Mistress Fiona gives the word. Oh yes, and you can come all you like, girlie – no restrictions this time, just so long as you do a good job on him!'

Events were beginning to develop on their own and going a lot further than Amaarini had intended, but there was no way she could communicate this to Higgy. And he was, she thought desperately, only really doing what she had asked him to do. The original idea had been for her to try to assimilate some of the basic early experience of a new pony-girl and to try to discover if there was anything to explain why almost always the girls came around to an acceptance of their new lifestyle in a fraction of the time that would reasonably be expected.

So far, however, there were more questions than answers and some of those questions were becoming unsettling. How was it, for instance, that whilst the original tacking up experience had been almost chilling in its clinical efficiency, the sudden introduction of the dildo into the equation – and at a stage where it was too late for her to redefine any of the parameters – had produced a surge of excitement in her, albeit an involuntary and inexplicable one, that had been accompanied by a sense of total outrage?

Pulling the sulkie had been quite boring in comparison, although walking and trotting had meant that the deeply embedded rubber phallus had produced unaccustomed friction that had in turn produced the beginnings of reflexive reactions, but Amaarini had found these not too difficult to control by focusing her mind on the reality of her situation. If she could do it, why could the human girls not, also? But then, of course, she was better than human, so the answer was really quite simple.

What had been stranger had been the way in which her nudity being taken for granted – what was one more pony-girl among so many pony-girls after all, no matter how fine a figure she cut? – had started those other feelings, the ones she could not control so easily. Why, for instance, had she suddenly felt so angry at this? And why had the anger been followed by a compulsion to impress and a desperate desire for people to actually take notice of her, when normally she would have been mortified to have women, let alone men, see her in what was really such a shameful situation?

The proposed race was, of course, taking things a lot further than she had envisaged and her initial reaction had been one of horror. Listening to the conversation with Sassie's driver, Amaarini had willed Higgy to refuse with every ounce of her concentration and had almost cried out through her bit gag when he finally accepted the challenge. Her? Race against an inferior species? She had nothing to prove where humans were concerned. Why, with this body she could probably outrun most fit human males, so being pitted against Sassie was an insult.

But then pony-girls grew as used to insults as they grew used to praise. In fact, Amaarini mused, as they trotted on to the side of the race circuit, they grew used to so many things, learning quickly that they had no option, no opinions and, when they were in harness, expected to have almost no minds of their own. They existed and had been created to serve their masters and mistresses and he or she who held the reins and the whip made all the decisions for them.

It would be interesting to race, she decided after all. Not that there would be any real contest; she could beat a fully fit Sassie, of that she was absolutely certain. Sassie as she was now, overworked since her arrival and with little or no sleep, would not be the star she had proved to be on the previous evening. In a curious way, Amaarini found herself feeling sorry for the human girl.

Colin and Anna stood expectantly on either side of the pony-girl as she stooped awkwardly, pointing the end of the projecting stick towards the dampened patch of earth.

'Right,' Colin said. 'We need to keep this simple, or else we'll run out of time, like I said.' He paused, thinking. 'Now, we already know she knows Lachan, so let's not waste that one,' he suggested. 'How about this – Jessie, do you know what happened to Lachan?' The girl gave a brief nod and started to press the point into the surface.

'No, wait a minute,' Colin interrupted her. 'Just nod or shake your head. Did you know that Lachan is dead?' This time the pony-girl shook her head

172

violently and Colin grasped her shoulder, afraid that the news might have come as too much of a shock for her, and realised he might have made an error in being so blunt.

'He apparently died in an explosion aboard his yacht, Jess,' he said, gently, but again she shook her head and tried to shrug his hand aside. 'Do you know anything different?' he tried. This time his question received a firm nod and the girl gestured towards the damp area with obvious impatience.

'Let her write, Colin,' Anna said, and then, to the girl: 'Jessie, how did Andrew Lachan die? Do you know that?' Immediately, the girl began to scratch in the muddy area, starting with the letter 'I'. It was plainly not easy for her with the stick strapped to her otherwise useless hand and the corset girth made it difficult for her to bend properly, but she shuffled slightly sideways and began again.

' "A",' Colin translated, as the letter took shape. 'And "M" is that?' The girl nodded and continued scribing.

' "I am",' Anna said, quietly. Three more letters appeared, followed by a fourth and then a fifth. Colin peered closer, puzzled. The sixth letter came as no surprise to either himself or to Anna, but the complete sentence . . .

' "I am Lachan",' he read aloud. 'That's a bit Zen, isn't it? You mean you belong to Lachan, Jess, is that it? It must be a form of brainwashing, Anna,' he concluded, turning to the tall Norwegian girl. 'Maybe she can't accept it, or something. Maybe she's trying to tell us he was or is her reason for being.'

He opened his mouth to say more, but was cut short by Jess shaking his shoulder with her free hand and shaking her head even more vigorously than before. She jabbed the stick back at the three words and then used her left mitt to point towards herself. Then, as if suddenly inspired, she reached down with the stick, scratched a line through the word 'AM' and carefully wrote the word 'WAS' above it.

'What the hell are you trying to tell us, Jessie?' Colin scratched his head and turned to Anna again, but Anna shook her head, apparently as baffled as he was himself. However, the pony-girl seemed to have had a further thought and was already writing again. Colin and Anna stood in silence as the next message took shape.

I AM NOT JESS.

'You're not Jess?' Colin let out a long breath. 'But you look like Jess, or did I get it all wrong last night? The light wasn't good, but it wasn't *that* bad, I didn't think.' 'Jess' was scratching in the mud again.

CLONE appeared, followed by a jab of the stick towards the corrected message that now read I WAS LACHAN. There was another pause and the exasperation showed in the girl's eyes as she strove to fit another message into what remained of the soft patch.

I LACHAN – IN CLONE BODY.

'I think she's lost it completely,' Colin muttered. He looked at the beautiful pony-girl and now it was his turn to shake his head. 'No,' he said. 'No way. This is one crazy place, but not that crazy. Listen, you daft wench, we want to know what happened to Lachan, so stop your nonsense.' The girl was making a final effort to cram some letters into the one remaining available corner.

SARA, she wrote.

'Does she mean Sassie?' Anna asked. The girl looked blank and jabbed the stick towards her final message. Colin's eyes narrowed.

'Sara was Lachan's wife, wasn't she?' he said, evenly. The girl immediately shook her head again.

'No, sorry, she was his sister,' he lied. The girl stamped one hoof hard on the ground and again her mane of hair flew from side to side. 'His lawyer?' This time the girl just stood and stared defiantly back and Colin felt a cold chill in the pit of his stomach.

'His mistress?' He was determined not to make it easy for her. 'Yes, she was his mistress and you were jealous of her,' he said. The look on the girl's face said it all.

'Right,' Colin decided. 'One final try. Raise your left hand if she was Lachan's secretary, or your right hand if Sara was his dog.' The girl raised her right hand, but immediately shook her head. Then, raising her right hand, she gave a shrug and, with her other hand made a vague so-so gesture. Colin looked down at the scratched letters, which now filled the entire dark area – a dark area that was rapidly becoming lighter as the warm sun dried it.

'Dammit!' he said. 'We need more room. Jess – or whoever you are – can you manage to pee the way Anna did?'

There was no time for her to answer, for a strident female voice had both himself and Anna scraping their feet over the original marks and he turned, trying not to look guilty, to see two pony carts approaching: the first driven by a masked woman, the second by a grey-haired male. To Colin's surprise, he saw that the pony drawing the second cart was unmistakeably male and that it was being followed by a trio of brightly garbed females who were almost certainly slaves rather than mistresses, judging by the revealing cutouts in their costumes.

'Want to join our party?' the woman driver called. 'We're heading for the race track, so the more the merrier. Your girl looks like – good lord, it's Jessica, isn't it? Well, I'd heard she was available, but I thought it was just gossip. Her usual master lost interest in her, or what?'

She turned and addressed the male driver behind her.

'You know about Jess, don't you, Vaughan?' she said. 'She's a pretty useful performer, so if our friend here is willing, this could turn into an intriguing little session. I'll be interested to see how she races without her usual owner in the driving seat, I must say!'

'I've been over most of this island at one time or another,' Celia said. 'It's not that big, after all, but no one ever comes up to this part – at least, I've never seen anyone up here and I've never been here myself.'

'I'm not surprised,' Millie panted. 'These rocks are hard going and it's damned steep.' The two women were moving along the lower slope of the tor that rose from the western end of the island. The undergrowth was thinner here, but the tree cover was still extensive and the chunks of broken rock made progress slow.

'Not quite pony country, is it?' Millie joked. Her foot slipped on a sloping piece of rock that was all but hidden by a clump of overgrowing grass and her knee banged against the side of the larger rock they were working their way around. She swore, rubbing the injured spot.

'These shoes should carry a health warning,' she muttered. 'One of these heels is going to go on me any minute now, I just know it.'

'Just keep your voice down and watch where you're putting your feet,' Celia said. She pointed up towards the top of the tor. 'They usually have a couple of lookouts up there, especially on clear days,' she warned. 'I'll have a hard job trying to explain what we're doing here if anyone spots us.'

'But what exactly are we looking for?' Millie whined. 'No one's actually said, yet.'

'That's because none of us knows,' Celia retorted. 'Just anything suspicious – damn!' This time it was her foot that slipped and she had to clutch at an overhanging branch to keep her balance. 'Oh, why the hell did I let myself get dragged into this? I can think of a thousand things I could be doing that all have a lot more appeal.'

'Me too,' Millie agreed. 'Uh-oh, watch out – the ground seems to drop away just in front of you.' Indeed, it would have been very easy for them to blunder into the steep cleft in the ground, for it tapered inwards to a sharp point, and the innermost several feet were all but hidden beneath a combination of overhanging grasses and straggling thorns. Only the way in which the trees fell back from either side of the edge had alerted Millie to the fact that there was something wrong.

'Well done,' Celia said. 'That's quite a nasty drop there, by the looks of it. Yes, look, it opens right up and that's the water. This is the Ailsa equivalent of the edge of the world, I reckon.' Millie had already dropped to her knees and was inching forward along one edge of the precipice, peering over the side.

'Wow!' she exclaimed. 'This is really something – and look, there's even a little beach down there and it's got sand, for fuck's sake! I thought it would be all rocks and stones here.'

'Yes,' Celia agreed, working her way along to join the younger woman. 'But look, the rock goes round and out on either side, like a small cliff on either side of a cove. That's why it's sandy down there still – the tide probably doesn't run right to wash stones ashore here.'

Fifty or sixty feet below them as they peered over the edge was a circular area of water, all but enclosed by the miniature cliff-faced promontories on either side, with just a narrow gap that was perhaps thirty feet wide, through which the sea ebbed and flowed. There was a narrow stretch of beach running around two thirds of the cove, which was at its widest just below them, and the innermost point of the inlet. Closer inspection showed that there were actually plenty of stones on this beach, but in between them, as Millie had said, sand shone with a yellowish glow.

'Oh, isn't it pretty!' Millie exclaimed. 'It's like something out of a fairy story. Do you think we can get down there?' Celia was already scanning the almost sheer face beneath them and, after a few seconds more, she shook her head.

'Not from here,' she said. 'The sides are almost vertical and even where they slope a bit, I wouldn't want to risk trying it, not even if we had the right sort of footwear. These rocks up here are all loose, so God knows what it's like further down. Bits could break off under foot and without ropes it would be suicidal to even think about it.'

'There doesn't seem to be much evidence of rock falls,' Millie replied. She was clutching an exposed tree root and had leaned out further for a better view of the beach immediately below them. 'No really big chunks of rock down there. Just a few big stones and a lot of smaller pebbles.'

'Probably been sheltered from the winds and rain over the years,' Celia mused. 'Bit of freak geology – there's a lot of that in these parts. But we're still not going to try it, okay? Apart from anything else, even if we did manage to get down in one piece, what about getting back up again, eh?'

'I wasn't serious about climbing down,' Millie giggled. 'But it is pretty, don't you think?'

'Yes, very,' Celia agreed. 'But we still haven't – shit, get your head down and shut up!' As she spoke, she reached out and grasped Millie's right arm, hauling her backwards.

A moment later, Millie saw the reason for her alarm. From somewhere under the rock face, a *Healthglow* security guard appeared. He was holding a long, semi-rigid driving whip and was walking with a peculiar sideways gait, as if concentrating on whatever was behind him at the same time as watching where he was putting his booted feet.

Sure enough, a second or so behind him appeared a second figure, then a third, a fourth and a fifth. Eventually, the two women were able to count eight naked, brown-skinned females. All were chained: metal collars about their necks supported vertical chains, from which, at waist height, hung shorter chains attached to wrist manacles. Connected to the lower end of the vertical chain were short ankle hobbles, so that the girls were only able to take small, shuffling steps.

'Who are they?' Millie hissed.

'How should I know?' Celia retorted. Below them, a second guard appeared; he too carried a whip and, judging from the cowed attitude of the girls, neither whip was for show.

'Get them into the water and make them sit down!' the first guard called, his words echoing up to Celia and Millie clearly. 'They stink, the filthy little animals. Probably haven't washed themselves in months – if ever. Let them have a good soak here and then we can run them through the showers afterwards.'

'Be fair, Orrie,' the other guard laughed back. 'The poor little bitches have been cooped up in a bloody submarine for several days and I'll bet those bastards never thought to let them wash themselves.'

'Why would they?' his companion retorted. 'I mean, look at them – they're not much better than animals.'

'Arrogant bastard!' Celia snarled, not quite under her breath. Beside her, Millie was watching the straggling procession to the water's edge with wide-eyed bemusement.

'It's like something out of *Roots*,' she whispered. 'This isn't like the other stuff we've seen here. No rubber, no leather, no costumes of any sort. This lot are real prisoners.'

'Yes,' Celia said, quietly. 'They are – and I reckon I know where they come from, if nothing else. Remember that girl Anna came over to talk to the lads about? Well, I reckon this lot come from the same part of the world – South America. They're Andean Indians, all of them.'

'I thought Anna said the girl told her there were just the two of them?'

'As far as I remember, that's true,' Celia said. 'But that was a good few days ago now. From what "Smiler" down there just told his buddy, I'd say this bunch has only just arrived.'

'By submarine, yes,' Millie nodded. She shuddered. 'Ugh, the thought of being under the sea for days on end . . .'

'And not knowing where you're going, nor what's going to happen to you when you get there,' Celia said. 'No wonder they all look so pathetic. They must be frightened out of their wits, poor little mares.'

'I reckon they're running a real slave racket here, as well as all the spoof stuff,' Millie said. 'Like the Arabs used to do when they raided the African coast hundreds of years ago. This time they're bringing them the other way.'

'Could be,' Celia nodded. 'But it's a lot of trouble and expense to go to, shipping girls across the Atlantic in a submarine. Even if there were more than just these, there's a limit to how many they can bring in one trip, and submarines don't run on fresh air.'

'Less chance of being found out than if they brought them over on a surface ship, surely?' Millie said. Celia shook her head.

'Maybe, but I'm not so sure. I shouldn't think modern day slavers worry too much about being intercepted. If any official ships get too close, they just heave their cargo over the side with weights chained to their ankles. Cheaper to go back and grab another load later, plus they still have their regular cargo to cover the cost of their trip.'

'You're kidding me!' Millie gasped, horrified. Celia grunted.

'You don't have the first idea of what a nasty, rotten world we live in, do you?' she snapped. 'As long as you can play in your nice, safe, fantasy world, that's all you care about. There's more than one kind of slavery in this world, missy, and most of them don't end in a nice hot shower and a few drinks at the pub on the way back to an interior sprung mattress!'

There were not as many people around the track as there had been for the racing during the previous evening, Amaarini saw; the day was becoming quite hot now and most of the current visitors would have sought the shade offered among the trees. Nevertheless, there were several interested spectators, many of whom recognised Sassie from the night before. The appearance of Jessie – a familiar figure on the island, and without her ever present master Lachan – also turned several heads.

Amaarini, in turn, recognised Jangles who, it appeared, had been pitted to race against the girl everyone assumed was Jessie. That, she thought, would be interesting – only she and Higgy knew the true identity of that particular pony-girl and neither she nor Jangles was an experienced racer.

181

There was a good deal of discussion between the respective drivers as to the duration of the race. Fiona Charles favoured a long race and Amaarini seethed as she listened to the woman arguing. Any driver with sense should have realised that a day like this called for a sprint event, no more than two laps at the most, but then Fiona, Amaarini knew, cared little for the welfare of anyone other than Fiona.

The new guest, Anderson, appeared to have more idea and he seemed less than keen to race anyway. Of course, as Higgy had told her earlier, the man was apparently falling under Jess's spell in much the way Lachan had before him and Lachan had always been concerned with his pony-girl's welfare before anything else. She smiled inwardly at the irony of it. As Bambi, regardless of what was going on inside his head, Lachan was the image of Jess and was now exerting on others the same magic Jess had exerted on him. And they said beauty was more than skin deep! Men, Amaarini reflected, especially human men, were almost terminally stupid at times and deserved everything they got.

Vaughan came strolling up, having left Sol in the custody of his three girls, who were taking it in turns to tease the helpless pony-boy's permanent erection, much to the amusement of several of the female guests.

'Can't you sort something out, Higgy?' he suggested. 'That stupid bitch seems intent on running those girls into the ground and the guy won't have any of it. At this rate, we won't get any racing before sunset.' Higgy nodded and began walking across to where the two drivers were still arguing. Vaughan turned to Amaarini, looking her up and down appreciatively.

'You look like a spirited filly,' he said. 'Amazes me where they get you all from. So many stunning

182

examples of the feminine form in one place. Must cost them a fortune. Mind you,' he chuckled, 'they charge us well enough for the privilege.'

He reached out and cupped Amaarini's breasts in his hands, squeezing them gently. Amaarini bristled and sucked air in through her nostrils. Vaughan smiled.

'Ah! Real spirit, eh? No wonder Higgy's still training you.' He began to massage her breasts, his thumbs pressing against her rigid nipples, the bells tinkling against the back of his hands. Amaarini stiffened even further, willing the tiny warm darts that were shooting through her body to stop.

'Good and firm,' Vaughan observed. 'Very nice indeed. I might just ask Higgy if I can book you out myself tomorrow. The girls will like you, too. You'll get the sort of day you won't get here that often, I can promise you, and you'll sleep well afterwards, that's for certain.'

At the edge of the track, the argument over the impending race was quickly settled. Fiona's grim set mouth showed that the outcome was not to her liking, but Higgy's ruling was official and, as head groom, only a very senior member of staff could overrule him when it came to his pony-girls.

'Three laps,' he said to Vaughan, as he sauntered back. 'That's probably one lap more than's sensible, but there's a breeze starting to come up, so they should be all right.' He sighed. 'That bitch is a menace, if you ask me, but don't tell anyone I said so.

'At least our friend Harvey understands.' He appeared to be speaking to Vaughan, but Amaarini sensed Higgy's remarks were more for her benefit. The groom patently did not like the television woman and he was trying to tell Amaarini that, in his opinion, she was being allowed too much free rein.

He was quite right, she thought, and made a mental note to talk to Major about that particular situation at the first opportunity.

Vaughan, meanwhile, was still fondling her breasts and Higgy was making no attempt to stop him.

'I like this one, Higgy,' he said. 'Look at her eyes, the way they go all distant. Ye gods, but she must have sensitive tits. I'd like to take her out tomorrow, if that's okay?'

'Well, er . . .' Higgy hesitated. 'I'll have to check that, sir,' he said, recovering his composure quickly. 'She's still only a novice and we have strict rules about letting them out to guests too soon.'

'I'll accept responsibility if anything goes wrong,' Vaughan chuckled. He leaned forward and brushed a kiss across Amaarini's lips. 'I'll pay whatever extra might be involved, too. I get the feeling this one will be worth it!'

Amaarini closed her eyes and bit hard into the rubber between her teeth. Inside her, the dildo seemed to have grown in size and she could almost have sworn that it was trying to move. Her nipples tingled and there was a faint buzzing in her head and she knew that her body was on the verge of betraying her. The walls of her vagina began to spasm involuntarily and she fought to bring them back under control, snorting at the same time and trying to step backwards. To her relief, Higgy finally intervened.

'Best leave her for the moment, sir,' he said, gently, though his tone made it clear that it was more than a suggestion. 'Can't have her losing it just before a race. The more experienced ones can handle that, and even coming during a race don't seem to affect them, but same as you said, Diamond here is raw. You take her over the top now and she'll be useless out on the track.'

184

Seven

Major had dismounted and was leading Tammy by her bridle now. Even in the shade of the overhanging trees, the temperature was steadily rising and the humidity was starting to increase alarmingly. Tammy was grateful for his concern, but her thoughts were in such turmoil that she barely noticed the conditions.

Inside, her body now felt completely different and she was only too well aware why. Most of it, she was sure, was in her head, for it was far too early for any physical changes to manifest themselves and yet there was a definite feeling that something had changed, the body's knowledge that the seed that had been placed into it had already begun its work.

Tammy was already pregnant, of that she had no doubt. Her fertile womb – Major had chosen the moment with deliberate precision, as he had told her beforehand – had conceived, the waiting egg embracing the winning sperm willingly and, in a few months – would it be the normal nine of a human gestation period? – she would give birth to Richard Major's child.

The thought should have horrified her, she knew. Only weeks ago the prospect of becoming a woman, let alone having children, would have been anathema to the young fisherman, but this body they had given him was doing something to his mind. He should have resented that, too, but now, as they came to a halt under an overhanging canopy of leaves at the edge of the race circuit clearing, Tammy just felt contented and fulfilled.

She was going to have a baby. No, she corrected herself and would have laughed had she been able to. No, she was a pony-girl, so she was going to have his foal. The thought amused her even more and, smiling around her bit, she tried to lean her head sideways and place it on her master's shoulder.

'Get down!' Celia grabbed Millie's arm again and dragged her back into the bushes. A moment later, two more security men appeared on the trail below them and to their right. They appeared to be wandering aimlessly, but Celia knew they would ask questions as to why the two women were so far away from the regular tracks. They had come back down the slopes now, but were still a little way from where the ground flattened out completely and in an area that would normally not be used, especially for pony carting.

Celia raised a warning finger to her lips, even though the two men had sauntered past their hiding place and were already several yards down the trail back into the central area of the island.

'Keep well down,' she whispered. 'We'll wait a while to make sure those two are well clear and then we need to move ourselves. Sooner we get back on the flat, the happier I'll be.' She began fumbling inside the small bag and drew out a pair of wrist cuffs.

'Get one of those on your wrist,' she ordered. 'They're snap locks, so you can do it yourself. If it looks like we've been spotted, get your hands behind your back and snap the other one on. I'll just have to swear blind I brought you out here for a bit of open-air punishment work. Those heels of yours should convince them – I hope,' she added, raising her eyebrows. She shook her head and Millie could see that she was more than just worried.

'Sooner we get back and find the others, the better I'll like it,' Celia said. 'And then we're getting the hell out of here. I'm starting to get a bad feeling about everything on this island. Games are games, but what we saw back there wasn't for fun, Millie. That was for real and not very nice at all.'

The race between Alex and Lachan – Jangles and Jessie as far as the spectators were concerned – ended in an anti-climax that could have turned into a disaster.

The real Jessie, though not possessed of the sort of sprint finish that the harder raced girl often displayed, was a seasoned veteran and would have used the warm day to her advantage by setting a hard enough pace to sap her opponent's strength well before the final lap. Lachan, however, whilst looking like his former pony-girl lover in every way, had never yet been raced in competition and had also to rely on a completely untried driver in Colin.

Alex, in her turn, was scarcely more experienced and Fiona, her driver, was far too heavy-handed and convinced that zealous application of the whip could compensate for anything. The final result, Amaarini thought afterwards, was almost inevitable and the only surprise was that neither pony was badly hurt in the ungainly melée of arms and legs as they went down together on the fifth bend. As it was, when Higgy and the other volunteers who ran to their aid had finally disentangled everything, Lachan had to be led away, hobbling badly on a twisted ankle and supported by her driver and his woman slave.

A quick inspection from Higgy confirmed that the unfortunate girl would not be racing again for a week or two, let alone today. He waved over the two security guards who had been watching proceedings from beneath the trees and they called in via walkie-talkie for one of the junior grooms to bring out the wheeled stretcher wagon.

'It was the Charles woman's fault,' he snarled. 'Bambi had the inside and she deliberately cut right across her. Even an experienced driver would have been pushed to avoid hitting her wheel like that. By the way,' he added, 'when you beat Sassie, you'll be running against your Jangles. Nothing I could do about it,' he added, apologetically. 'They're running their own book out there now.

'Don't worry,' he said, patting Amaarini on the shoulder. 'Sassie's all but out on her feet and Jangles took a knock on the knee just then. It's not that bad, but it'll stiffen up by the time you face her, believe me.'

Tammy had watched the racing on the oval circuit before, but always with a feeling of distance mixed with distaste. Even her efforts of the previous evening had been made only because the consequences of not trying had been made only too clear to her. Today, however, she found she was viewing the proceedings with an entirely different perspective, for the girls out there on the track were her sisters; proud, eager to please, beautiful and so loyal to their masters that it made her want to cry.

'You are as beautiful as any of them, Tammy,' Major said, quietly, sensing the change in her. 'Perhaps you, too, would like to race? Race properly,

I mean, not just to make up the numbers for some Philistine driver? Perhaps with a beautiful tail and some brightly coloured purple plumage?'

He continued, thoughtfully: 'Not today, of course – that would be hardly fair, but I think I shall instruct Higgy to begin some preliminary training with you. Apparently you showed considerable natural talent last night and the opinion among the grooms is that you could become a true champion.'

Tammy breathed in as deeply as her girth permitted, her chest swelling with pride and anticipation. Yes, it would be good to race and she would give everything to make her master proud of her. The past was past and fast fading from her memory now, whereas this was the present and the future stretched almost endlessly ahead of her. As long as she continued to please her master, that future would be rosy, of that she was certain now.

'I see Higgy has a new girl over there,' Major said, speaking as much to himself as to Tammy. 'She must be one of ours if he's driving her out, but I wasn't aware we had any novices in the stables at present. Business must be even more brisk than Amaarini told me, I suppose.' He fell silent again as the first race began.

Tammy recognised Jangles as the two sulkies went by on their first circuit and she also recognised Jangles's opponent's features as those of either Jessie or Bambi, concluding that it had to be the former. Bambi, like herself, had never received any proper race training and, because of her still unreliable attitude, had never yet been permitted even to set hoof on the circuit, as far as Tammy was aware. Knowing what she did now of Bambi's background and former identity, it was hardly surprising that she showed such rebellious reluctance and it would be

189

taking an unnecessary risk to allow her into competition in the hands of a visiting driver. Alongside her, Major was becoming agitated, apparently at the tactics of the woman driving Jangles.

'Damn fool!' he cursed. 'Doesn't she realise how valuable these girls are? It's that Charles woman, the mindless moron. Amaarini will make life hell for her if she injures the Jangles girl – she's the first of our Jenny-Anns she's ever shown any interest in, for some reason or other! And Jess, too – luckily she has the experience to keep out of trouble, at least.'

The words were scarcely out of Major's mouth however when the collision came, as Fiona Charles forced Jangles to cut across her path as they were half way around a bend just yards from where Major and Tammy were standing. Both girls went down and it was a miracle that neither vehicle ended up on top of them.

Immediately, Higgy and several of the spectators rushed towards the carnage and Tammy sensed that Major only just restrained himself from joining them. For a few minutes there was much consternation and uncertainty, but eventually both pony-girls were helped to their feet and Tammy heard her master's sigh of relief. He did not seem so pleased however when he saw how Jess was now unable to place any weight on her right hoof and muttered darkly to himself as she was helped away to await a stretcher.

'Idiot woman!' he snarled. 'Higgy and Amaarini both tried to warn me. Well, that's it as far as she's concerned. She's driven her last day here, believe me, but it won't be the last she sees of this race track.' He patted Tammy's arm, gradually regaining his composure.

'We shan't be able to allow her the opportunity of trying to get back at us for banning her from the island,' he explained, quietly. 'We have lots of "material" that ought to prevent her from opening her mouth, but the woman is unstable and she may well throw caution aside if she feels slighted. No,' he continued. 'I think I shall have Boolik and Amaarini organise an unfortunate accident for her when she returns to the outside world. She won't really die, of course, but it will be the last she sees of that body. She'll wake up here in a nice new one and then she can have all the racing she wants – except this time she'll learn how to do it properly.

'Aha,' he continued, seeing the next two contestants trotting out towards the starting line. 'I see Higgy is racing the new filly. He must think she shows promise to do that this early, but then there are few who know how to bring the best from a novice the way he does. This should be most interesting, Tammy. I'm sure you'll remember the other girl from last evening?

'Strange, though,' Major continued, raising a hand to shade his eyes from the bright light. 'There's something very familiar about that other girl of Higgy's. Maybe she's another of the upper level slaves who's volunteered for part-time in the stables; that mask makes it impossible to identify her, of course, but I'm certain I've seen her somewhere before.'

SASSIE

I was really far too tired to race, but what alternative did I have? I could not speak to explain how exhausted I felt and I suspected that even had I been able to, Master Harvey would have given my protestations little consideration. After all, unless he was a complete idiot, he must surely have realised my condition without the need for any words from me.

He was, I decided, a heartless brute and I was only glad that I would soon be out of his clutches, wishing only that 'soon' was not such a relative term.

My opponent, I learned from the snippets of conversation I was able to overhear, was a complete novice and this was her very first time on the track, which was why Higgy was driving her. On the other hand, I knew it was unlikely she had been overworked and abused to the extent I had suffered, so she would be much fresher than I was and I myself had already proved just what a keen amateur could achieve in the right hands. I had had Celia to bring out the best in me, and she, Higgy.

And now I had Harvey, a brutish Neanderthal who apparently cared nothing for any living creature other than himself. The fact that he was also several pounds heavier than Higgy only added to my feelings of foreboding. At least, I consoled myself, the mad-woman driver who had been responsible for causing the accident to Master Colin's filly was not in the equation, though she would be waiting in the final run-off for whichever of us triumphed in this race.

Despite my naturally competitive nature, I found myself hoping it might not be me . . .

'Higgy's girl is definitely a novice,' Major said. 'See how she runs, Tammy? She's certainly not had much practice in those hooves.' Tammy nodded, remembering the first time she had tried to walk in her own hooves, her feet forced into a ridiculously elevated position, virtually no support for her heels, forcing her to move with her weight kept forward and over her cramped toes. How anyone in a normal human body could manage to endure such torture was beyond her and yet the other girl on the track, Sassie, seemed to have mastered the knack easily enough.

Today, however, it was obvious that Sassie was not at her best, for what remained visible of her features were flushed by the time she passed them for the first time and Tammy could hear the sound of her laboured breathing even from a distance of several yards. She was leading Higgy's pony by a cart-and-a-half length, but Tammy guessed that was probably only because the shrewd groom was allowing her to make the pace and wear down her reserves of energy even further.

They completed the first lap at what even Tammy could tell was a very ordinary pace and started on the second with no change in their order. Round the bend they came and past her and Major for the second time, breasts bouncing high, bells and harness buckles jangling and clinking, hooves scrunching on the fine gravel surface. It was, Tammy thought, a fine sight and suddenly wished that she was out there with them right now. Her own nipples tingled and there was a hot cramping sensation in her lower stomach.

'Higgy's girl will win this, novice or not,' Major said. 'The other one is flat out already and I'll bet she doesn't have a finish left in her.' As if on cue, the two girls turned into the back straight and Higgy, guiding his pony wide, asked her for an effort. There was a brief hesitation of a few more paces, but then she responded and drew easily abreast of her opponent, passing her well before they arrived at the next bend.

'She's raw but strong,' Major commented, nodding. 'One of the taller ones, too, so she's got a very long stride. Dammit, but I feel I should know who she is. We'll have to walk round after this race and I'll ask Higgy about her. Whoever she is, she's going to be a popular addition to the stables. Our dear guests will be fighting each other for the chance to race her.'

193

SASSIE

By the end of the second lap I knew I was beaten and no amount of urging from Master Harvey, let alone his liberal and frantic use of his driving whip, was going to coax another yard of speed from me. My legs felt like lead and my breasts, which had bounced so prettily the evening before, now ached – the rings and bells each feeling as if they weighed a ton, rather than an ounce or so.

My opponent may have been raw, but I could see that she was naturally fit, slightly taller than we and with much longer legs, or so it seemed to me in my exhausted state of mind. Gradually, despite my best efforts, the gap between us was opening up, so that by the time we came into the back straight on the final circuit, I was trailing by maybe six or seven lengths – something like twenty yards – and an impossible distance to pull back in the time remaining, even if I had any reserves left to draw on.

The result, I could see, was a foregone conclusion now and I would have eased up, sparing myself any more punishment, except that I knew Harvey would be furious and my back and shoulders were already smarting from his spiteful ministrations. And so I kept on, hooves rising and falling, my bells seemingly now mocking my failure, adding hollow music to my humiliation. Oh, how the mighty was fallen and what a difference a few hours had made.

And then it happened.

Unbelievably, for the pace of a pony-girl race is only relative and any fit teenage girl in training shoes could have beaten even a champion pony-girl easily, Higgy's girl leaned too far over to the side. She was under no pressure whatsoever, for Higgy must surely have known what I did and that the race was theirs, but maybe he relaxed or maybe it was just her inexperienced over-eagerness to please.

Anyway I saw her left hoof sliding in towards her right, as the steel shoe beneath lost its traction. Then, instead of throwing her weight outwards, against the bend, she tried to compensate with the next stride of her right foot and succeeded only in tripping herself. She went down as if in slow motion, but the catastrophe appeared to have caught Higgy by surprise and, instead of applying the elementary brake, he allowed the cart to slew sideways and was catapulted forward, straight on to his sprawling filly.

Her flailing hoof, already in mid air, crashed into the side of his head – I heard the crack of steel on bone and winced, even as Master Harvey began guiding me to the outside of the track. As we moved past the scene, I saw that Higgy was already out cold, lying sprawled across his girl's legs, face down to the track.

I wanted to stop, to see that the groom was all right and to wait for the men to come to his aid, but my driver had his mind set on but one thing, finishing the race. At least, I thought grimly, as we completed that final bend, there was no further need of his whip and I was able to slow to little more than a walk as we approached the winning line.

Behind me, I heard his shout of triumph, but there was none of the sense of elation I had experienced when winning the previous evening. Instead, I felt cold all over, my stomach knotted, and even the dildo embedded within me seemed to have shrunk into insignificance. Worse still, I thought, as he guided me on to the grass, winning, even by default, meant that I would be expected to race again: this time against a more experienced opponent and a driver who seemed even more brutal and unfeeling than my own.

It was all too much for me to bear and, as I drew to a stop, I began to retch uncontrollably. Just in time, my own dear master, Colin, came running to my side, wrenching the bit from between my teeth a moment before I was violently sick. I did not care, I thought miserably, as hands sought to release my tongue snaffle, whether I ever saw a harness again, let alone a race track, and all I wanted was for Colin to take me away and rid me of my bells and hooves forever.

Amaarini groaned as the two men lifted her back on to her feet and took a deep breath before trying an experimental step forward. Her hip and the tops of both thighs had been grazed in the fall, but miraculously nothing had been badly damaged and there were certainly no bones broken. The tough leather of the hoof boots had done its work and now she was more worried about Higgy than she was about herself. One look back to where two more men crouched over the fallen groom was enough to tell her that his participation in the day's events had come to an end.

'He's out cold,' she heard one of the men say. 'Better get him to a doctor.'

'I *am* a doctor,' his companion growled, 'but even a doctor can't see through solid bone. He needs a hospital and an X-ray. There could be serious brain damage, judging from the way her hoof cracked against his skull. Lucky he's not already dead.'

'We have the facilities here.' Amaarini started at the sound of Richard Major's voice and, despite her mask, turned her head away. 'I've given instructions for our own doctor to come out here and he'll arrange for Higgy to be taken back to the sanitorium. It's very well equipped and Higgy will receive the very best of attention, I can assure everyone.'

196

Amaarini allowed herself to be led away from the upturned sulkie. One of the women guests had somehow managed to produce a bottle of what felt like iodine and a clean cloth and began to dab at the broken skin on her hip and thighs. It stung, but Amaarini barely felt it. She was far more worried about Higgy, and not just for his welfare.

With the trusted groom unconscious, maybe even dying, there was no one here who knew the truth about her and no way she could communicate with anyone. As far as these people were concerned, all she was was a pony-girl, anonymous behind her mask and defenceless in her harness and bridle. If only one of the grooms would appear to take her back to the stables for proper treatment. It would mean her secret would have to be shared further, but the grooms lived in terror of her and the threat of her retribution would be enough to ensure that it travelled no further.

Any such hopes, however, were quite shortly dashed. Harvey, the victorious driver, was clearly unhappy about something and now Amaarini saw that her opponent was clearly in a very much worse condition than she was herself. The wretched girl had been sick and was only standing now because her own master was supporting her. If she raced again today it would be little short of miraculous and even if she did, from what Amaarini had seen of her during their race, she wasn't going to win anything.

Fiona Charles was making her own thoughts heard.

'If she can't race, the victory is mine!' she asserted, looking round the assembled faces. 'Jangles qualified for the final, fair and square.'

'I'm not so sure about that,' a male voice called out, but Fiona ignored the jibe and rounded back on

Harvey. 'Either declare your pony fit for the final, or else pay up like a man.'

'She can't race in that state.' Apparently even Harvey could not miss the obvious, especially not when it was as obvious as a pool of vomit and a near-swooning pony-girl.

'No, she isn't racing any more today,' Colin said, looking up from Sassie for the first time. 'Sassie is my pony-girl and I'll not permit her to run again. She shouldn't have been raced this afternoon anyway, not after last night. She was probably already exhausted before the race started – you all saw how she ran, compared to last night.'

'Perhaps,' Major intervened, 'you should have thought of that before, Mr Anderson. However, what's done is done and you have every right to withdraw your own girl.'

'So where does that leave me, eh?' Harvey was almost beside himself with rage now. 'I'm not paying out to this bitch, not just because that bitch can't stand the pace. If I'd known she was in that state, I'd never have raced her, not for money, anyway.'

'So, take the other one,' Fiona said, suddenly, pointing to Amaarini. 'She's only got a few grazes and it looks like she's got her wind back. Another ten minutes and she'll be right as rain.'

'But she's a bloody novice!' Harvey stormed. 'Any fool can see that!'

'And any fool can also see that she had the beating of my girl until she fell,' Colin said, his voice calm but very icy now. 'If you want to race, race her, assuming she is fit enough.'

'What about the pony-boy?' Harvey said sulkily, turning to where Sol stood between the shafts of his own cart, the three brightly clad slave girls forming a tight semi-circle around him. Fiona shook her head.

198

'You can't race my own pony against me,' she declared, firmly. 'I've got him booked for five full days and that's that. He stays where he is and he can fuck the losing filly afterwards, which is about all he's useful for anyway.'

'He's certainly got a big enough cock,' the woman who had been tending Amaarini said, sniggering, and there was a wave of laughter agreeing with her observation. Fiona squared up to Harvey.

'Well?' she said. 'Are you going to race Diamond against my Jangles, or not? I could just claim the race if your own girl is ruled out, so you can't say I'm not giving you every chance.'

'You're all fucking heart,' Harvey spat, venemously. He looked around for support, but met only vaguely amused expressions or blank masks of rubber and leather. 'Fuck it!' he snapped, seeing that no one was prepared to back him. 'Okay, I'll take the damned novice. But I demand a weighting allowance. I must way thirty pounds more than you do.'

'I'll add twenty-five pounds of weights to my sulkie,' Fiona sneered, 'but that's as good as it gets. You reckon you're such a damned good driver, Harvey, so now's your chance to show it. You were only too fucking keen to show how good you were when you had me between the shafts, weren't you? Well, I can tell you now, you're the worst fucking driver I had during the days I was playing pony and I'm going to beat the crap out of you on the track, just to prove it.

'And to show you how confident I am, if you win, you can shag me in the middle of the track, in front of everyone here, as long as you agree to a forfeit yourself if you lose.'

'What sort of forfeit?' Harvey demanded, clearly suspicious. Fiona snickered.

'If I win,' she said, 'you strip off and walk three times around the track naked and at the end of it, you can kneel down, kiss my boots and I'll piss in your ugly face, you bastard!'

Richard Major's earlier good mood had evaporated completely now. Two accidents on the track in such quick succession were bad enough in themselves, but the injury to Higgy was even worse news and the groom, although still breathing and with a steady enough pulse, was still unconscious when the two orderlies arrived with their stretcher trolley to take him back to Lineker's sanatorium. Leading Tammy by her bridle, the empty sulkie bumping along in her wake, Major accompanied the solemn-faced party back as far as the tunnel entrance, where a groom was waiting to take charge of her.

'Higgy will be all right, Tammy,' he said, with more assurance than he felt. He could see that the girl was upset by the events she had witnessed and he did not want her becoming too distressed. He turned and addressed the groom, a sandy-haired youth named Jacko, who Tammy knew had only been working in the stables for a few days.

'Take good care of her, Jacko,' he instructed. 'I want her to have a proper shower and ask Jonas to arrange for her to have the special quarters next to Jess's, though not for tonight. She could do with some company and there's no one better than Jess. Put Bambi in an ordinary stall for now, but give her a decent mattress to rest on whilst her leg's still sore. Jonas can work out something permanent later, as I doubt Higgy will be back at work for a few days, at least.

'And let her have her voice back, once she's stabled – Tammy I mean, not Bambi.' He stroked Tammy's shoulder. 'I'll come back down and see you again as soon as I'm free,' he said, soothingly. 'In the meantime, try to relax and not worry.' He looked meaningfully down at her girth. 'Whatever else, we don't want you getting yourself stressed, not now.'

Amaarini was horrified by this latest turn of events; after the collision and Higgy's sickening injury, she had assumed that the racing would be abandoned for the day, but the man Harvey and Fiona Charles were so self-obsessed that they appeared to have no room for compassion, nor any consideration for anyone but themselves. Not that any of the spectators seemed much better.

Desperately, she looked about her, seeking some way out of her predicament, but apart from the woman who had tended to her abrasions, no one seemed to be paying her any attention and the woman herself soon lost interest and drifted away to talk to a small group of other visitors. The nearest security men, Amaarini saw, were away on the far side of the clearing, keeping well in the shade and not really that interested in the proceedings during this enforced lull. As for grooms, there were none at all to be seen.

'Well, Diamond, I believe.' Amaarini spun round awkwardly at the sound of Harvey's voice behind her and almost lost her balance in doing so. The man's eyes, she saw, were burning with intensity, which did not bode well for her.

'Now, girlie,' Harvey hissed, between clenched teeth. 'You're going to learn how to really run – and I do mean really run. No more stupid accidents like the last one. That was just plain carelessness and I don't tolerate carelessness – from anyone, let alone a stupid pony-girl whose main asset is big tits.' As he finished speaking, he reached out and grasped Amaarini's breasts, squeezing them painfully. She winced, but inwardly, willing herself not to show any pain, whilst all the while her mind was racing, trying to work out a way to stop this happening.

'You're going to win this race for me now,' Harvey said, coldly. 'If you don't, that freak over there is going to fuck you in front of all these people; but then a slut like you will probably enjoy that, so I'm going to add a little incentive of my own. You lose and when Champion the Wonder Stud has finished with you, I'm going to whip your arse and then take you out into the woods and leave you strung up from a tree all night and give every man I meet directions of where and how to find you.

'By morning, you'll be so sick of sex that you'll never be able to look at a cock again, I promise you!'

Amaarini felt her pulse quickening and it was all she could do to prevent herself from drawing back and kicking Harvey with all her might, but she knew that such an action would only make things far worse than they already were. Pony-girls who became violent towards masters and mistresses were given short shrift indeed and there was a special dark, sound-proofed cell, deeper even than the stables, where any girl stupid enough to demonstrate that sort of defiance would find herself incarcerated for days on end. Eventually, of course, someone would realise the mistake, but that would mean the entire island learning of her misadventure and a potential end to her authority. It did not bear thinking about, she knew.

As Harvey led her back to the sulkie and began securing her between the shafts, Amaarini considered her alternatives. There really weren't any, she concluded, beyond trying her hardest to win this damned race, after which it would depend on how events continued to unfold. With luck, Higgy might regain consciousness and at least send someone to rescue her; Jonas probably, who could be relied upon to keep his mouth shut, if only because he had only just been promoted temporarily as Higgy's deputy and the final decision on whether he kept that position, along with the status that brought, would be up to Amaarini herself.

And if Higgy didn't come round soon, eventually someone would realise that she was missing, though that might not be for some hours, as she had let it be known that she was retiring to her private quarters to sleep and did not want to be disturbed until mid-evening. Even then, she realised, forlornly, who would think of looking for her among the ranks of the pony-girls?

There was one other possibility, she thought, as Harvey finished buckling the last strap to her girth. If she could manage to make the sulkie flip over, maybe Harvey would end up in the same way as Higgy. If she did it right, no one could prove it was her fault, Harvey would be carted off to the sanatorium and she would probably be returned to a stall for the rest of the day and night, by which time . . .

But flipping the sulkie was easier said than done, unless she wanted to risk the possibility of serious injury to herself. She had been lucky earlier to escape as lightly as she had – a second time was pushing that luck beyond all reasonable bounds. Besides, if she tried and failed, all she would be doing was handing the race to Jangles anyway.

Jangles. Jangles, Amaarini knew, was scarcely less of a novice racer herself. She had been out on the track a few times and she had certainly had plenty of time to accustom herself to walking and running permanently in her hoof boots. But she was unused to competition and besides, whilst her body might be roughly the equal of Amaarini's, her brain was only, after all, a human brain. Out of fear and inexperience, she would probably follow Fiona Charles's instructions absolutely and Fiona was not the driver she liked to think herself.

If Amaarini could keep her wits about her and ignore Harvey and his whip, she could run her own race and, whilst today was her first personal experience of the race track, she had certainly watched enough pony-girl races to have absorbed as much tactical knowledge as the best drivers and the most successful ponies. Grunting to herself, Amaarini allowed Harvey to lead her around in a wide practice circle, loosening her stiffening thigh muscles and reaccustoming her to the required balance of her hooves.

Yes, she thought, grimly. Yes, she could do this and win the race despite Harvey, not for or because of him. That would not be the end of her predicament, she knew, but at least she would be buying herself more time. And time, right now, was very precious indeed.

SASSIE

Colin accompanied me back as far as the tunnel entrance, but there, to my surprise and despair, he handed me over to one of the junior grooms.

'Make her comfortable in a stall,' he told the lad. 'And make sure she's not bothered, not by anyone. No bit and no snaffle, and check in on her every ten minutes or so to make sure she hasn't been sick again.

'I'll be back for her in an hour or so and I'll probably take her back to my own quarters, but there's something I have to attend to urgently.' I watched him go, tears forming in my eyes. How could he abandon me like this and what could possibly be so urgent that he would leave me in the hands of this mere lad?

Anna, I thought to myself, bitterly. Yes, Anna. That would make him rush back the way he had. I had seen the way he had been looking at her ever since she had appeared in that unbelievably bizarre guise and now he was intending to take advantage of her indisposition to ...

I shook my head, refusing to picture the possible scene and turned back towards the tunnel entrance. The stable lad, who had waited patiently for me to watch Colin out of sight, patted me gently on my buttocks.

'Don't look so sad, lass,' he said, softly. 'He'll be back. I'll look after you in the meantime and I promise to take good care of you.' Free of both bit and snaffle for the first time in what seemed like half a lifetime, I was finally free to make something of a choice for myself. I looked him up and down – he was a nice enough looking youth, still wiry rather than muscled, with features that life would some day harden, and the most incredible deep green eyes.

'What's your name, stable boy?' I demanded. The lad, apparently not realising my snaffle had already been removed, looked taken aback, but quickly recovered his composure.

'I'm Harrison,' he grinned, 'but everyone calls me Harry.' I smiled back at him. He didn't look as if he could be any more than eighteen at most and, in my towering hooves, I stood at least two inches taller than him, maybe three.

'Have they let you fuck a pony-girl yet, Harry?' I said. Harry looked even more shocked.

'Well, no – no, not yet,' he admitted. 'But then I only just started down here, so I didn't expect –'

'Never expect anything, Harry,' I interrupted him. His lower jaw seemed to drop as if the hinge had suddenly broken. 'If you don't expect anything, then you never get disappointed, first rule of life, I reckon.' I stood up, proud and straight – even though my arms were still pouched uselessly behind my back – and deliberately thrust my breasts towards him, jiggling them so that my nipple bells tinkled.

'Expect nothing, Harry,' I repeated. 'But take anything and everything that's offered. They say never look a gift horse in the mouth and I reckon the same goes for gift ponies, don't you?' I grinned and laughed, harshly, shaking my head at the same time. 'Well?' I said, seeing the confusion in his eyes and the blank expression on his features. 'What are you waiting for, Harry-boy? Why don't you just find us a nice secluded stall and fuck your first pony-girl? All of a sudden I feel a whole lot better, but I reckon I could do with some extra personal attention, don't you?'

Amaarini could not believe how heavy her legs felt as she walked towards the starting line. Every step seemed to require a tremendous effort and the steel shoes on her hooves scraped awkwardly on the gravel surface. She tried to steal a sideways look at Jangles, to see if she also looked tired, but Harvey snatched spitefully at her reins, jamming the bit painfully back in her mouth and jerking her head back straight.

The sun now felt hotter than ever and, although the cloned bodies had been refined to a stage where they rarely sweated, Amaarini could see that there was now a damp sheen covering both her breasts. Her heartbeat sounded and felt as if it was all over the place; the blood was pounding in her temples, her knees felt weak and her stomach cramped. She shook her head and breathed in, willing herself to become calm and focused, recognising the symptoms of fear.

She would not lose, she *could* not lose. She was Askarlarni, she was strong. She repeated this litany over and over in her head, trying to block out all thoughts of failure, picturing only herself flying across the winning line with her opponent trailing forlornly in her wake.

And then they were racing.

With the advantage of the inside draw, Amaarini went into the first bend slightly ahead, refusing to be intimidated when Fiona Charles tried to force Jangles past her, hanging so close that she knew the wheels of the two vehicles must be almost touching behind them. Halfway round, her perseverance paid off: realising that staying upsides was asking Jangles to run several lengths extra, Fiona abandoned the effort and hung back, allowing Amaarini to set the pace into the back straight and for the remainder of the opening lap.

Trying to ignore the discomfort of her freely-bouncing breasts, Amaarini set her teeth into her bit and concentrated on trying to establish a good rhythm, listening to the sound of her hooves as they pounded on the hard surface, her nipple bells playing a steady descant. Harvey, however, clearly wanted more from her, even at this early stage.

'Pick it up, you lazy pony slut!' he roared, scything across her shoulders with the whip. Amaarini bit down harder, blocking the stinging pain from her head and resolutely continued at the same pace. Again Harvey tried to whip her to accelerate, but again she ignored him, knowing that to go faster now would drain her remaining energy far too quickly in this heat.

'Move it, you insolent bitch!' This time the whip cut horizontally, slashing against her cheek. It was a most vicious action and one which no self-respecting driver would even contemplate. In a human body it would have brought blinding tears to the eyes, but a red mist descended in front of Amaarini's vision instead.

Unable to see anything now, she had to rely on instinct and Harvey's dubious driving skills. The top bend was coming up again, she knew, but how far? A violent jerk on her left rein told her that they were not only there, but she had started to run far too wide, almost running off the track altogether and, as she started to move back left to correct this, she heard a loud exchange of obscenities from behind.

Seeing the gap on the inside, Fiona had tried to push Jangles through it and Amaarini's move back had all but forced her off on that side. Amaarini forced herself to blink, trying to clear her sight again and eventually shapes and shadows began to re-materialise, enough for her to hold something approaching a steady line around into the back straight again. Behind her, Harvey was flailing indiscriminately with his whip and further behind again she could hear Fiona Charles's raucous screechings loudly enough to know that Jangles was still hard on her heels.

Harvey's overuse of the whip was beginning to take a toll of its own now. No matter how much she tried to blot out the pain, each time the stiff braided leather cut across her skin, Amaarini found she was gasping instinctively, ruining any chance she had of establishing an even breathing pattern. Her chest now rose and fell raggedly and oxygen-starved muscles were already complaining.

Past the finish line for the penultimate time and the start of the top bend now seemed a mile away. All she could do was keep going, hoping that Jangles was suffering as badly, knowing that all she had to do was to keep going, round that bend, down one more straight and the race would be as good as over. If she remained ahead into the final, bottom bend, Jangles would never have the finishing speed to get around the outside of her.

She risked a slight acceleration into the top bend. If Fiona had any ideas about pushing to overtake there, the manoeuvre would throw her and also dishearten Jangles, forcing her into a true sprint far too early. The tactic seemed to work and Amaarini came into the back straight for the final time, still ahead and still plodding doggedly on.

Suddenly, to her horror, she realised that Jangles was drawing alongside her!

Desperately, Amaarini tried to accelerate a second time, but her opponent had already established her stride and was passing her, leading her, and the bottom bend almost upon them. Seeing this, Fiona deliberately hauled hard on the left rein, dragging Jangles across, just as her sulkie wheel came level with Amaarini's hip.

The protruding hub clipped Amaarini's right leg in mid stride and she stumbled, veering away, staggering on to the inside grass as she fought to stay upright. She managed it, barely, but the damage was done. Already Fiona and Jangles were ten or twelve yards ahead and still drawing away, so that by the time Amaarini had regained any sort of rhythm, the gap was insurmountable.

A desperate, animal roar tore itself from the depths of Amaarini's throat, ripping past the gagging bit, as she recognised the inevitability of defeat. Behind her, Harvey had seen it too and began laying into her frenziedly, but Amaarini now felt nothing, nothing

209

but the shame of defeat and the even greater shame and horror of what she knew was still to come . . .

Colin returned to the track just as Jangles was crossing the finishing line, but he was no longer interested in the outcome of the race. With Sassie out of the running for the rest of the day at least, he needed to make the most of the remaining time to see if he could find anything that would ultimately justify a full-scale raid on the island and so far as that was concerned, the day had been a waste of time up to this point.

He found Anna standing where he had last left her, shaded by a tree, standing tall and erect, drawing plenty of attention from the race spectators but so far still on her own. Now the racing had finished for the moment, Colin knew that she would not remain unmolested for long and he was even a little surprised that none of the masters and mistresses had bothered her yet.

'They're not quite sure of my status,' Anna whispered, when Colin mentioned it to her. 'I'm standing so they can't see my wrists are connected to my belt and nobody's come close enough to get a proper look anyway. The man, Harvey, he knows of course, but he's had his mind on other things. His girl just lost in the final, in case you're interested.'

'Not really,' Colin sighed. 'Unfortunately, I've got too many other things on my mind.'

'How's Sassie?' Anna's expression remained as blank as before, but her eyes showed her concern. Colin shrugged.

'She'll be okay,' he said. 'Just the heat, that's all. I told one of the grooms to take care of her and let her rest. The stables are nice and cool, so a sleep will do her the world of good.'

'Lucky her,' Anna sighed. 'So – what next?'

'Next we take another look round, only this time we try a bit further afield. I'm going to put your leash back on you and then act like I'm taking you for a walk. I want to try to get right to the shore and see if there's anything there that might give us a few clues. If this lot are importing and distributing drugs, which is the most likely scenario, they'll need to have somewhere to come ashore.'

'That could be on the other island,' Anna pointed out. Colin nodded.

'Yes, I know,' he agreed. 'But that might be a bit risky, don't you think? Unless all the visitors here are in on it, which I seriously doubt, they'd need somewhere they could be sure wouldn't be discovered, for loading and unloading.'

'And you think that somewhere is on Ailsa?' Anna said. 'And you also think that the two of us would just be allowed to walk up and find it, just like that? They'll have guards looking out for stray guests, I should imagine.'

'Of course they will,' Colin snapped back. 'We'll just have to be on the lookout ourselves and try to find a way around them, won't we? Now, come on – we're running out of time.' He reached out and clipped the chain leash on to Anna's collar. She allowed herself a wan smile of resignation.

'Sure you wouldn't like to gag me as well ... master?' she added, sarcastically. Colin grunted.

'Don't tempt me,' he said.

They walked casually away towards the nearest trail and set off up it, pausing after a few minutes to try to get their bearings. The tall trees all around made accurate navigation difficult, but the sun was penetrating enough to cast helpful shadows.

'We need north,' Colin said. 'The sun must be just about due south right now, so we need to try to get

211

over that way.' He pointed a finger, but unfortunately the path they were on continued away at an angle from it.

'We'll keep going and see if there's a branch off,' he announced. 'If not, I think we can assume that we'll end up finding the sea eventually, whichever direction we go in.'

'Elementary, my dear Watson,' Anna said, softly. Colin gave her a hard look, but she continued to regard him passively, her breasts rising and falling gently, drawing his gaze away from her eyes before he could stop himself.

'Yes, me too,' she whispered. 'Some master you turned out to be, letting a girl get all dolled up like this and then virtually ignoring her all day. At least you could find us somewhere comfortable to sit down, if only for a few minutes. These heels are crippling my feet.'

'Yeah, sure,' Colin said. 'Let's just walk on a bit, shall we? Get as far away from people as we can and then we can think and pool our suggestions.' At last, Anna smiled at him properly.

'If that's what you want to call it, that's fine by me,' she said. Her eyes went down to his breeches and Colin felt himself growing hot with embarassment. 'I won't even ask you to untie me,' she continued, looking up again. 'After all, I don't need my hands free for *thinking*, do I?'

Richard Major peered down at the inert figure and then across at the bank of monitors that stood on a mobile stand to one side of the bed. The electronic bleep sounded regular and steady enough, but the pallor of Higgy's complexion told him that all was far from right with the groom.

'How is he doing?' he asked.

The young Askarlarni nurse looked glum. 'We're not sure, Rekoli Maajuk,' she said, nervously. 'The pulse is strong enough and the brain scan shows no damage, but he shows no sign of responding to – oh my!' The girl jumped visibly as Higgy's eyes jerked open.

'Get Lineker!' Major snapped. 'Quickly now!' He leaned over, placing his face directly in line with Higgy's vision. 'Higgy? Higgy, can you hear me?' The groom's eyelids flickered and his pupils moved hesitantly from side to side, but they were dilated and completely unfocused.

'Take it easy, Higgy,' Major said, softly. 'You're going to be all right. You had a fall and a nasty bump on the head, but there's no damage done. Just try to relax and everything will be all right.' Higgy's lips began to move and finally a word formed.

'Amaa – rini!' Higgy croaked. Major laid a soothing hand on his shoulder and nodded.

'She'll be here,' he promised. Higgy's devotion to Amaarini was well known among all the Askarlarni and she, in turn, was as fond of him as she had ever been of anyone; allowing him the sort of latitude and occasional familiarity that she would never permit from anyone else. 'As soon as the doctor gets back, I'll go and find her, I promise,' Major said. 'They tell me she went to her quarters to rest and gave orders not to be disturbed, but I know she'll want to be here for you.'

'No!' Higgy gasped. His features contorted in an effort to concentrate, but the rest of his body, Major noted, remained totally immobile, despite his obvious agitation. 'Pony!' Higgy grunted. 'Pony-girl!'

'Your pony-girl is fine,' Major tried to reassure him. 'Just a few bruises and minor cuts. She was up and about straight away and apparently fit enough to run again.'

'No!' The word came out as a strangled gasp and Higgy's features contorted in apparent pain. 'No . . . she . . . pony . . .' His eyes closed and he fell silent again, but the lids were moving still. Eventually, he forced one of them up. 'Pony . . . Diamond.' His chest rose and fell with the effort of speaking. 'Amaarini!'

'I'll get her. I'll get her now,' Major said, as the door opened and Lineker appeared. 'She'll be right down here, I swear.'

'We need to talk.' Colin tugged at Anna's leash and guided her off the trail and through a gap between two straggly bushes. Behind them, around the base of a stunted pine, was a small patch of clear ground.

'Lie down,' Colin instructed her. Anna chuckled.

'I thought you were never going to ask,' she said. Colin sighed.

'I said talk,' he told her. 'If anyone comes along, we're master and slave doing what masters and slaves are supposed to do. No, don't worry, there's no sign of cameras or mikes in this area.' Carefully, Anna lowered herself, first into a sitting position and then stretching out on her back. Colin dropped to his knees beside her.

'I want to try to get in to see Jessie again,' he said. 'For some reason or other she couldn't speak earlier, but if they have used some sort of paralysing agent on her, it ought to wear off eventually.'

'Yes,' Anna agreed. She stretched her long brown legs out straight, pointing her toes. 'Like everything else wears off, I suppose.' Colin looked at her, puzzled, but continued with what he was saying.

'We know she knew Lachan very well,' he said. 'That means she's still our best chance of finding out what really happened to him. I don't know what all that nonsense in the dirt was supposed to be about and I don't intend to waste time trying to work out if it meant anything, either. My opinion is that the girl's brain is a bit addled – maybe they drug them here to keep them from making trouble.'

'And yet you still want to question her again?'

'I don't see what other options we have,' Colin retorted. 'We can go on snooping around, yes, and we certainly will, as long as we don't draw attention to ourselves, but I get the feeling you are probably right. Anything incriminating will be well hidden and well guarded.'

'Then why bother even looking for it?'

'Because there's not much else to do just yet,' Colin said impatiently. 'They've taken Jess off for treatment, which is going to mean she won't be alone for a good few hours yet and besides, if it was some sort of drug that was stopping her talking, we need to give it time to wear off.'

'So, between now and whenever,' Anna said, testily, '– you expect me to totter around after you in these shoes, looking like this, is that so?'

'I'll take the shoes off for you, if you prefer.'

'Oh, you're a gentleman, master,' Anna said, her expression and tone mocking. 'And then I end up with cuts all over the soles of my feet. I had another option in mind.'

'Like what?' By way of an answer, Anna slowly spread her legs, revealing the gaping pink slash of her sex.

'Like what do you think, you silly English policeman?'

'You mean you want me to –'

'Fuck me, yes,' Anna finished for him. She smiled, but it was clearly an effort. 'Listen, I know this is all still pretty new to you, but surely you must realise what all this has been doing to me?' Colin tried to avoid her eyes, pretending to scan the undergrowth for potential trouble.

'Why don't you tell me?' he suggested. Anna nodded.

'I shall,' she said. She took a deep breath. 'Back home I belong to a sort of club – oh, it's nothing so large or organised as this, just a few like-minded people who get together every two or three weeks for some innocent play.'

'Well, I guessed that the bondage thing wasn't exactly a complete revelation to you,' Colin said.

'No, it wasn't,' Anna confirmed, 'and neither was all the pony-girl stuff. It's not so popular in my country as it seems to be here, possibly because our climate is not quite so accommodating. But we have our devotees and yes, before you ask, I have played at being a pony myself.'

'Among other things, presumably,' Colin added, quietly. Anna nodded again.

'Among many other things,' she agreed. 'Sometimes I play the dominant role – it helps with my being tall, you see – but I tend to prefer to be submissive. My analyst tells me it is because I have authority in my job that I feel the need to pass that authority and all responsibility to someone else, if only for a few hours.'

'Yeah, well I've heard that theory somewhere before,' Colin said. 'But where's this leading us to?' Anna smiled again and sighed heavily.

'You really don't undertstand beyond the obvious, do you?' she said. 'Look at me, will you? What do I look like?'

'Well, I . . . er . . .'

'I look like most men's ultimate fantasy. Nearly naked, almost completely helpless and yes, immodestly, I must add that I know I am fairly beautiful.'

'No "fairly" about it,' Colin said. 'You're one very tasty lady.'

'Tasty? Ah yes, I understand the expression. 'Yes, Master Colin, I am very tasty, a very tasty dish, all served up ready for the eating and yet you appear not to be hungry.'

'Well, yes . . . I mean, no. I mean, well, I'm trying to concentrate on other things right now.'

'And I am too,' Anna said, urgently. 'But spending so long like this, watching everything I've been made to watch, I am getting the hot and sticky feelings.'

'Ah.'

' "Ah" he says,' Anna echoed, mockingly. 'It is more than just an "ah" situation. I don't care what you do afterwards – you can walk around this damned island until you drop dead from exhaustion, but please, surely you can spare just a little time for me first?'

'You mean –?'

'Fuck me? Yes, that is exactly what I mean. And I am sorry if my directness shocks you.'

'You mean just like that?'

'Just like what? I mean just what I said. I'm supposed to be your captive slave princess or whatever and I think I have played the role admirably, and yet my conquering master ignores me as if I'm some plain serving wench in an ankle-length smock.'

'I'm not sure I can –'

'Take off your trousers,' Anna said. Colin's eyebrows shot up.

'Hey!' he protested. 'I thought I was supposed to be the one giving orders around here?'

'Then give the right orders,' Anna retorted. She ran her tongue along her top lip. 'But take your damned trousers off first and lie down next to me. Lie on your back, if you prefer and leave everything to me. You don't have to sweet-talk me, play games, anything.

You have only one thing I need just now and I can't get it if you're going to keep it hidden away.'

The scattering of spectators had suddenly somehow grown into quite a crowd, Amaarini saw. News of the various wagers and forfeits had apparently spread to the guests spread throughout the woods and now they had filtered back to form an expectant audience, awaiting the finale with a mixture of anticipation and bawdy good humour.

The good humour, however, had not touched Harvey and his expression was thunderous as he was forced to wait whilst Fiona gloated over her victory and milked the moment to its full potential. Eventually, however, she was ready to exact her vengeful pound of flesh.

'Well, Harvey,' she smirked, sauntering up to him. 'Are you ready to pay your dues? I've wiped my boots in the grass, as you can see –' she said, waving one foot towards him, '– so no one can say I'm not being fair-minded. I'm sure you'll choke badly enough anyway, without me forcing you to swallow mouthfuls of Ailsa's dust.'

'You're too kind, I'm sure,' Harvey snarled. 'I'm sure you've made enough people choke in the past anyway.' Fiona smirked triumphantly and jabbed a finger towards the centre of the race track.

'Out we go then, Harve old boy,' she said. 'Out there, where everyone can see you. I presume there's no need for me to insist on you being cuffed for this?' Harvey gave her a venomous stare.

'You wish,' he rasped. 'Just get your arse out there and let's get this over with.'

'I couldn't agree more,' Fiona laughed. 'My poor bladder is fit to burst and I can't stand around here with my legs crossed for much longer.' She half turned, enjoying the amused looks on the surrounding faces. 'You go first,' she instructed. 'And down on your knees, ready and waiting. One kiss for each boot and then – well, you know what to expect. Shame you don't have a shower cap handy!'

'No, I don't need my hands for this, *Master* Colin,' Anna whispered. She shuffled herself across, positioning herself between Colin's widespread thighs and looked down at his semi-erect penis. 'One pair of hands is more than enough,' she said. 'And yours are free, aren't they? Just close your eyes and relax now. Remember, I am your slave, after all.'

She bent forward, lowering her head, her mouth seeking his organ, her tongue already flickering. Colin groaned quietly as he felt the heat of her, the rough surface caressing the base of his shaft, sliding over the sensitive skin of his scrotum. The effect was almost instantaneous, for his cock began to swell rapidly, stiffening to full erection within seconds.

Anna rocked back on her heels and inspected the results of her efforts with a cat-like smile of satisfaction.

'Perfect,' she purred. 'Absolutely perfect.' She began to shuffle forward on her knees and, to Colin's astonishment, managed the difficult feat of straddling him without even once looking as though she might be in danger of overbalancing. 'Relax, master,' she whispered. 'This is why you have a slave.'

Carefully, she lowered herself until the yawning lips of her sex were just resting on his rigid length. Then, with a measured precision, she began to slide back and forth, lubricating his shaft with her juices and at the same time stimulating herself, until her clitoris emerged from beneath its hooded sanctuary.

'These tits are not just for show,' she said, wriggling her hips and sending little darts of white fire spearing up into Colin's stomach. He gasped, but instinctively his hands were already reaching for the two waiting orbs, first grasping them tightly, then, as she leaned forward to him, relaxing their initial grip and slowly kneading them.

'Oh yes!' she sighed. 'Oh yes indeed!' Colin bit hard into his lower lip, tasting blood and salt, fighting to preserve the moment, knowing that, for all Anna's bondage, he was no longer the one in control. Anna knew it, too.

'Hold it up for me,' she whispered, leaning further forward and nibbling at his ear lobe. 'Your cock, I mean. Yes – that's it. Ah, can you feel me, feel my heat? Feel my hot little cock-eating pussy?' She giggled, wriggled her hips and suddenly dropped on him, swallowing his entire length into her until she was grinding against his pubic bone.

'Hungry little pussy, isn't she?' she chuckled. 'Look how she's eaten your poor cock, master. You should feed her more often, I think, take her in hand and save her from being so greedy!'

She had begun to rock backwards and forwards as she spoke, but now Anna added a gentle up and down motion. Colin, fists balled, teeth gritted, tried to fight against it, but he knew it was no contest. The warrior princess, bound slave or not, had added another conquest to her battle honours and, as he finally surrendered to the defeat, Colin knew that this was not going to be the first battle in a war that he had already lost, before it had even been begun.

Amaarini had watched Harvey's humiliation still secured between the shafts, hoping against hope that Fiona would forget about her, but as the losing driver finally got back to his feet and stomped off towards the entrance to the stables, his conqueror let the front of her brief skirt drop back into place, turned to the crowd and raised her arms in a gesture of triumph.

'And now, folks,' she cried. 'For your further and final entertainment this afternoon, we have a game but losing filly, Diamond!' She turned further and extended her arm, pointing at Amaarini. 'Good losers are all very well, but this game is all about winners, and second place counts for nothing. Now, where are those two grooms?'

From the back of the crowd, two of the young stable lads came forward and Amaarini saw to her horror that they were carrying between them a piece of equipment that Higgy referred to euphemistically as the 'mating frame'; a lightweight tubular contraption that was regularly used by the grooms to subdue novice pony-girls and reluctant top side slaves alike. It was also a favourite among certain guests for the way it reduced their chosen subject to a state of complete helplessness.

It was simple but extremely effective in its design, with two semi-circular side lattices supporting a central transverse connecting bar, the centre of which dipped to support a padded rest at waist height. The unfortunate female could be bent forwards or backwards over this and her wrists and ankles secured as and if desired, holding her in either one of two ideal positions for her master's ultimate enjoyment.

The two young men placed the frame at the track side and checked that it was on level ground, turning to give polite salutes to Fiona and then stepping back to await further instructions.

'This is a rare treat this afternoon, ladies and gentlemen,' Fiona laughed. She walked the few paces to stand beside the frame and leant on it, as if making a further test of its stability. 'You've all seen my new pony-boy, I know.' She gestured to where Sol had

221

been released from between the shafts and was now standing with the twins, Maisy and Daisy, flanking him on either side. Behind him, the black girl, Lou, stood grinning broadly.

'Well, as I said earlier, I was prepared to offer myself as forfeit to Harvey, had I lost,' Fiona continued. 'But I knew there was no real danger of that. Superior skill won the day and I see that my opponent has conceded that, as well as his pony-girl, who will now pay the second half of the agreed forfeit.

'I know from experience that Solly has something of a penchant for pony-girls and, although he is currently under punishment, I am going to give this one to him.' Fiona laughed and nodded to the twins, who each grabbed one of Sol's elbows and began to march him forward.

'However,' she continued. 'Sol *is* under punishment, so maybe we shouldn't allow him to enjoy himself too much, so I have also decided to use this.' She held up what at first Amaarini took to be a solid and very lifelike pink dildo, complete with scrotum with very generously proportioned testicles, but then, with a quick flick of her wrist, Fiona sprung the thing open, revealing that it was in fact hollow.

'This –' she said, smirking, '– fits tightly over the pony-boy's own equipment, preventing any real sensation and thus, of course, any enjoyment on his part. Also, unfortunately for our Diamond here, it means that his male equipment is enlarged somewhat, but that cannot be helped. Such a pity.' Her mocking tone made it only too clear that Fiona did not consider this a pity at all and Amaarini shuddered.

Only a matter of a day or so ago, she herself had fitted the prosthetic, or at least one very like it, to Sol and watched him as he was forced to couple with two slave girls belonging to one of their regular German mistress visitors. The two girls had been old hands, but even they had squirmed under the ensuing onslaughts. Now the same fate was to befall her. She closed her eyes, willing Higgy or anyone else to come to her rescue before it was too late, but already the final seconds were ticking away at all too alarming a rate.

'You're sure there's no one in her quarters, Boolik? No one at all?' Richard Major's brow furrowed. The Askarlarni security chief shook his head.

'As certain as I can be, Rekoli,' he replied. 'She is not answering her house line and the man I sent to her door cannot get any response either.'

'Her personal communicator?' Major suggested. Again Boolik Gothar shook his head.

'Switched to messages,' he said.

'If she was sleeping . . .' Major replied, dubiously. 'But if there was no reponse from her, then . . . oh no, surely not!' His pallor suddenly became a deathly grey and his hand went to his temple. Boolik stared at him in alarm.

'What is it?' he demanded. 'You have remembered something, Rekoli?' Major looked past him, staring into space.

'It surely cannot be . . .?' he began. For two or three seconds the Askarlarni stood as if frozen to the spot. 'I should have realised,' Major said, in a hoarse whisper. 'But why would she . . .? It makes no sense, except that Amaarini is a law to herself at times.' He grasped Boolik by the shoulder.

'Come with me,' he said, urgently. 'Call the security desk and have them check *all* available monitors in the meantime, to see if they can spot her, and have them call you back if they come up with anything. And ask them to – no, it doesn't matter . . . one pony-girl looks very much like another.'

'Pony-girl?' Boolik asked, as he started after the already retreating Major. 'I don't understand.'

'I'm not sure I do, either,' Major retorted. 'I hope I'm imagining things. Just get on to them and have them start checking anyway. We must hurry. The foolish female may well have got herself into something she didn't bargain for, whatever her original motives!'

Amaarini's natural instinct was to struggle against the two grooms when they began to unhitch her from between the shafts, but she knew that it would be a futile gesture. Young or not, the lads would already have had plenty of practice at handling unwilling pony-girls, and the junior hands were often quicker than the older heads to use their short discipline whips to enforce their authority.

Her glistening breasts rose and fell, her heart pumping furiously as they led her out and turned her towards the waiting frame. The spectators were pressing closer now, forming an untidy semi-circle from which to watch the proceedings, and Amaarini could not fail to see the hungry expectation in most of the eyes that followed her progress.

'Put her over,' Fiona ordered. 'Standard mare mating position.' The grooms pushed Amaarini between the ends of the two side support frames, each of them now standing outside the curving support legs and holding her between them. One reached across and seized her bridle, dragging her head down, pressing against the small of her back until her stomach was forced against the padded support. Immediately, his companion drew a wide securing strap across the small of her back and buckled it tightly, preventing her from standing upright again.

She now stood bent, with her upper body parallel to the ground, her breasts swinging beneath her with their dangling bells swaying and tinkling softly. Her arms were still trussed in the pouch behind her back, so that there was no need for them to employ the wrist straps, but now they dragged her feet further apart and, taking one of her ankles each, quickly strapped them to the tubular supports.

Hands now began to tug at the buckle of her crotch strap, where it was secured to the back of her girth and now this dropped free between her legs. Her stomach and vagina muscles contracted involuntarily with her fear and, to her chagrin, Amaarini felt the now slippery dildo slipping from her to fall almost soundlessly on the grass between her legs. There was a titter of laughter from the watching gallery, but Amaarini scarcely heard it.

The thundering in her head had increased to storm pitch, as she waited helplessly for what she knew now she could not escape. Her teeth drove hard into the rubber of her bit and she closed her eyes, waiting for the inevitable and trying not to admit to herself that she was now beginning to understand more than just the fear and helplessness that came with the rigid discipline of the bridle . . .

The two Askarlarnis almost ran headlong into Harvey in the tunnel between the stables and the open air. Major, almost frantic now and looking as Boolik had neither seen nor ever expected to see his leader, grabbed the man by the shoulders and began to shake him. Harvey, almost as surprised as the security chief, stepped backwards in surprise.

'Where is she?' Major all but screamed at him. 'What have you done with her?'

'The pony-girl, man!' Boolik added, seeing Harvey's utter lack of comprehension. Harvey grunted and tried to push Major away.

'That stupid little slut?' he sneered. 'I left her back at the track. Hopeless bitch – I should have given her a good thrashing for refusing to run properly.'

'You'd better not have hurt her!' Major roared. Harvey raised both eyebrows in an expression that was both surprise and scorn.

'Hurt her?' he echoed. 'She was perfectly all right when I last saw her. I don't understand what all the fuss is about – she's only a bloody pony-girl, when all's said and done.'

'And that makes it all right, does it?' Major snarled. 'Who did you leave her with?' he demanded, as he pushed past Harvey. Harvey, turning to watch the two departing figures, shrugged.

'That bloody Fiona woman has her,' he called after them. 'We had a bet and I lost, so now –' he paused, '– now her bloody pony-boy is going to fuck the silly mare,' he finished quietly, realising that neither Major nor his companion were still listening. Harvey continued to stand staring towards the daylight for several seconds after their silhouettes had disappeared from view.

'Bloody madhouse,' he muttered to himself. 'You pay good money and they tell you "do whatever you like" and then they start panicking and complaining when you do what you've paid for. Madhouse,' he repeated, finally turning away. 'Headcases, all of them. Fucking headcases!'

Colin was only vaguely aware of the pressure on his arms and made no real effort to resist, his tired and sleep-fuddled mind failing to register that it was not Anna seeking to continue where they had left off before he had fallen into the sated doze, but the double snap of the locks that brought him suddenly wide awake.

He realised, even before he had his eyes open, that his wrists had been cuffed behind his back and that he had been rolled over on to his stomach and could not believe that he had not woken earlier. Kicking his legs, he rolled himself back over, stopping when he realised that to continue would mean lying with his full weight on his now helpless arms.

'Wakey-wakey, sleepyhead.' Celia stood, legs astride, looking down at him, a mocking smile on her deep-red lips. Beside her, Anna stood quietly, a strange expression on her exotically adorned features. The rubber covered silhouette of what he presumed was Millie stood in the background.

'What the hell . . .?' Colin began. 'Oh yes, very funny,' he snapped. 'Very funny and very clever.' He struggled into a sitting position, but Celia raised one booted foot, placed it in the centre of his chest and pushed him on to his back again.

'Hey!' Colin exclaimed. 'What's the game?' Celia pursed her lips.

'Same game as before,' she replied, evenly. 'Slaves and masters – or should I say slaves and mistresses. Needless to say, I'm the mistress.'

'Wha –? I don't understand.'

'There's a lot you don't understand,' Celia said. 'There's a lot I don't understand, either, but I do have some information for you and now I think our little arrangement is nearing its end.'

'You haven't told anyone?' Colin felt a cold chill of alarm, but Celia quickly dispelled that particular fear.

'No,' she said. 'I've kept my part of the bargain. Millie and I did some exploring and we stumbled on something you and your people can probably make use of, but I shan't tell you what it is until we're safely off these islands.'

'But we've hardly had time to –'

'It's time enough,' Celia stopped him. 'I was never keen on bringing you here anyway, but you forced my hand, so I had no choice. Now I do. I've made an arrangement with one of the security people and I'll be receiving some very revealing stills as a reminder of our short stay here – a reminder for you, I hasten to add. I know there's nothing actually illegal, but then nothing I do at the farm is illegal, as we all know, but the pictures show you obviously enjoying yourself with a variety of different companions, so I don't think your threat of publicly exposing my little operation will hold much water now, do you?'

'We'd never have actually done that anyway,' Colin protested. 'It was only a threat.'

'I don't like threats,' Celia said, quietly. 'And I've never appreciated anyone telling me what to do. I went along with you because I had to, but now it's over and it's nearly time to go. You've been fairly careful, but almost not careful enough,' she added.

'Too many questions, even innocent sounding questions and people start to notice you,' she continued. 'Which is asking for trouble, so I've decided we're getting out. However, before we do leave, I think you need teaching a little lesson.'

'What? What do you mean?' Colin tried tugging at the leather cuffs, but realised immediately that there was no way he was going to break free from them using brute strength. As he talked, he tried slipping his hand out – squeezing his thumb to elongate and narrow it – but Celia had made sure the straps were far too tight for that.

'Where's Sassie?' Celia demanded. Colin looked up at her.

'Back in the stables,' he said. 'She was sick.'

'So I hear,' Celia drawled. 'And so you just hand her over to some stable lad and screw with Princess

Policewoman here?' She jerked her thumb at Anna, who continued to stand impassively by her side.

'Quite a little holiday you're having yourself, isn't it?' Celia continued. 'Millie, Sassie, Jessie and now this one. Well, there's one person you seem to have overlooked. Me.'

'You?' Colin looked at her in surprise. Celia smirked.

'And why not?' she challenged him. 'Maybe because you think I only like girls, is that it? Well, I must admit I do prefer them, but I'm still not averse to the occasional healthy male, as long as he's suitably submissive and properly prepared.'

'Properly prepared?'

'You'll see, slave boy,' Celia laughed. She turned to Anna and began unclipping her wrist restraints from her belt. 'Get him on his feet,' she said. 'And take off his boots and breeches. There's also a knife in the bag there that Millie's carrying. Cut that top off him, too. Let's have him naked – and pass me the bag while you're doing that. I've a few little presents in there I think will suit our new slave.'

Behind her, Amaarini could hear Sol shuffling forward and she tensed herself, knowing that she was completely helpless, held splayed and ready for him to take her with the awful phallus that Fiona had fitted to him. Her eyes were wide now and she stared like a cornered animal around the faces she could see, but everywhere she looked she saw only lust, mockery and anticipation. If any of the watching crowd understood what she was feeling now, their intent expressions and eager eyes did not show it.

'In order to encourage Sol –' she heard Fiona saying from somewhere just behind and to the side of her, '– I shall give him three cuts with my whip every minute that the pony slut doesn't come.' There was a ripple of laughter at this. 'I think that will keep him up to his work. Now, let's have you, pony-boy!'

Amaarini guessed, without seeing, that Fiona had grasped the rearing dildo, dragging Sol in the last few inches and positioning its tapering tip against her tightly-pressed labia. She felt the first pressure as the hard plastic probed for an opening and clenched her muscles again, but it was a hopeless struggle and the first dildo had left her wet and slippery anyway. With a sigh of surrender, she forced herself to relax again – it would make his entry easier, she knew, and lessen the pain involved for herself.

The head of the phallus moved slowly inside her now, pushing back the swollen lips on either side and Amaarini whimpered into her bit. Beneath her, she felt a gloved hand massaging one of her dangling breasts and looked down and backwards to see that the fingers were most definitely female.

'Like a cow, aren't you, pony-girl,' Fiona whispered, close to her ear. 'With udders like these, they should milk you twice a day! Now, Solly!' she snapped, suddenly. Amaarini gasped and groaned as the remaining length of the dildo slid deep into her in one movement, Sol's pubic bone grinding against her, his stomach crushing against the soft globes of her naked buttocks.

The first dildo had felt unnaturally large, even though she knew Higgy had selected one of the smallest available sizes, but this monster was in a different league. She felt stuffed, stretched, filled beyond belief and yet her body's only response seemed to be coming from the insistently throbbing little nubbin as the pressure against it began to exert its influence.

'There, pony cow,' Fiona chuckled, as the watching audience burst into applause and ragged cheering.

'That wasn't so bad now, was it? Who knows, you may even enjoy this after all.' As she spoke, Amaarini felt the long shaft beginning to withdraw again, but she knew only too well it was not going to be removed altogether. She had seen too many such rituals herself to entertain any false hopes now and she knew that any moment now the real trial would begin for her.

She closed her eyes and waited, understanding now just what it might be that could turn an ordinary female into a humbled, dutiful pony-girl. It would not happen to her, of course, that much she did have to cling on to, but for those weaker than her . . .

Sol pressed forward again, steadier this time, filling her, withdrawing, filling her again. A weaker mind, she thought, desperately . . . a weaker mind, yes, but not her. She was strong, stronger than this, stronger than anything. She was Askarlarni. She could rise above this, beat it, control . . .

With a stifled groan, Amaarini made her final, superhuman effort and then, as her first shattering orgasm took over, she arched her back and screamed at the sun, even the bit and the snaffle unable to prevent the sounds of her final surrender echoing around the clearing.

Eight

'You can read this whilst we're waiting, if you're bored.' Frearson dropped the manilla folder into Geordie's lap. 'It's a bit wordy, I'm afraid, but that's civil servants for you.'

'What is it?' Geordie turned the folder around and opened it, revealing a sheaf of closely printed A4 sheets of paper.

'A report, of course,' Frearson grinned. 'An analysis of certain aspects of illicit trading in Central and South America – slave trading, to be precise. I can give you the short version, if you'd prefer?' Geordie squinted at the lengthy paragraphs and small typeface and nodded.

'It might be better,' he said. 'Certainly quicker.'

'Well, all that little opus tells us is what a lot of people already know,' Frearson said. 'Young women – and men, for that matter – go missing from the more remote areas of Latin America on a regular basis. Hundreds of them disappear every year, and that doesn't even count the street kids who beg in the big cities.'

'And the authorities don't bother doing anything about it, I presume?' Geordie sighed. Frearson shrugged.

'The fact is, there's so much of it they don't have the resources. And a cynic might also say that it leaves them with fewer mouths to feed anyway.'

'You're thinking about those two girls, I suppose?'

'Yes, I am.' Frearson paused. 'The girl they picked up out of the water was definitely from this region here.' He reached down, turned over the bulk of the papers in the folder and extracted a single sheet on which was printed a coloured map. 'Here,' he said, jabbing a forefinger at it.

'Mountain country,' Geordie observed. Frearson nodded.

'Mountains and jungle,' he said. 'Bloody awful place, from what I've heard about it. But over here –' he said, tracing an invisible line across to the Pacific coastline, '– the mountains become hills. However, the area is hard to approach overland, because of what surrounds it.

'There's one small town on the coast here but it just so happens it's controlled, to all intents and purposes, by one of the usual rebel factions that we read about every day. The government forces, for what they're worth, give the place a very wide berth and let the locals get on with whatever it is they get on with. Which,' he continued, 'is very handy for anyone wanting to ship things in or out of the country, because the town stands on a very deep estuary and would make a perfect jumping-off point for a submarine. Or any other bloody boat, for that matter,' he added, as an afterthought.

'It's a long way around from there to the Atlantic,' Geordie pointed out.

'True, but it would be very safe and they could travel on the surface for most of the way. Most of the countries in that area have out-of-date navies – they buy all our old wrecks usually – and mostly they can't afford the fuel to send them far anyway, so it's all just for show.'

'So you think our submarine stopped at Ailsa to drop off a consignment of slaves, is that it?'

'Well, it stopped for something and it doesn't look as if it was drugs,' Frearson said. 'Plus, we already know the two girls were taken to the island in what was almost certainly a submarine. What we don't know is whether they were the only ones.

'The girl told the Eriks that there were just the two of them this time, as far as she could tell, but there could well have been earlier trips and what we saw may well have been a later batch.'

'So, maybe this *Healthglow* crowd have decided to start playing the game for real?' Geordie mused. 'Maybe they started off with something like Celia's operation and now they've graduated to the serious stuff.'

'Well, there are people who'd pay good money for that serious stuff,' Frearson said. 'It's a wicked old world out there in places, I can tell you.'

'No need,' Geordie said. 'I've seen enough of it myself, believe me.'

'Yes, I'd almost forgotten,' Frearson said, quietly. 'You'd been through quite a rough old time before they moved you up here out of the way.'

'A nice quiet little break, they told me,' Geordie laughed. 'And I was daft enough to believe them.' He shook his head and slowly closed the folder. 'I'll save this for a sleepless night,' he joked, placing it on the side table. 'Right now, I'm starting to feel really hungry again.'

'Well, I know where we can get an excellent beef sandwich,' Frearson said. 'Might as well take advantage of this lull in the proceedings. We can't really do much more until that girl gets here and even then we're really waiting for Colin to get back. I can't wait to hear what he has to tell us.'

'Me neither,' Geordie muttered, under his breath. 'Me neither.'

* * *

'Call this my fee for services rendered,' Celia chuck-led, as she buckled the thick collar about Colin's neck. Behind him, he felt the dangling strap between his shoulder blades, the weight of the attached cuffs feeling unnaturally heavy against the small of his back.

'I shouldn't even bother trying to struggle,' Celia warned him. 'I'm a lot stronger than you might think and Millie will do whatever I tell her. She always has. Millie, get your lazy backside over here and help me.'

In fact, although the original cuffs had to be removed in order to fit Colin's wrists into the new ones, there wasn't really much opportunity to resist anyway. Whilst Celia gripped his arms, Millie effected the replacement with skill and speed born of long practice. Celia then began adjusting the vertical strap, hauling it through the buckle until Colin's arms were forced as high up his back as his joints would allow.

'If you had tits, of course,' Celia mocked him, '– this harness would make them stick out beautifully. Would you like tits, slave boy?' Colin glared at her, refusing to rise to her baiting, but Celia was not going to be thwarted. 'He'd look good with tits, wouldn't he, girls?' she said. 'Maybe nice brown tits, like yours, Princess.' To Colin's annoyance and complete chagrin, he saw Anna smile at this, whilst Millie, apparently gagged under her mask, let out a muffled giggle.

'Mind you,' Celia continued, reaching down to cup his balls and penis in one hand. 'We'd have to do something about these, wouldn't we? A girl with a cock – well, it'd be a novelty, anyway. Cuff his ankles, Millie.'

The rubbered slave girl stepped forward and knelt down, placing the leather cuffs about Colin's ankles, buckling them and slipping in the locks that would prevent the buckles from being undone again. Peering down, Colin was just able to make out the few inches of chain that now prevented him from taking anything more than the shortest of steps, but Celia was far from finished in that department.

From the bag she now produced a pair of bright red, women's high-heeled sandals, passing them to the still kneeling Millie, who proceeded to lift each of his feet in turn and force them into the precarious footwear.

'Very fetching,' Celia said. Anna's smile did not waver. 'And now this.' Celia held up a curious assemblage of short, thin straps, at the centre of which was a shiny, stainless steel ring. Colin shuddered, understanding its purpose immediately.

'Strap him good and tight, Millie,' Celia said, passing the harness to her. The slave girl nodded and slid the ring over Colin's flaccid penis, pushing it down as far as it would go and then buckling the first strap round and behind his pendulous balls. A second strap was then drawn forward and buckled snugly about the top of his scrotum, stretching the skin and forcing his testicles into prominent relief. A final strap was then pulled down between his testicles, forcing them apart.

The effect was most uncomfortable and yet, to Colin's horror, he realised that he was beginning to get hard and the discomfort quickly began to turn into genuine pain.

'Damn!' he gasped. 'Take it off, please! At least loosen it a bit!'

'Cry baby!' Celia taunted him. 'Just a little bit of pressure to stop you coming too quickly, that's all that is. We don't want to go to all this trouble and have you shooting off straight away, do we? Give me that tail, Millie.'

Millie picked up the bag from Celia's feet and delved into it yet again. This time her hand came out holding a bright-red nylon tail and, when Colin saw what it was fixed to, he groaned out loud.

'No, not that, please,' he begged, but Celia was not listening. She took the tail and its tapered butt plug and waited whilst Millie found the next item – a small tube with a long, thin nozzle.

'You can have that dubious pleasure, Millie,' Celia said. She reached out and grasped Colin's ear, forcing him to bend forward at the waist. He winced, but there was no point in trying to resist, as there was no point in trying to resist when Millie pushed the nozzle of the tube into his anus and proceeded to squeeze in the lubricant.

'Relax and it'll be easier,' Celia advised, as Millie thrust the point of the plug against the puckered opening. 'Tense yourself and it'll hurt,' she cautioned. 'And don't even think about trying to expel it afterwards. It's shaped so that your sphicter muscles will close over the end and it'll have to be pulled out by hand afterwards.'

'That's it, mistress,' Millie announced, eventually. Colin's stomach felt as if something were pressing up into it and the slightest movement made the trailing tail brush against the backs and insides of his legs. 'Is that all, or do you want to gag him?'

'We'll gag him later, I think,' Celia decided. 'First he can thank you for your efforts. Down on your knees, boy, and get your tongue ready. Poor Millie's had a most boring day so far and I think she deserves just a little diversion, at the very least. After that, we'll put a mask on him and he'll just be any other old slave.

'People here aren't ever surprised by anything, especially role swapping, but it'll save having to stop for unnecessary questions and I want to get him back to my room as quickly as possible. The sooner I do what needs to be done and we all get off this island, the happier I'll feel.'

Amaarini opened her eyes slowly and tried to focus. Her head was throbbing and she felt sick and stiff. The dream images had continued into wakefulness with her. She found she was shivering and trembling and her entire body felt cold.

'Don't try to sit up.' Richard Major's face swam into view above her, though she had to use all her powers of concentration to sharpen the image of his anxious features. 'We gave you a mild sedative,' he was saying. 'You were very agitated and we didn't want you injuring yourself or doing anything that would reveal your true identity. It'll wear off quite quickly, but I think you should try to lie still for a while yet.'

'What happened?' Amaarini closed her eyes, but the images were too raw and she quickly opened them again. Major reached down and took her right hand in his own.

'I think you know what happened,' he replied, softly. 'Higgy was trying to tell me, but I didn't understand until too late and we couldn't reach you in time.'

'We?' A pang of alarm stabbed through Amaarini, but Major patted her hand reassuringly.

'Myself and Boolik Gothar,' he said. 'No one else, apart from Higgy, of course, knows it was you. We did not remove the mask until we had you safely back in my quarters here. I have sworn Boolik to absolute secrecy, naturally. We can trust him, I know.'

'Yes,' Amaarini sighed, relaxing again. 'Yes, he's a loyal man. A good man.' Though she knew he would keep this to himself only as long as it suited his purposes, and then he would use it over her for its maximum advantage. Loyal as Boolik was, he was also ambitious and Amaarini would be a useful ally to that ambition, willing or not.

'What I don't understand was what you were trying to do and what on earth you thought you could gain from such a risky venture,' Major was continuing. 'I presume none of the other grooms knew? No, I thought not. But why, Amaarini? Why?'

'I'm not sure myself, Rekoli,' Amaarini sighed. 'I was trying to understand something that I think is beyond true understanding, trying to find a logical reason for something that defies logic. I didn't realise that then, of course, but I think I do now.'

'You wanted the experience of being a pony-girl yourself?' Major's eyebrows rose. Amaarini avoided his direct gaze.

'I didn't want the experience for myself,' she replied, carefully. 'I wanted to see which parts of the experience had what sort of effects on the human psyche. I did not for one moment expect it would have any such effect on me. I am Askarlarni, after all.'

'In your mind, yes,' Major agreed. He hesitated. 'But what about in your body – did you think of that?'

'My body,' she said, pensively, closing her eyes again. 'Yes, my damned body.' She sighed. 'I want a new body, Rekoli.' Her voice had dropped to a barely audible whisper now and Major was forced to bend closer to hear her.

'Please arrange for me to have a new body, Rekoli.' The silence hung heavily over them and, when Amaarini finally broke it to speak again, she sounded like a small girl on the point of bursting into tears, though tears were something she knew she could never shed . . .

'I don't want this body any more, Rekoli,' she sobbed. 'Please say you'll allow me to have another. Please, Rekoli?'

The mask was almost identical to the one Millie had been wearing all day and disguised Colin's identity completely, but the feelings of helplessness and humiliation he experienced at being led back across the island, past dozens of people, visitors, slaves and staff alike, were like nothing he had ever imagined he could experience.

His nudity and even the spontaneous erection that the harness had triggered and now retained, hardly drew more than the most casual of passing glances, but this was almost worse still to Colin, almost worse, even, than the fact the the one person who showed the most interest in his condition was male, overweight and almost certainly elderly, though his own mask made that difficult to tell for certain.

'He seems to like you, slave boy,' Celia chortled, as the man passed behind them and out of earshot. 'Maybe I should call him back and ask him what he's willing to pay for an hour of your services, eh? No? Well, I wonder how much Sassie enjoyed being left in the stables for anyone who'd paid their fees, eh? I bet she was thrilled.'

'We were supposed to be here to do a job,' Colin hissed, from the side of his mouth. 'I needed to talk to Jessie. She started trying to tell me something, but it didn't make sense and she couldn't talk and then we were interrupted and –'

'And she wasn't Jessie,' Celia interrupted him. 'I overheard one of the grooms talking about her after she got injured.'

'Of course she was Jess,' Colin snapped. 'I should know. I –'

'I asked,' Celia said. 'They were a bit embarrassed that I'd overheard what they were saying, but apparently someone thought it would be funny to do the old twin-swap routine on you. The girl you got is called Bambi and the lads told me she's Jess's twin.'

'Shit!' Colin made as if to stop, but Celia prodded him on with the short crop she was carrying. 'I wonder if Lachan knew there were two of them?'

'Does it really matter? They're not the only twins on this island and there are even triplets, which is quite a feature for some people, believe me.'

'I thought she couldn't speak,' Colin muttered. 'I never thought it was a case of wouldn't speak. All that pantomime with the stick in the mud. It was just a bloody wind-up.'

'Probably,' Celia agreed. 'Though I haven't the faintest idea what you're talking about and I really don't want to know any more. And, as for not being able to talk, that reminds me. Pass me that gag harness, Millie, and let's have some peace and quiet.

'You, my boy,' she said, as she prised his mouth open and forced the pear-shaped rubber wedge between his teeth, '– have done all you're going to do with your mouth.' She pressed deliberately against him, crushing his throbbing organ between their bodies.

'I know you think I'm probably past my sell-by date and I know you'd rather fuck your princess there, or even Millie, but this is my game now, and I'm going to have my share before we go, believe me.' She finished buckling the strap at the back of his neck and reached down to squeeze his burgeoning flesh.

'Just think yourself lucky I'm in a hurry to get out of here,' she grinned. 'Otherwise, the fun I could have with you over the next few days – it hardly bears thinking about. And do try to walk properly on those heels, otherwise I'll have to ask Millie to whip your pretty arse for you!'

She stopped and looked up at the sky, sniffing the air.

'Just as well we are going,' she sighed. 'I can smell a storm brewing somewhere. This old nose of mine is never wrong.'

Epilogue

From the front page of the *Southern Standard*, Friday 9 September, 2000:

GO-GETTER GIRL GONE BUT NOT FORGOTTEN

Family, friends and former colleagues of television's all-action girl Fiona Charles filled the tiny sixteenth-century parish church at Minston Cross, Wiltshire, for an hour-long memorial service to the thirty-year-old presenter, who died in tragic circumstances two weeks ago and who was buried after a private service on Monday.

Thousands of grieving fans brought traffic to a halt for miles around, with tailbacks as far as the M4 motorway. Local police described the chaotic scenes as their 'worst nightmare', but family friend, Leo Ottinger (53) said that the overwhelming show of affection for their daughter had proved a great help to Fiona's parents, George and Margaret, in their darkest hour.

'Fiona was a lovely girl,' said a sad Leo. 'She was born and brought up in the village here and we all knew and loved her; as a devoted daughter, a loving friend, or as a cheery and helpful neighbour. She spent a good deal of time raising money for local charities and was a regular visitor to the local old folks' home,' he added.

George Charles told our reporter: 'I think it would be fair to say that not a single person who ever met our daughter ever had a bad word to say about her. The television image was just that, an image. Underneath that she was a gentle soul.'

Former fellow presenter on GTV's *How The Heck?*, Jason Foster-Graham, added his own tribute on the steps of the church.

'Fee was a joy to be around,' he said. 'Professional and hard working, she set herself high standards and was always eager to encourage others less fortunate to achieve greater things.'

Police investigating the road crash in which Miss Charles's BMW plunged seventy feet down a Cornish hillside this morning announced that vehicle inspectors had discovered a badly-worn brake pipe, which was almost certainly the cause of the accident. No other vehicles were involved, but Inspector David Moss of Cornwall's Traffic Division is still appealing for any witnesses who might have seen the tragedy to come forward.

(Full report and pictures on Page 7)

'Sounds *just* like the girl we knew, doesn't it?' Colin Turner folded the newspaper and dropped in back on to the table. Anna, her features still brown from Celia's skin dye, had accepted his offer to stay at one of the local hotels with him: an offer made after Sassie had announced that she was returning to London and Frearson had told them all that it would be several more days before they would know whether the go-ahead had been given for a proper move on Ailsa and Carigillie. He had not sounded optimistic.

246

'This thing is so big –' he said, the exasperation in his voice unmistakeable, '– that now they're talking about setting up a new task force to deal with it and we'll end up playing second fiddle to a load of jumped-up university graduates and gung-ho ex-special forces officers. And the politicians will have their four pennyworth, too. What they're saying now is that this crosses national boundaries and we don't want to go upsetting the wrong banana republics, do we?'

'It all seems so, well, remote now, doesn't it?' Colin mused. Anna smiled and pointed at her face.

'Not when you've got something like this to remind you,' she laughed. 'Celia said it would fade quite quickly, but I can't say I've noticed any difference since we got back. If she was lying to me, I'll give her a taste of her own whip she'll never forget.'

'If you can find her,' Colin said. 'She didn't waste any time in heading south again, did she?' And neither had Sassie, he thought to himself, but then she was a free agent and a very independent person and probably had her reasons.

'Well, she's fulfilled her part of the bargain,' Anna pointed out. 'And it *was* her who found out about those native girls. I wonder if they came from the same place as our little one?'

'Most likely,' Colin said. 'And they're probably all as crazy as she sounds.'

'I thought she seemed remarkably self-possessed, considering what we know she's gone through,' Anna replied. 'Very intelligent, too. Her English is improving at an astonishing rate.'

'Shame about her imagination,' Colin retorted. 'Either that, or she's gullible as hell. Geordie was quite positive and so was everyone else I've talked to. That body they cremated was definitely Alex

Gregory, so she's either mad, or lying, when she says Alex is still alive.'

'And that pony-girl?' Anna reminded him. 'Bambi, wasn't it, the one we first thought was Jess?'

'Mad as a hatter,' Colin replied. 'Probably jealous that her twin sister was having it away with Lachan and she was left out of it. All that nonsense about being Lachan. Lachan was blown to smithereens in that explosion.'

'Which meant no body,' Anna reminded him. Colin shook his head firmly.

'Maybe not, but wherever his body might be, it certainly never looked like hers and never will do. No, I tell you the girl was mad. That place is enough to send even a shrink round the bend, if he spent enough time there.' He sighed and sat back in his chair, lifting his feet up on to the low table.

' "I am Lachan",' he quoted. 'Well, if that gorgeous piece of totty was Andrew Lachan, then I'm Cleopatra. Unless you want me to believe that someone's found a way of transfering minds into other people's bodies – and I'd rather believe in the Tooth Fairy than that!'

Amaarini peered through the hidden observation port at the figure huddled in the corner of the specially padded room, that was one of three used to keep new Jenny-Ann girls from harming themselves during whatever period of readjustment was required after their transition. The girl was completely naked, her head shaved and her ebony-coloured skin shone under the harsh overhead lighting. She sat with her knees drawn up against her massive breasts, her face buried against her folded arms.

'She's black,' Amaarini observed, stating the obvious. 'And I didn't think your new batch would be

248

ready for hosting for a good while yet?' Beside her, Keith Lineker, still wearing his white laboratory coat, smiled in a self-satisfied fashion.

'That body is nothing to do with Valerez's Andean girls,' he said. 'It's something we started working on at the beginning of the summer. Apparently one or two guests expressed surprise that we had no ethnic minorities represented among our resident girls and suggested that might not be quite politically correct. I presume he was joking, but the point was well made.'

'Knowing human nature as I now do,' Amaarini growled, 'I shouldn't be surprised if the fool was serious. Not that it matters.'

'Indeed not.' Lineker thrust his hands into his pockets. 'Well, what do you think of her? Isn't she a beauty?'

'Aren't the breasts just a trifle over-developed?' Amaarini suggested. Lineker shrugged.

'Large breasts feature in so many human male fantasies,' he sighed. 'So we thought we'd see just what we could do on that score.'

'You don't think maybe you've taken it just a little to the extreme?' Lineker shrugged and pursed his lips.

'They'll support themselves fine, as long as she does the right exercises,' he said. 'The musculature involved has been strengthened beyond normal, so there should be no premature sagging.'

'And how is she taking it now?' Lineker sighed.

'Well, obviously she suffered a severe shock when she came round and she became very traumatised, as you know, but we've been keeping her sedated and the new drug is working quite well. She's passive enough now, though there are still signs of her former rebelliousness, obviously. Would you like to go in and talk to her?'

'Will that upset her again, do you think?'

Lineker hesitated. 'Possibly a little,' he replied, cautiously. 'If you'd rather –'

'No.' Amaarini cut him short. 'No, a little upset won't hurt her, not after what she did. If it hadn't been for her malicious stupidity . . .'

'I understand,' Lineker replied, softly. 'The whole episode must have been very disturbing for you, though I still don't understand why you –'

'It doesn't matter what you understand,' Amaarini interrupted him for a second time. 'I had my reasons and they were very sound, scientific ones. If she hadn't caused Higgy to be injured like that . . . well, enough said. She's starting to pay for that now.'

The black girl looked up as the heavy door swung open and her eyes narrowed as they focused on the figure of Amaarini framed in the opening.

'You!' she said, her full top lip curling back to reveal a row of perfect and brilliantly white teeth. 'This is all down to you, isn't it, you bitch!'

'It was my idea, yes,' Amaarini replied, smiling down at her. 'But I can't take the actual credit for your fine new body. That goes to Doctor Lineker and his team and I must say, up close I can see they've done an even better job than I had first thought.'

'You're all monsters!' the girl screamed, her eyes wide with a mixture of anger, fright and confusion. 'How can you do something like this?'

' "The appliance of science", as one television advert once put it, I believe,' Amaarini said, smoothly. 'Your brain has been transferred to a body specially cloned and genetically modified to as near perfection as the human gene pattern will allow.

'It's not all bad, either. You'll be fitter than before, stronger than before, you almost cannot get ill and you'll probably live for up to four hundred years from the day of your transition. Not quite immortality, but a passing semblance.'

'Four hundred years!' The black girl gasped, her eyes rolling. 'Four hundred years of *this*?' She spread her hands feebly, indicating her body and the room about her. Amaarini smiled again and shook her head.

'Not four hundred years of this,' she said. 'You don't think we'd keep a sentient creature locked up in a place like this for the rest of her life, do you? No, you won't be kept here much longer, I promise you. As soon as the doctor thinks you're ready, you'll be moved down to the stables.

'Remember the stables? All those poor defenceless pony-girls you were so quick to berate and mistreat. Well, Miss Fiona Charles, now it's your turn again. You had a few days to experience the other side of the equation before, didn't you, yet still you refused to learn?

'Well, I'm afraid this time it's for good. I've ordered a nice white girth, bridle and harness for you and I see you've already been pierced for your pretty bells. The white will form such a striking contrast with your new skin tone, too, don't you think?

'And you'll be popular, too, I can assure you – Ailsa Ness's very first resident black pony-girl. There will be others coming along soon, no doubt,' she added, 'but for the moment you will be quite the star attraction, I'm sure.'

'This is some kind of joke, isn't it?' Fiona moaned, burying her face again. 'You've given me some kind of hallucinogenic drug, that's got to be it.'

'Oh no, Raven – that's your new name, by the way – this is no hallucination. What you see, what you feel, that's all quite real, I can assure you. But it's nothing to what I'm going to make sure you see and feel in the future, believe me and, until Higgy makes a complete recovery and can return to running the stables, I intend to personally supervise your induction and training.

'I'll make sure your hooves fly with the best of them, Raven, and by the time we've finished with you, you'll be the champion of champions, the fastest girl on the track and the most willing slave off it.'

'Never!' Fiona hissed. She worked her new lips, trying to form something to spit at her tormentress, but her mouth had gone suddenly dry and all she could do was glare balefully up at her. Amaarini smiled again and turned back into the corridor.

'Never –' she said, as the door began to swing closed, '– never say never, my dear Raven. Not when we have such a long future together. It may not be forever, but I'll be doing my damnedest to make sure it feels like forever to you!'

'It won't be forever, Higgy,' Richard Major said, his tone conciliatory. 'Doctor Lineker and his people are still working on the male cloning problems and he anticipates a year or two at the most, and then you can be transferred again.'

'A year or two like this?' Higgy, sitting propped up in bed in one of the small side wards that were part of the island's sanatorium, looked down at his new body morosely. Beneath the lightweight gown, the swelling breasts and their darker nipples were clearly visible and the face, he knew, would not have looked out of place anywhere in the stables above – anywhere, that is, except on a male groom like himself.

'How the hell am I expected to look those lads in the face again, sir?' he growled, except the growl came out as a rather husky and sexy purr. 'This ain't me, is it?'

'I'm afraid it is for the moment, Higgy,' Amaarini said, entering the room and walking up to the side of the bed. 'We're sorry, but there wasn't any other option, short of letting you die. The crack on the head was bad enough, but it was disguising the injury to the base of your neck and there was also kidney damage from the fall itself.

'Apparently you must have landed on one of the girl's hooves before the other struck your temple. Doctor Lineker considered restorative surgery for your spinal cord, but the other injuries made that too risky, so it was safer to just give you a new body.

'It's a good body, though, probably just as strong as your old one and you'll be up and about in it in a few days. The doctor reckons you'll even be able to return to your duties in another week or so.'

'Not like this I can't!' Higgy snapped, hating the contralto voice that now echoed inside his head.

'Why not?' Amaarini said. 'Just let me know when you're ready and I'll help you sort out a suitable uniform and teach you just how a woman keeps a bunch of brainless young males in order. You can even have a new title, at least until you can change bodies again – Stablemistress of Ailsa,' she grinned. 'How does that sound to you, Higgy?'

'Not as appealing as I know you'd want it to, miss,' Higgy sighed. 'And not as fucking amusing as those young bastards are going to find it. I do thank you and I will do my best, as always, but I'll not be easy until I can be rid of this body again, believe me.'

Amaarini nodded and reached down to squeeze the slender hand.

'Me too,' she whispered, softly. 'Me too.'

AND ON THAT NOTE ...

... we must leave Ailsa yet again, perhaps with the feeling that all life is but an act anyway, and that none of us are really anything but role players. No less a person than The Bard of Avon himself suggested as much, don't forget, and I wouldn't dream of arguing with anyone who still sells as many books as he does.

But, meanwhile they also say that we are all ultimately judged by our acts, rather than by our thoughts, so, until the next time, play kind, play safe and try to make at least one person smile every day, even if it's only me and you can do that by visiting my website:

THE STORYBOOK WORLD OF JENNIFER JANE POPE

www.avid-diva.com

or e-mailing me to let me know if you've enjoyed this latest chapter in the *Slave* saga at

jenny@avid-diva.demon.co.uk

You can also ask to be placed on my special notification list and be among the first to know when the release date is announced for the next book in this series, *Slave Judges*.

Thank you again and happy reading.

NEXUS NEW BOOKS

To be published in February

PEACHES AND CREAM
Aishling Morgan
£5.99

Peaches and Cream follows the story of Charlotte Bomefield through the 1920s from her days as the lover and plaything of the strong-willed Cicely St John. From the decadent joys of London's invert society, to the rustic pleasures of Somerset, her beauty and compliant nature are taken advantage of again and again, by lovers both male and female, conventional and peculiar. None, however, are so peculiar as her own guardian, Colonel St John, who expects fellatio with his bedtime story each evening and takes girls' milk as his preferred tipple.

ISBN 0 352 33672 2

THE TAMING OF TRUDI
Yolanda Celbridge
£5.99

Coming to sexual submission is not to be rushed. You start at the beginning, and develop at your own pace, often understanding what appears on your canvas only after it's there. Sometimes Trudi Fahr, a 22-year-old nubile from America's West Coast, lies awake at night, awed by her own desire to be punished, humiliated, teased and shamed. To punish her tormentors, and herself too, she wants them to hurt her even more. Trudi's that wildest of animals, a tamed girl.

ISBN 0 352 33673 0

BRAT
Penny Birch
£5.99

Natasha Linnet is the perfect modern girl – single, successful, independent and capable of putting men in their place with a single word. Yet she has a single desire, and not one that she could ever admit to her smart friends. She wants to be spanked, and not just by a girlfriend or any of her male admirers. Instead she needs proper discipline, and from someone strict enough to take her across their lap, pull down her expensive silk panties and slap her bare bottom to a glowing pink ball. First, though, she has to find someone who will see her not as the aloof young woman she appears to be, but as what she is underneath – a spoilt brat. A Nexus Classic.

ISBN 0 352 33674 9

To be published in March

DIRTY LAUNDRY
Penny Birch
£5.99

Natasha Linnet is back, and with her pet dirty old man in France, she is feeling deprived of kinky sex. Unfortunately, Gabrielle Salinger, the therapist from hell, has found out about Natasha's sex life. Not wanting to end up as a case study in perversion, Natasha tries to keep her nose clean, and walks straight into the flabby embrace of the awful Monty Hartle, whose main joy in life is the humiliation of women. Before long, Natasha finds that she really can't handle the filthy Monty, and that what Gabrielle *really* wants is not work-related at all! That leaves only one way out, and Natasha exploits it to the full.

ISBN 0 352 33680 3

TEASING CHARLOTTE
Yvonne Marshall
£5.99

Young debutantes Charlotte and Imogen are about to come out for the London season. The girls, however, feel little need for the company of the stuffy and reliable bankers and diplomats to whom they're introduced. They're fascinated, instead, by the legend surrounding the mysterious Kayla, a society beauty infamously caught on camera doing a very special favour for an unidentifiable but clearly very important man. But when they get close to the heart of the mystery, the truth proves more bizarre than gossip ever could – in ways that even Charlotte and Imogen's fertile imaginations can scarcely have prepared them for.

ISBN 0 352 33681 1

DISPLAYS OF INNOCENTS
Lucy Golden
£5.99

The twelve stories in this collection reveal the experiences of those who dare to step outside the familiar bounds of everyday life. Irene is called for an interview, but has never before been examined as thoroughly as this; Gemma cannot believe the lewd demands made by her new clients, a respectable middle-aged couple; and Helen learns that the boss's wife has a wetly intimate way of demonstrating her authority. For some, it widens their horizons, for others, it is an agony never to be repeated. For all twelve, it is a tale of intense erotic power.

ISBN 0 352 33697 X

If you would like more information about Nexus titles, please visit our website at www.nexus-books.co.uk, or send a stamped addressed envelope to:

Nexus, Thames Wharf Studios,
Rainville Road, London W6 9HA

BLACK LACE NEW BOOKS

To be published in February

GONE WILD
Maria Eppie
£5.99

Zita's a 21st-century girl – sassy, and smart enough to know it's a mad world. To survive it, you've got to know the unwritten rules. She enjoys a life of innocent hedonism at Tanglebush, the old pile that friends – including the sexy, feral Cy, his airhead girlfriend Elain and mad Ivan, a once-famous Russian film director – are squatting prior to demolition. But matters become inevitably more complicated as relationships intertwine. When Ivan offers temporary escape on a research trip to Cuba, sparks fly. Sassy erotic fiction from an exciting new author.

ISBN 0 352 33670 6

RELEASE ME
Suki Cunningham
£5.99

Jo Bell is a feisty music journalist with just one weakness – her sexy boss Jerome. When he sends her on an assignment to the remote stately home, Hathaway Hall, she finds herself caught up in a world of titillation and control, where the hidden desires of the past mingle with the decadent sex of the present. In this world where degradation becomes addictive and punishment is its own reward, can Jo come out on top – and does she want to?

ISBN 0 352 33671 4

JULIET RISING
Cleo Cordell
£5.99

Nothing is more important to Reynard than winning the favours of the bright and wilful Juliet, a pupil at Madame Nicol's exclusive but strict 18th-century ladies' academy. Her captivating beauty tinged with a hint of cruelty soon has Reynard willing to do anything to win her approval. But Juliet's methods of persuasion have little effect on Andreas, the academy's rugged gardener and object of her lustful obsessions. That is, until she agrees to change her spoilt ways. A Black Lace Special Reprint.

ISBN 0 352 32938 6

To be published in March

SWEET THING
Alison Tyler
£5.99

Jessica Taylor is a sultry brunette with strongly defined cheekbones, a striking mouth, and deep-set blue eyes. Men lose themselves in her gaze, fantasising about starring in the visions they see there. Currently, several are auditioning for a permanent role in her love life. What Jessica most wants is to be a big-time reporter. Dashiell Cooper is Jessica's Editor-in-Chief. And what he wants is Jessica. Intriguingly to Dashiell, the young writer refuses to be easily trapped. Putting her journalistic skills to use, Jessica discovers where, when, why and how her heart falls for one particluar who.

ISBN 0 352 33682 X

DEMON'S DARE
Melissa MacNeal
£5.99

Kentucky, 1895. Traded as payment for her aunt's gambling debts, Vanita is whisked to Harte's Haven, a decaying plantation mansion where Franklin Harte and his albino twins are quite happy to have her. She is to marry Damon Harte, whose interest in his sister Desiree, and in creating erotic clockwork friends, plunges Vanita into their forbidden world of gender-bending and illicit secrets. To reclaim her lost estate, she must escape Franklin's obsessive humiliation and Desiree's designs on her. And yet she has yet to meet the darkest demon of them all.

ISBN 0 352 33683 8

ELENA'S CONQUEST
Lisette Allen
£5.99

On a summer's day in 1070, 22-year-old Elena is gathering herbs in the garden of the convent where she leads a peaceful, but uneventful, life. Lately, she's been yearning for something sinful: the intimate touch of the tautly muscled blond Saxon who haunts her dreams. But when Norman soldiers besiege the convent and take Elena captive, she is chosen by the dark and masterful Lord Aimery le Sebrenn to satisfy his savage desires. Captivated by his powerful masculinity, she is horrified to discover that she is not the only woman in his castle. Will Elena triumph over Lady Isobel, her cruel and beautiful rival, or will she be banished to a life of innocence and mundanity? A Black Lace Special Reprint.

ISBN 0 352 32950 5

NEXUS BACKLIST

This information is correct at time of printing. For up-to-date information, please visit our website at www.nexus-books.co.uk

All books are priced at £5.99 unless another price is given.

Nexus books with a contemporary setting

ACCIDENTS WILL HAPPEN	Lucy Golden ISBN 0 352 33596 3	☐
ANGEL	Lindsay Gordon ISBN 0 352 33590 4	☐
THE BLACK MASQUE	Lisette Ashton ISBN 0 352 33372 3	☐
THE BLACK WIDOW	Lisette Ashton ISBN 0 352 33338 3	☐
THE BOND	Lindsay Gordon ISBN 0 352 33480 0	☐
BROUGHT TO HEEL	Arabella Knight ISBN 0 352 33508 4	☐
CANDY IN CAPTIVITY	Arabella Knight ISBN 0 352 33495 9	☐
CAPTIVES OF THE PRIVATE HOUSE	Esme Ombreux ISBN 0 352 33619 6	☐
DANCE OF SUBMISSION	Lisette Ashton ISBN 0 352 33450 9	☐
DARK DELIGHTS	Maria del Rey ISBN 0 352 33276 X	☐
DARK DESIRES	Maria del Rey ISBN 0 352 33072 4	☐
DISCIPLES OF SHAME	Stephanie Calvin ISBN 0 352 33343 X	☐
DISCIPLINE OF THE PRIVATE HOUSE	Esme Ombreux ISBN 0 352 33459 2	☐

MAIDEN	Aishling Morgan ISBN 0 352 33466 5	☐
NYMPHS OF DIONYSUS £4.99	Susan Tinoff ISBN 0 352 33150 X	☐
THE SLAVE OF LIDIR	Aran Ashe ISBN 0 352 33504 1	☐
TIGER, TIGER	Aishling Morgan ISBN 0 352 33455 X	☐
THE WARRIOR QUEEN	Kendal Grahame ISBN 0 352 33294 8	☐

Edwardian, Victorian and older erotica

BEATRICE	Anonymous ISBN 0 352 31326 9	☐
CONFESSION OF AN ENGLISH SLAVE	Yolanda Celbridge ISBN 0 352 33433 9	☐
DEVON CREAM	Aishling Morgan ISBN 0 352 33488 6	☐
THE GOVERNESS AT ST AGATHA'S	Yolanda Celbridge ISBN 0 352 32986 6	☐
PURITY	Aishling Morgan ISBN 0 352 33510 6	☐
THE TRAINING OF AN ENGLISH GENTLEMAN	Yolanda Celbridge ISBN 0 352 33348 0	☐

Samplers and collections

NEW EROTICA 4	Various ISBN 0 352 33290 5	☐
NEW EROTICA 5	Various ISBN 0 352 33540 8	☐
EROTICON 1	Various ISBN 0 352 33593 9	☐
EROTICON 2	Various ISBN 0 352 33594 7	☐
EROTICON 3	Various ISBN 0 352 33597 1	☐
EROTICON 4	Various ISBN 0 352 33602 1	☐

Nexus Classics

A new imprint dedicated to putting the finest works of erotic fiction back in print.

✂ -----------------------------

Please send me the books I have ticked above.

Name ....

Address ....

....

....

.... Post code ....

Send to: Cash Sales, Nexus Books, Thames Wharf Studios, Rainville Road, London W6 9HA

US customers: for prices and details of how to order books for delivery by mail, call 1-800-805-1083.

Please enclose a cheque or postal order, made payable to **Nexus Books Ltd**, to the value of the books you have ordered plus postage and packing costs as follows:

UK and BFPO – £1.00 for the first book, 50p for each subsequent book.

Overseas (including Republic of Ireland) – £2.00 for the first book, £1.00 for each subsequent book.

If you would prefer to pay by VISA, ACCESS/MASTER-CARD, AMEX, DINERS CLUB or SWITCH, please write your card number and expiry date here:

....

Please allow up to 28 days for delivery.

Signature ....

✂ -----------------------------